PRAISE FOR ABIGAIL HING WEN'S LOVEBOAT SERIES

"If you've ever wanted to feel as if you're breaking all the rules without actually breaking any rules, then this is the book you need to read."

—STEPHANIE GARBER,
#1 *NEW YORK TIMES*–BESTSELLING AUTHOR OF *CARAVAL*

"An entertaining and heartfelt debut that takes readers on a roller-coaster ride of romance and self-discovery."

—*KIRKUS REVIEWS*

"Refreshing and exciting . . . YA readers will love the mix of romance, defiance, adventure, culture, and friendship."

—*SCHOOL LIBRARY JOURNAL*

"From tea eggs to snake blood sake, the energy of Taipei in the summer provides a winning backdrop to this joyful debut about a young American dancer who finds love and freedom by exploring her Taiwanese roots."

—*PUBLISHERS WEEKLY*

"An inspiring look at the strength of family and the importance of art, and how both can influence how we see ourselves and the world around us. Plus, it's just wonderfully romantic!"

—MARISSA MEYER,
#1 *NEW YORK TIMES*–BESTSELLING AUTHOR OF *INSTANT KARMA*

"What a sheer delight . . . Full of familiar faces and new friends, revelry, romance, and self-discovery, Abigail Hing Wen has crafted another confection you'll want to devour in a single sitting."

—GAYLE FORMAN,
#1 *NEW YORK TIMES*–BESTSELLING AUTHOR OF *IF I STAY*

Kisses, CODES, AND CONSPIRACIES

ABIGAIL HING WEN

FEIWEL AND FRIENDS
New York

A Feiwel and Friends Book
An imprint of Macmillan Publishing Group, LLC
120 Broadway, New York, NY 10271 • fiercereads.com

Our books may be purchased in bulk for promotional, educational,
or business use. Please contact your local bookseller or the Macmillan
Corporate and Premium Sales Department at (800) 221-7945 ext. 5442
or by email at MacmillanSpecialMarkets@macmillan.com.

Library of Congress Cataloging-in-Publication Data is available.

First edition, 2024
Book design by Ellen Duda
Feiwel and Friends logo designed by Filomena Tuosto
Printed in the United States of America

ISBN 978-1-250-88323-0
1 3 5 7 9 10 8 6 4 2

For my siblings

Chapter 1

Tan's back hit the front door with a thud. Overhead, a tapestry of stars shone in the Palo Alto night sky, but they were lost on him. His senses were overpowered by Winter's soft mouth. She tasted sweet, like the red gummy bears they'd devoured too many of tonight. As her fingers tightened in his hair, a jolt of sensations sparked down into his toes.

Fumbling for the doorknob, his thumb found the biolock. Even at an angle, a beep sounded. Dad's good work. Mouths still locked, they tumbled inside into a cozy darkness. Their dress shoes sailed off into the shared collection of Lee family and Woo family shoes.

"Your room," she whispered, which was the farthest from his sleeping parents—not to mention her bed lay in half of a partitioned suite she shared with her mom.

Winter clung to his arm, and they fumbled across the dark hall-way, over the silk runner, and into his room. Sana's bedroom door stood ajar across from Tan's, but fortunately, his five-year-old sister slept like a log. Winter shut his door silently. Moonlight flashed on the pearl pins in her coiled black hair as they crashed together again.

The world inverted. On his bed, his tuxedo pants legs tangled in her bare ones. He felt drunk on the strawberry scent of her skin and the petals of his magnolia blossom boutonniere shredding between them. As he cupped the smooth line of her jaw, an ache burned inside him.

He'd been wanting to tell Winter how he felt about her. It had been building slowly inside him over months. It was right there, on the tip of his tongue. But at the moment, her tongue was in the way. And he wasn't in any rush to change that.

"Winter." He breathed her name into their kiss. His lower lip grazed hers. She shifted against him, and then the thud of something hitting the carpet reached his ears.

The dull sound was like a splash of water on Winter. She pulled away, creating a space between them that filled with cool air. Her brown eyes, rimmed with soft black lashes, opened wide and startled.

"What are we doing?" she whispered.

"Kissing," he whispered back.

Winter rolled over to the far side of his bed and hung her legs over the edge. She gazed down at the floor, at whatever it was that had fallen.

"We can't do this, Tan."

Tan sat up, too. His lips burned from Winter's mouth. They felt tender and slightly sore, in a delicious way he'd never felt before.

"I'm sorry," Winter said. "I guess . . . I guess I got carried away."

So had he, obviously. But their whole world was self-restraint, trained from the cradle. Didn't it mean something that they wanted this so badly?

Winter bent over, and when she rose again, she was holding a vase in her hands. Moonlight caught the delicate gold lines on its peacock-blue painted surface. Rebecca, his ex, had given it to him, not for any reason. Just because. She was a gifts person.

It's not there because it matters to me, he wanted to explain. It was there—on his bedside table—on the side he didn't sleep on—because he hadn't gotten around to moving it somewhere else.

But Winter beat him. "You're still hung up on her."

"I'm not," he protested.

Winter's face was obscured by shadows. He couldn't read her eyes, which bothered him. He usually could, and he didn't like not knowing how she was feeling. Especially right now.

Their kiss had started nearly two hours earlier. At prom, which they'd agreed to attend together at the last minute, after tickets opened up to sophomores.

After Winter asked Tan.

After Rebecca had ghosted him for four months and he'd sunk into a bleak, Rebecca-shaped depression.

After he finally made contact with her and found out she was dating another guy.

"I'm not hung up on her," he repeated now. Which felt like the truth. And yet, why did he also feel like he wasn't being entirely honest?

"Your parents are our *landlords*, Tan."

Technically true. After Winter's father passed away last summer, Fannie and Winter found the Lees' in-law suite for rent on Craigslist. It was a spare bedroom with a bathroom between it and Tan's room, intended for Mom's widowed mother one day.

Their parents had become fast friends. So had he and Winter. Everyone thought Winter and Tan going to prom was sweet and adorable and the perfect way for him to return to life "AR" (After Rebecca).

But he'd never anticipated the magic of tonight. The way his entire body shook with laughter as their teppanyaki chef tossed a savory cooked shrimp at Winter, who caught it in her mouth—and he'd captured it on camera. How right it had felt when she tucked her hand into the crook of his arm on their way into the decorated gym.

And as they danced on the floor with her head pillowed on his shoulder and his arms wrapped tightly around her waist, prom seemed like the perfect moment to let her know the truth of what she'd come to mean to him. They'd left the gym, hand in hand, and headed for his car. Inside, he wasn't sure who'd initiated this kiss. Both of them, it seemed.

And then they hadn't stopped. Even for most of the drive home.

"I don't think of you guys as our tenants," Tan said. "Neither do my parents. You guys are like . . . like family now."

She ran her hands over her rose-colored gown, smoothing down the satin folds. "How could I be so selfish?"

"Selfish?" He wasn't following. Winter was possibly the most unselfish person he had ever met. "Winter, I don't think you need to—"

"If we got weird, whose side would your parents take?"

"Got weird? What, between us?" Tan frowned.

"Finding your house was a fresh start for my mom. I can't ruin that. God."

"Ruin that? You mean, if this didn't work out? As in, my parents would kick you guys out? No way!" Winter was looking far, far ahead into the future. That was so her. "They're not like that—" he began, but then he realized what she was saying:

Tan's family was *Winter's landlord.*

That meant Tan was in a position of power over her, even if it didn't feel that way. Winter and her mom had lost everything when her father died. Their house. All their furniture and most of their possessions. They'd been living off savings ever since so Winter's mom could go to law school.

Tan gripped his cotton sheets. He'd read enough stories in English classes about entitled sons taking advantage of people in their household. He wasn't as rich as them by far. But he was never going to be *that guy*.

And now that he thought about it, if their parents got even a whiff that he and Winter were attracted to each other, they might insist the Woos leave.

"I get it. It's cool." Tan held up his hands and slid off his bed. His feet pressed into the soft pile of his carpet, and he squeezed his toes together, trying to stay grounded. "No problem. You're right. We just got . . . carried away."

A silence fell. Then Winter rose to her feet. "I guess it was inevitable," she said. "Hormonal teenagers living in the same house." She gave a short laugh. "Going to prom together."

Tan felt as though she'd smacked him. Was that really all that had happened? Some function of biology or brain chemistry or circumstances?

It didn't feel that way. Not to Tan.

"We just need to make sure we're never alone from now on," she continued. "Okay?"

"Okay," he said, because there wasn't anything else he could say.

Then she left his room, her kisses still burning on his lips.

Chapter 2

Tan managed to avoid Winter the rest of their sophomore year and into the summer. Winter was busy with her internship at the Peninsula Youth Theatre, and Tan was busy coaching middle school kids on solving mind benders at a camp at the Community Center. He hung out with his friends on the weekends.

He needed to respect Winter's wishes, and that meant keeping his distance, no matter how hard it was. He barely saw Winter and had to resort to rewatching her shrimp-catching video. And he tortured himself wondering: Was the whole landlord thing an excuse? Or was Rebecca the real reason Winter had backed away? Was she right? Had they simply been hormonal teenagers caught up in the music and lights of prom?

But he always came back to the same point. No matter what, he couldn't jeopardize things for Winter and her mom. Renting their rooms enabled Winter to start sophomore year at Palo Alto High School, one of the best public ones in California, while her mom got back on her feet. Palo Alto housing was otherwise impossible to afford. Not to mention, having a boarder was how his parents pulled off buying this four-bedroom home in the neighborhood, too, until the day they could hopefully afford it on their own.

At school, Winter had formed a tight group of friends through theater and even landed a leadership role as an executive editor for the yearbook. Transferring schools would disrupt her entire life, and Tan would never forgive himself if he was the cause.

He'd upended an existence once before—Rebecca Tseng's.

The memories played through his mind on Labor Day as he walked to Walgreens to pick up a trifold board for a major presentation later in the year. He passed Timothy Adams, Rebecca's favorite hot chocolate shop. He and Rebecca had dated sophomore year, after she'd arrived at Palo Alto High School last September, same as Winter. Rebecca was all extremes: the sleekest black hair, the softest skin, the most satiny clothes. Elegant pearls dangled from her ears. She was a parachute kid, meaning her parents lived in Shanghai, and she lived on her own in a designer-everything apartment on University Avenue—the nicest part of town. An education consultant checked in on her a few times a week. And that was it for supervision.

They'd met in English class. She'd asked for his help with an assignment on idioms. After school, they headed to Timothy Adams for hot chocolate, and soon after that, they were a thing. He liked her openness to learning another culture and her artistic flair. Her style, alluring accent, and gracious way with words quickly made her one of the most popular girls in their class. He woke up every morning and fell asleep every night to a text from her, and he felt amazed that, miraculously, this glamorous girl had picked him.

But it all ended with Rebecca's parents visiting in December and forcing her to literally *flee the country*—to get away from Tan.

That wasn't how Winter saw the whole debacle. She thought Rebecca's parents were monsters. But that was definitely how Tan saw it.

And that was how Tan had completely upended Rebecca's life.

Inside Walgreens, the ceiling and shelves fluttered with BACK TO SCHOOL signs and discounts. Tan found a collection of ten different trifold boards with ten different prices and features. A big red sticker even promised an A+.

He picked it up, frowning. No matter how Winter spun what had happened, Tan had been the catalyst. He'd dated Rebecca for three months. Her parents had dined with him for an hour. The length of a serious job interview. Tan wasn't secretive or complicated. He had medium-length black hair, regular brown eyes, and twenty-twenty vision. What you saw was what you got, and the Tseng family knew pretty much all there was to him.

And they'd evaluated him and found him lacking.

And then, Rebecca was gone.

He set the A+ trifold back with a thump. This presentation wasn't for a grade. It was for an encryption project to showcase at a local science fair in November. Recruiters for major summer internships would attend. It was mostly targeted at college students, but some high schoolers participated, and Winter had encouraged him to submit a project. So he'd signed up. But that was a lifetime ago. Before prom. Tan and Winter hadn't talked about it since.

Bags of gummy bears, Winter's favorite, hung from the shelves directly beside the poster boards. The same brand Winter and Tan had eaten at prom. Suggestive selling: homework and sweets. It was effective. Tan automatically reached for a bag. Then his hand fell. This project was going to be a lot of work. A lot of hope that might only be dashed. Tan wasn't sure he could take much more of that.

Leaving the candy behind, he grabbed the closest trifold and headed for the register.

Along with the start of junior year, fall arrived with a chill to the air and a graying of the sky. It was harder to avoid each other. Despite the in-law suite, the house wasn't that big. One living room, one garden, one small kitchen. If she was studying on the couch, he went to his room until one of their parents showed up from work. If she was in the garden, he stayed in the kitchen.

On Winter's end, she'd started to dress in baggier clothes since prom. Was that for his benefit . . . to cool things off? If so, it didn't help. Winter's baggy clothes couldn't hide how pretty she was. Or the fact that Tan knew what her mouth tasted like. And every month, Winter seemed to get hotter, a feat he would have thought impossible, and that turned the weirdness up another notch.

But the good thing was, Winter's and Tan's parents were home-bodies. Having them around was a good buffer. The three of them loved weeding the garden and cooking elaborate meals together. Their families ate dinner together around their modest dining table almost every night. You didn't exactly think about kissing someone when her mom was asking you to pass the potatoes.

Tonight, they'd cooked a particularly elaborate meal. Everyone dug in as Sana prattled on about how she was teaching Morse code to her classmates in kindergarten. After Mom cleared the plates, Dad brought out a lemon meringue pie. He cut huge slices and dished them out.

"Is something going on?" Tan asked suspiciously.

"Just because I made pie? Does that mean something is going on?" Dad brushed a slight dusting of flour off his forehead, pretending to be wounded.

"Yes," Tan and Sana said together.

Their parents exchanged a three-way smile.

"We have an announcement," Mom said. "We've decided to go on vacation—together!"

"Vacation?" Tan choked down his sweet and tart mouthful. He avoided looking at Winter. They'd never been on vacation together. What would they do? Wander museums? Stay in cozy hotels? Tan already knew it was a bad idea. "For what? Thanksgiving?" It was less than a month away. Time enough to divert this disaster-in-the-making.

Winter got up to grab an extra napkin and leaned against the counter. She folded her arms over her chest, wrinkling her oversize button-down shirt. Her thick black hair was pulled casually back from her face with a purple bandanna.

"Where are we going?" she asked cautiously.

"Not you guys. Us." Mom flashed the dimples that only Sana had been lucky enough to inherit. "James and I were invited to speak at a conference in Maui next week." Mom and Dad both worked at the same digital-currency exchange based in Palo Alto. "With Fannie finishing law school this quarter, we thought she could come along to celebrate. Tickets are incredibly cheap if we leave Friday."

"Friday!" Tan said, alarmed. "That's the day after tomorrow."

"Yes, we're going a few days early to enjoy the island."

"It's so thoughtful of you," said Winter's mom. Her black hair was more gray-streaked than when they'd arrived, probably because for the past few years, she'd redefined what it meant to burn the midnight oil, taking online night classes and working as a legal assistant during the day. "I haven't traveled since before Noah passed away. And I'm psyched for an excuse to spend my signing bonus." She'd landed her first job at a law firm. "More wine?" She tipped the bottle of merlot toward Mom, who held out her glass for the ruby liquid.

"We have so much to celebrate," Mom said as they clinked their glasses.

"Ahh! Seven whole days of piña coladas." Dad leaned back and stretched his long-limbed arms, showing off his favorite In-N-Out Burger shirt. "Maybe I'll pick up surfing!"

Great that they all were so happy, especially Mom, whose tea-brown eyes had crinkled at their corners with her smile. But this was not good news. If the kids weren't going on vacation with the adults, it meant he and Winter—

"You three will be on your own!" Mom said.

Tan gulped. Alone in the house with Winter. With no parent buffers, roadblocks, or distractions.

"Are you sure about this? You've never left us alone before," Tan said, hedging.

"It's not that hard to keep house with all hands on deck," Dad said.

Keeping house . . . would they have to shop for food together? Cook together?

Talk to each other? A charge crackled in the air.

It was practically like . . . well, being together for real.

This time, Tan met Winter's gaze across the kitchen. Her brows knitted together. Winter was an aspiring actor, which might explain why her face often said everything she was feeling inside. And right now, her dark brown eyes reflected all the worries Tan was feeling, too.

This was a recipe for disaster.

And he was doomed.

Chapter 3

"Tan, you and Winter will be in charge," Mom said. "Keep things tidy. Water the garden. And, most important, of course, look out for Sana."

"I don't need looking out for," Sana said with an exaggerated eye roll that took her head along with it. She was five going on eleven, with long black hair in messy braids over a pink T-shirt and jean shorts. "I'm in *kindergarten*." *Kindergarten* was where she'd picked up the eye roll. And about a dozen other irritating habits. She was constantly trying on new personas.

"You and Winter are pretty much on autopilot walking to school and activities," Dad said.

"And you're seventeen," Mom said. "You've babysat for years. The Kellers are on call if anything comes up." The Kellers were the elderly neighbors next door, on the other side of the high stone wall that ringed their house.

"It's about time you learned to take care of someone besides yourselves," Dad concluded cheerfully.

Tan popped a bite of graham cracker crust into his mouth, chewing to stall any answer. Their parents were so excited, and Winter's mom deserved this vacation more than anyone Tan knew. Winter caught his gaze and gave a tiny nod.

It was just seven days. They could make this work.

Tan forced himself to shrug, nonchalant. "We got it. Babysitting is easy."

"Especially for Sana," Winter added.

"All we need is the TV. And if Sana won't go to bed, she'll eventually pass out anyway."

"No, I won't!" Sana said.

Tan's mom opened the pantry door, then pulled out her favorite travel bag for her medications and vitamins. She smiled. "I know you'll find plenty more than TV to occupy yourselves."

A bite of Tan's pie went down hard. He chased it with a glass of water. That was exactly the problem. If they knew about The Kiss, Tan doubted they'd suggest he and Winter stay home on their own and . . . *occupy themselves*. Their parents simply never considered that they could be interested in each other. Possibly because Tan started dating Rebecca just a few weeks after the Woos moved in.

"I don't need a babysitter. *I'll* babysit Winter and Tan," Sana declared with a ferocious scowl. Dad ruffled her hair, laughing, as everyone began to stand up and clear the table.

Tan laughed, too, a little relieved. Of course Sana would keep things in check. Nothing could happen while they were busy babysitting. Right?

"We'll work it into the schedule," Winter said confidently, stacking plates. She was much more the typical Palo Alto High School student than Tan: juggling classes with not just yearbook, but volleyball and theater. Tan was more streamlined—he enjoyed the satisfaction of cracking a cipher and the way patterns emerged in cryptography when he was sinking his mind into a complex problem. But between the two of them, she was the one who kept to her calendar. "We can leave ten minutes early to drop Sana off at school."

"We can get dinner at Panda Express." Tan carried their emptied glasses to the sink, where Dad was rinsing dishes. "Best thing about where we live."

"Panda Express?" Winter scoffed, amused.

"All the Asian fast food—give me a little credit." He smiled. Bantering with Winter felt a little like old times. And they were safe in the presence of their parents. Tan set the glasses by Dad's elbow. "It's only a week. What could go wrong?"

All Thursday, the house buzzed with a frenetic blur of activity. Tan returned from school to find Dad cooking an enormous oxtail stew to ration out while he was away. Fannie was meticulously polishing every surface and vacuuming the floors. Mom was processing the backlog of paper ads and envelopes addressed to their double-lucky 88 Grove Avenue, a single-story bungalow with blue shutters, ringed by a stone wall that hid it from view.

Mom and Dad were American-born, like Tan. They swore they weren't really into Chinese numerology. But they'd bought 88 anyway, and for the most part, it *had* been a lucky place. It had brought Winter Woo and her mom into their lives.

Now, with their parents' readying for their trip tomorrow, Tan would take any shred of luck that came his way.

Tan fished out Winter's unfinished math homework on the floor under the couch. She'd have missed it and not turned it in. They were all slightly absent-minded. Probably a reason their families got along. They could put up with each other's forgetfulness. She'd gotten the first problem wrong. He stuck a Post-it tab to it and jotted a tip: *prime numbers*.

"Tan, let's run through the emergency contacts," Mom called from the home office. He headed over and paused in the doorway. She was sitting at the desk in Dad's oversize shirt and her old sweatpants. "Come in. You're blocking all the light," Mom joked.

Tan moved in. He'd shot up a few inches this year, and at five-foot-eleven—six feet if he counted his thick, slightly overgrown hair—he was now officially the tallest in the house. He dropped into a seat at the big, rectangular table his parents shared.

Their home office was lemon-scented from a recent cleaning, tidy and uncluttered. DigitalWallet, where they worked, was like a very safe bank for converting digital currencies into cash. All their work was in software, so all they needed was a laptop each. And a big screen, because Mom's eyesight was going bad from too many hours before it. But contained in each laptop was the technology to securely process trillions of dollars a day. It was pretty impressive.

Still, Tan couldn't help feeling a little resentful. It wasn't easy having parents who were leaders in their field. They'd come from humble roots. His grandparents had emigrated from Shandong Province in China to San Francisco without a penny to their name. His parents had built on their sacrifices. They had great jobs. They even got invited to speak at conferences in *Hawaii*.

Even their marriage of twenty years was great. They debated big ideas, fought, made up. Mom was in a lifelong battle with depression, and Dad supported her against the dark clouds that pressed in on her, despite all the good things going on in her life. She was surviving. They were best friends.

Every generation was supposed to do better than the one that came before. Tan wanted to make his parents proud. But deep down, Tan was sure he would never live up to them. Who could?

"Are you attending the internship fair at Menlo School tomorrow?" Mom asked.

"I'm going to enter the science fair in a few weeks," Tan reminded Mom. "It's basically the same thing." Only way more work.

"You should take every opportunity you can. Which includes sending out résumés and applications."

"Right," Tan said. "So you've said." And so had Winter.

It wasn't that Tan *didn't* want a summer internship in cryptography. He did. The prospect of getting to do mind-bending challenges and cracking ciphers for a living was thrilling.

But trying to crack the big bad world of internships—walking aisles of recruiters assessing and finding him not good enough—was not his top choice for how to spend an evening.

"The fair will expand your horizons," Mom said. "There are lots of jobs out there besides what your dad and I do at DigitalWallet."

"Didn't Dad say DigitalWallet owes me a big bonus for solving their problems?" he asked. "That time we were playing with the Go stones at the coffee table?" Games were their thing. He was only twelve at the time, and he wasn't even sure what he'd done—something related to prime numbers—but Dad had slapped his own leg and said to Mom, *That's it!*

Now Mom smiled. "Yes, you solved one of the biggest encryption issues for DigitalWallet. Dad still reminds our colleagues. They call it the Tan Encryption Scheme."

"Ha," Tan said. He didn't even know what problem he'd solved—it was all top secret. Like the CIA. Which was Tan's secret dream job, not that he'd even consider applying. That was so pie in the sky that he was embarrassed to admit it, even to himself. "So if I'm so valuable, maybe DigitalWallet should just hand me a job on a silver platter. They don't even have to pay me."

"Very funny." Mom didn't bat an eye.

That was the thing about his parents. Some of his classmates would get internships at places like Stanford and Meta through their parents, who were on the faculty or worked there. But Tan's parents absolutely refused to give him a referral or recommendation. They wanted him to do it the pure way. So if he was going to get an internship in cryptography, he was on his own.

"You wanted to give me the rundown of emergency contacts?" Tan said pointedly.

"Yes, you may change the subject—for now." She flashed a smile and went through the list—the pediatrician, the dentist, the pastor.

"That should be everyone," Mom concluded. "And here's the list of hotels and Airbnbs we'll be staying at each night. We're moving around quite a bit. That's your dad for you."

"Can't keep a good Dad down," Tan quipped.

He followed Mom back to the living room, where Dad was rolling two big suitcases from their storage shed. Winter was there now, helping Sana with homework. One hand played with her silver necklace, a heart charm, a gift from her father. She waved her calc homework at Tan and mouthed thanks, then dropped her gaze. Tan was glad she'd found it.

"If you need to reach us, call," Dad said as Mom hung her lists on the fridge door. "We're not bringing our laptops or checking email."

"Your garden doesn't have a cell phone," Tan observed, fetching a pencil stuck under the rug. "It's going to need you most."

Dad laughed. "True enough." Dad's deepest passion was coaxing his garden to grow, despite the perpetual California drought. "Thank you in advance for looking out for it."

"Email is a new evil in the world," Fannie declared, snapping the lid onto a Tupperware container. "It takes so little for someone else to create an obligation for you to respond."

Tan's mom gave Fannie an affectionate squeeze. "I'm *so* glad we're getting off the grid. A parents' getaway, a kids' week off. Or maybe it's the other way around?"

She smiled at Tan, who dropped his pencil at the same time Winter, across the room, dropped hers. He ducked to pick it up, schooling his face back to neutral. By the time he'd straightened again, Winter had returned to helping Sana.

Winter knocked on Tan's door that evening, a first since the night of prom. Tan let her in. Her eyes darted about the room, skirting Tan and his bed. She clutched her notepad, which was covered in six-digit numbers. Which meant she was nervous.

When Winter's father passed away, Winter and her mom had discovered they didn't have his iPhone passcode. Not because her parents hadn't shared passwords and bank accounts—they had—but for some reason, her mom hadn't known that one.

To their surprise, Apple apparently didn't provide passcodes, even to an heir or next of kin. The phone held precious family photos, but after nine failed attempts, they were on the verge of a permanent lockout. Nowadays, trying to come up with the passcode was more of a tic for Winter—and a barometer for Tan for how she was feeling.

"Thanks for the tip on prime numbers," she said now.

"No charge."

Her lips twitched, like she was trying not to smile. "We need to set some ground rules for while they're gone."

Ground rules. Tan dropped into his chair, which scraped against the floor.

"Sure," he said, feigning nonchalance. But inside, he was anything but. Their last encounter in his room had been The Kiss.

The night everything changed—and nothing changed.

Winter's eyes fell onto his rumpled sheets. Her cheeks pinked, and she chewed on her plump bottom lip, drawing Tan's attention to it.

"Ground rules. Totally agree," he said.

"We should divide and conquer," Winter said. "Pickup, bedtime, mornings. One person cooks, the other person sets the table, then we take turns cleaning. What do you think?"

Was this for making sure they kept apart? He was pretty sure it was, with bonus points for efficiency.

"Great. I'll take the first day's shift." He made himself yawn and busied himself fixing his comforter.

"We'll alternate days."

"I'll do trash duty," he said. Winter hated that one.

"Oh. Thanks." Her eyes fluttered, surprised. "Then I'll do dish duty. You hate getting cold food on your hands." True, too. Winter straightened suddenly. "Hey, Mr. Lee."

Dad rapped on the doorway. "Ready to adult for a week?"

Why were his ears burning? He and Winter were standing six feet apart with his door open, for crying out loud. Tan held up two fingers in a pledge to Dad. "No wild parties. No burning down the house. Scout's honor."

"You guys just please have an amazing time," Winter said. "I haven't seen Mom this excited since before Dad passed away."

"We're *all* excited," Tan's dad said. "What do you guys want from Hawaii?"

"Macadamia nuts," Winter and Tan said together. They glanced at each other, surprised. Macadamia nuts were Tan's favorite. He hadn't known Winter liked them, too.

Winter gave him a strained smile. "Have a good night," she said, and slipped off.

Dad took Winter's spot in the doorway, leaning on it in the same pose. "They're so terrific," Dad said. "Winter's been like a big sister to Sana. And I'm glad you two get along. That was our one worry when we decided to rent to them. Since you're classmates. I know you're not *best* friends, but you've made it work, and I'm proud of you both."

Not best friends. Was that how they came across? Maybe because they both worked so hard to hide what had been there.

Or maybe it wasn't actually there.

"Winter's cool," Tan said evasively.

"One thing, though, Tan. With you and Winter."

Tan straightened. "Yeah?"

"Winter's a great girl. But you have to remember your role. This is your house."

"Yes, I know," Tan said guiltily.

"Winter would never complain, but I don't want you letting her do the lion's share of the work while you play D&D online with your friends. We appreciate how much she pitches in, and she gets along so well with Sana. But *you're* the big brother, and the buck stops with you, especially when it comes to taking care of your own little sister. Okay?"

His shoulders relaxed a fraction. *This* was what Dad wanted to remind him about.

"Got it, Dad," Tan said. "The buck stops with me."

Dad picked up an empty can of seltzer water. "Maybe tidy up in here a bit?" he suggested.

After Dad left, Tan shelved a pile of books and moved laundry into a hamper. On his desk, behind his 8x8 Rubik's cube, he found the silk corsage he'd bought for Rebecca for the winter formal, because she was allergic to flowers. A corsage he'd never used.

He fingered the petals, feeling guilty. They smelled like jasmine—like Rebecca. He hadn't even realized it was still there. Had Winter noticed it that night? Along with the other Rebecca artifacts strewn around his room? Like the *Business as a Calling* book on his shelf, which he'd tried and failed to read several times. And the stuffed penguin she'd gotten him because he'd said the tux he'd rented for the formal made him look like one.

No wonder Winter had fled.

Tan collected everything he could find of Rebecca in his room. He dumped it all in a box and drove it over to Goodwill, which was just down El Camino Real.

He felt a little lighter as he returned home. He was worrying way too much about being stuck alone in the house with Winter. By the time the week was up, he was resolved to have moved on from all relationship woes. He would double down on his science fair project and be ready to hit his presentation out of the ballpark. And all the angst of the past year would be just like the penguin—left in a cardboard box at Goodwill.

Chapter 4

Friday morning, Tan's door burst open and Sana flew in, already dressed in her candy-print shirt and pink shorts, her pink headband in her hair.

"We're home alone!" She leaped onto his legs, narrowly missing him in the wrong place. "Let's go to Barnes and Noble for a cookie!"

"Too early," Tan groaned. "Nothing's open."

"Winter, wake up!" She darted off, yelling, her feet pounding on the floorboards.

Their parents had left just an hour before. Tan was tempted to fall back asleep, but Dad had said the buck stopped with him. And today was his day to watch Sana.

He hauled his ass out of bed and reached the living room just as Sana bumped into one of the elegant lamps Mom had found in a hotel rummage sale. As it tipped forward, Tan darted in to catch it.

"No tag in the house," he chided.

"Hide-and-seek, then!" she said, already darting off.

"No, wait! School first!" Tan moved to grab for her, but his arms were tangled in the lamp cord. Sana vanished down the hallway. Damn. He set the lamp back in place. On the coffee table was his dog-eared *Book of Codes*, which he'd read voraciously since he was six. Sana was now getting into it, starting with the simplest of substituting numbers for letters.

Under it, a brochure caught his eye: Shakespeare's Globe, covered in Winter's six-digit numbers. Wait, what? A summer theater camp . . . *in London?*

That was big. Why hadn't she mentioned this?

He frowned. Was this how it was going to shake out? Would they stay polite strangers until they graduated from Palo Alto High? Then he would go one way and Winter the other, and that would be the end?

"Can't find me!" Sana sang out from the direction of the hallway. Tan returned the brochure and went after Sana, but she had vanished.

Sana was a good hider. She moved between spots after he'd passed through an area. And she was so small that she could hide anywhere—under a bed, in any closet. Once, he'd even found her clinging like a monkey to the inside of the laundry chute that dropped a flight down into a half cellar outside. The whole incident had triggered a panic attack in Mom.

"Sana!" he yelled, growing impatient. "We have to go to school. You'll make us late." He was taking a science test first period. He couldn't afford to be late. "Sana!"

No answer. He gritted his teeth and kept searching. All the usual places were empty. His parents' bathroom cupboard. The broom closet. The pantry behind the big bag of rice that was large enough to shield her entire body.

Winter came out of the bathroom, her body wrapped to her armpits in a *very* short blue towel that barely passed her hips. Her hair was darkened and damp from a shower.

"Oi!" Tan yelled.

"Tan!" Startled, she ducked back out of sight. He closed his eyes, trying to get his body under control. But he couldn't unsee her long, bare legs or ignore the fact that she was totally naked under that excuse for a towel.

"I thought you were gone already!" she said, poking just her head around the bathroom door. She rubbed a second towel—he hoped it was a second towel—against her hair. "Shouldn't you be dropping off Sana now? You'll be late."

The scent of her soap and strawberry shampoo wafted over him, tantalizing and teasing.

"Sana's playing hide-and-seek," he snapped.

"Oh boy. I'll be right out."

He headed out the patio doors. Maybe he should crash at a friend's house—except Sana wouldn't want to sleep anywhere but her own bed. And leaving his own house because of Winter was just plain immature.

In the garden, he searched up and down all the rows of raised berry beds, in case Sana was lying flat on the ground beside them, silently shaking with laughter.

"Sana! Come out *now*."

Winter joined him, dressed in a striped sweater over jeans, and tucked her feet into a pair of straw slippers. Easier on Tan's eyes, though not by much. He averted his gaze and kept moving.

"Sana!"

"Sana, we aren't playing right now," Winter called. "We need to get to school on time."

No answer. Winter moved toward the back, where the washing machines sat in their sunken space.

"Where is she?" Tan was starting to worry. Would Sana have left the house? Normally, she wouldn't. But she was so excited to be on their own, imagining she was setting their own rules, and he'd never actually mentioned that she needed to stay put.

"Tan, I found her!" Winter called from the shed.

Tan rushed to her side. Their arms brushed. Her skin was heated from her shower. A shovel clattered to the ground as she jerked out of his way. For him to see better.

In the shed, lying in a fetal position on a bag of sunflower seeds and clutching her Hello Kitty doll, Sana had fallen fast asleep.

Tan was thirty minutes late after dropping Sana off at her elementary school. Since he needed to pick Sana up this afternoon, he had to reschedule his science test for an open period on Monday. But at least school was orderly. People his age, synchronized by the ringing of bells and everyone filing in the right directions. He didn't run into Winter, since they rarely frequented the same corridors at the same time. At lunch, he hung out with the guys he'd been eating with since first grade.

"You all going to the internship fair at Menlo tonight?" Neil asked the table.

"Yeah. Should be a good one," Will said. "You, Tan?"

He'd completely, conveniently forgotten about the fair. Or deliberately put it out of his mind. Maybe he could ask Winter to swap evenings with him.

"I'll do my best," he said.

Winter was leading Yearbook Club after school, so Tan picked up Sana on his own. This part was easy. He'd picked her up for the past few days, and they had the routine down. Sana rushed out in her candy top to hug him, squeezing him around the knees and tipping her head back to grin up at him.

"Hey, scamp." He tugged on her braids. She was so much smaller than him, not surprising given their twelve-year age gap. But the bright pink flush on her face, especially around her eyes, caused him to stop short.

"Oh no," he said. "We forgot the sunscreen."

"And my hat," she reminded him. "I was the only kid without one."

Damn. The California sun was relentless. Sunscreen and a hat were necessities. Sana must have been out on the playground unprotected all day.

"Does it hurt?" he asked.

"A little," she admitted, touching her nose. "We forgot my water bottle, too."

"I'm so sorry." He'd probably caused ten years of damage to her skin today. "We won't forget next week." He hadn't realized so much went into the morning routine. Tooth brushing hadn't happened, either. At least they'd grabbed breakfast—apple cereal bars their parents had left on the table.

Tan dug his own tube of sunscreen from his backpack and knelt to smear the cream liberally over her face. She wrinkled her cheeks under his hand, making an already-hard job—who knew her face had so many parts to it?—even harder.

"It stings!" She slapped at his hand.

"I'm sorry. But you need it." He hoped he'd gotten all of her. Capping the tube, he took her hand and headed for her favorite playground in the park.

"Can I play *Candy Crush*?" she asked.

His parents didn't like Sana spending time on his phone. He'd forgotten sunscreen, but at least he could put his foot down here.

"You should go play," he said, and ignored her pouting until she ran off to make a half dozen new friends on the jungle gym.

Winter wasn't around when Tan and Sana returned, which meant she was studying in her room. Before The Kiss, she'd have been working in the living room, and he'd have joined her. Now he could feel the wall of air between them like a physical barrier. He was determined to keep it that way. Divide and conquer.

Tan headed for the kitchen. Dad's big oxtail stew full of carrots and potatoes would last them at least a few days. All Tan needed to do was heat it up and set the table for three instead of six. Tan pulled the cast-iron pot out of the fridge, lifted it onto the stove, and turned on the burner.

He heard a loud crash from Sana's room.

"Sana, are you okay?" He rushed to her door, his bare feet slipping on the silk carpet.

Inside her room, Sana's big shelf of games and books had tipped over and was lying at an angle against her bed. A mess of plastic game pieces and picture books littered her comforter and floor. Sana herself was sitting on her beanbag chair, her arms around her legs and her face hidden.

Tan went to her first. "Are you hurt?"

She lifted her face. "I broke it!" she wailed. "I wanted my piggy bank."

She pointed to the smashed remains of her porcelain pig. A few dollars lay scattered among the shards. He was relieved she was intact, at least.

"Don't touch it, or you'll cut yourself," he said, moving toward her shelf. "What did you want to buy?"

"I want to go to Barnes and Noble for a cookie," she said in a small voice.

He let out a breath. "I have Dad's credit card and some cash Mom left us. We don't need to raid your piggy bank."

"Can we go now?"

He was wiped out. "Tomorrow."

He took hold of her shelf and righted it. A splintered crack now pierced its top corner. All this for a cookie, but then again, the bookstore was her favorite place in the world. Tan's, too. They'd spent most of their childhood reading in the kids' section. That was where he'd gotten his *Book of Codes*, which was now lying on Sana's floor. Tan retrieved it and set it on her dresser, out of harm's way.

"You could have been hurt," he said. "Ask me for help next time. That's why I'm here."

She bunched her lips into a bow, stubborn. "I can do it myself."

He groaned. "You know, Rebecca always said that." That was Rebecca: living in her own apartment without parents and attending school in Palo Alto—*I can do it myself.* Tan had been the exception to her independence, or at least it seemed that way.

"Why doesn't Rebecca like you anymore?" Sana asked.

Tan blinked, surprised by the question. Sana had met Rebecca the few times Rebecca had accompanied Tan to pick Sana up after preschool. He guessed he hadn't ever explained to Sana that they weren't together anymore.

Why, indeed, was the big question. Maybe he wasn't smooth

enough. Savvy enough. Rich enough. Ambitious enough. Whatever the criteria, the bottom line was, *Tan* wasn't enough. Which was why he'd gotten ghosted for months, oblivious to the fact that it was deliberate.

"I don't know," he said. "She ran around with important people. Kids of diplomats and business leaders. Maybe I'm not that important."

"Everything okay?" Winter appeared in the doorway, her school-issued laptop under her arm. She was wearing her oversize, ugly paisley pajamas, the ones Tan used to make fun of for making her look like a sloth that had been through a lawn mower. Tan appreciated that she was wearing it.

Her eyes grew wide at the sight of the chaos. Then she disappeared. Tan was gathering toys when she returned with a dustpan and broom. The piggy bank was swept away. She brought with her a fresh scent, like a breeze through the camphor trees. Her back was to him, and his arms itched to wrap themselves around her waist and bury his nose in her thick hair. Instead, he reloaded games onto the shelves, giving her a wide berth. They worked in a strained silence. Alone together.

"I can handle it," he said finally. "It's my day."

She dropped the dustpan by the door, no argument. "Maybe Sana can help."

"Yeah, I should get her." But speaking of his sister—

"Where is she?" Tan straightened suddenly.

"Oh no," Winter said.

It had been too quiet for too long. Tan brushed by Winter as he darted out the door and found the hallway full of smoke.

"The stew!" He rushed into the kitchen and grabbed the smoking pot off the stove. "Yow!" His hand stung, and he let go quickly. He turned off the flame, found a pot holder, and inspected the damage. Dad's stew was charred black and ruined. All their food for the next few days. The smoke detector began to wail overhead.

"Ugh!" Tan said.

"Just go find Sana." Winter was already opening the windows. Tan found Sana in the living room, where she'd dumped out a pink board game. Pink eye patches and wooden pirate ships were everywhere. And Sana herself was busy decorating Tan's science fair board with stickers, glue, and glitter.

"Sana, that's for my science fair project!" Tan yelled, louder than he meant.

Sana startled. She looked up at him with wide brown eyes. "I was trying to help."

"Well, it's *not* helpful." If he were less exhausted, he would have been more patient. But his burnt hand stung and so did his eyes from the smoke, and when he was hungry, he got irritated, and trying not to be around Winter was stressful, and now he'd have to go buy another board and redo the entire setup. "Your help is making everything worse."

Her lips trembled, and her eyes filled with tears. "I was waiting for you to play Pirates in Pink with me," she said in a quavery voice. A tear spilled.

Damn.

"Sana, I'm sorry," he said, but it was too late.

"I miss Mom and Dad!" Sana burst into loud sobs and ran to her room. Tan groaned. Divide and conquer clearly wasn't working. Sana was much bigger than a one-person job.

Tan returned to the kitchen, where Winter stood on a chair,

resetting the smoke detector. She climbed down as he entered, slipping her feet back into her bunny slippers. Avoiding his gaze, she collected her laptop and notebook from the dining table.

Then she paused before him, her arms tightening over her things. He was in her way, blocking the doorway.

"Sorry," he mumbled, and stepped aside.

But as she started past him, he put out a hand and touched her arm.

"Winter."

She jumped and faced him. They were in the doorway, not touching, but it felt like they were jammed together. The shock of their eye contact made him falter.

Why was this so hard?

"I need reinforcements," he said finally.

Chapter 5

Saturday morning was fun. Winter took Sana to her dance class while Tan went to martial arts. He was surprised when Winter appeared in a white sundress halfway through his class. She was holding Sana's hand, and took a seat among the parents and siblings. Sana must have insisted, or maybe Winter had suggested it.

Either way, Tan was forced to endure Winter watching him spar with the senior instructor, who routinely kicked everyone's ass. At least Tan was a black belt, first degree. He got in a few solid kicks . . . but then Tan was suddenly staring at his feet on the mat. His neck was trapped, noosed by an iron arm. He struggled to free himself from the headlock. He threw an elbow at the chest, gave a sharp twist, sent out a kick. His opponent hung on tight.

"A headlock is a very powerful hold," said Master Kwon belatedly. "It takes away your control. You must learn to defend yourself. Again." His opponent released him, and Tan gasped for air.

For the next half hour, Tan died of embarrassment as he got muscled into a headlock again and again under Winter's polite gaze and Sana's glee.

On their way out, Tan rubbed his chafed neck. "It's easier to put someone into one than to get out of one," he said. "I did it last week when I was on the offensive."

"Sure, Tan," Sana said, sounding suspiciously like Winter. "You go right on thinking that."

Winter just smiled.

Tan suggested lunch at In-N-Out Burger, which was one of Winter's favorites. Partway through the meal, Tan's phone rang with a video call.

"It's Dad," he said, answering. His phone bloomed with a window onto a sunlit picnic table, featuring Dad in a pastel aloha shirt, Mom with a purple lei around her neck, and Fannie showing off a big plastic bowl filled with a red-and-orange-striped mound.

"Aloha!" Dad said.

"What's that?" Sana asked.

"Shave ice!" Fannie lifted it higher into view.

"How's it going over there?" Mom asked.

"All good," Tan said. Except for his sprained dignity. "We're having lunch."

"In-N-Out, I see," Fannie said, craning her neck to get a better look at them. "Winter got to pick, I take it."

"All the food groups," Winter teased. "French fries *and* ketchup."

"Sana, are you getting enough rest?" Mom asked. "Don't forget your nap, or you'll turn into a monster after dinner."

"I'm not tired," Sana insisted. "No one else in kindergarten naps on weekends anymore."

"What are you up to?" Tan asked.

"We're headed on an overnight hike tonight," said Dad. A waiter arrived with whole pineapples on a tray, garnished with little paper umbrellas. Dad stuck one in Mom's hair, and Fannie took a photo.

"We're getting a lot of great photo moments over here," she said, then laughed.

Tan's parents worked hard, and he rarely saw them acting goofy like this. It was weird but nice. "All right, have fun, kids!" Tan said.

"Wait, that's my line," said Dad. "Glad you guys have everything in hand," he said, and they hung up laughing.

"Well, at least they're not worried," Winter said. Then she frowned. "Hey, I just realized—weren't you supposed to go to the internship fair last night?"

"I decided not to go," he answered. Sometime between burning dinner and asking her for help. Or maybe he never really intended to go. He wasn't feeling up to more failure at the moment.

"Why not?" She crumpled their paper wrappings, surprisingly upset. "It was a really good opportunity. If I'd remembered it sooner, I'd have taken Sana duty."

"Chances were low anyway."

"That's not true. You're really good at cryptography and ciphers. It's so easy for you, so you don't even realize how hard it is for the rest of the population."

"I still have the science fair in a few weeks." Although his trifold getting ruined was a good excuse not to enter after all.

Winter's frown deepened, as though she were reading his mind. "Are you actually going to submit a project? You haven't exactly made much progress."

"I said I would, didn't I?" He wiped ketchup off the table, avoiding her gaze. "If I get this presentation together."

"Tan, it's your chance to get the summer internship you've been wanting. Sorry, I know I sound like your mom. But she's pretty savvy."

"How do you know what I've been wanting?" He genuinely wanted to know.

"Oh please. I know you. You get this starry-eyed look whenever you talk about the CIA."

"I do not," he said automatically.

"The three-way cardboard display is so overdone anyway," Winter continued. "Why don't you do a video instead? You can play it on a loop for people who come by."

"How would that work?"

"I can interview you. I'll be the host."

"Oh," Tan said, surprised. A format like that would never have occurred to him. That was the thing about him and Winter. They thought about the world so differently. She was constantly catching him off guard with good ideas that shifted the ground under him a bit. "You'd make it so easy. You're so good on camera."

Winter's cheeks pinked, but she looked pleased. "I'm good at getting people to loosen up. We can work on it during Sana's nap?"

Why not? They needed something to *occupy themselves* when Sana wasn't doing that job. What better way to add ice to their relationship than a science fair project on encryption? It didn't mean he was committing to enter . . . although maybe that wouldn't be fair to Winter.

"If you help me, you need to get credit for it," he said tentatively. All science fair projects counted as extra credit in their science classes, even if it wasn't in the same field.

"I won't argue with that," she said.

"I colored on your cardboard," Sana pointed out. "I should get credit, too!"

"I wouldn't go *that* far," Tan growled.

"I'm not tired," Sana insisted when they reached the house. "I don't need naps anymore." Sana's eyes couldn't be more wide awake.

"Fine," Tan said. "Don't nap."

"Can we play hide-and-seek?"

"Didn't we play already?" Tan groaned.

"You promised!" Sana said.

Tan couldn't remember promising, but in Sana's case, everything Tan had ever said in her entire life was a permanent standing promise. And she held him to it: games, outings, piggybacks.

"Winter and I need to work. You can play in the living room. But stay out of trouble . . . please."

Sana executed her head-eye-roll. "I don't get into trouble," she said witheringly.

Tan and Winter sat at the coffee table—Tan on the love seat, Winter in the plush armchair—where they could keep an eye on her while they worked. Sana galloped her My Little Ponies over the green silk rug. That seemed safe enough.

"No rivers," Winter warned.

Tan looked up. What did she mean? Clearly Sana understood, because her mouth opened in a surprised O.

"Okay," Sana said.

"Did you just avert a flood?" Tan asked.

"It's my superpower," Winter answered. "Saving our asses."

He smiled. "All right. Let's do this." He opened his laptop and positioned his screen between him and Winter. They mapped out their presentation, starting with types of ciphers and where they were commonly used in modern technology: cell phones, laptops, espionage, banks.

"How hard do you think it would be to come up with a program to hack a cell phone password?" Winter asked.

"Like your dad's? Pretty hard," Tan admitted. "Any luck with cracking it?"

She shook her head. "I just spin my wheels on the same numbers. His birthday, my birthday, their anniversary. I even tried figuring out his astrological numbers, but he wasn't into those. Wow, Sana."

Tan followed her gaze. A whole Wild West diorama was spread across the floor, with ponies marching under the microsuede couches and chairs, along with more Oreo cookie crumbs than Tan had ever seen.

"Sana, when did you get the Oreos?"

"It's the dirt, stupid," Sana answered.

Tan grimaced. The kindergarten word of the week, and the nicest one so far, actually. Tan never knew when one would come out. He wasn't sure Sana always understood them, either.

"We can't leave food lying around," he said. "The ants, remember? Can you clean up?"

For an answer, she thrust a piece of paper into his hands, printed in her large, kindergarten script. It was a series of numbers, separated by spaces:

23 5 14 5 22 5 18 23 5 14 20 20 15 2 1 18 14 5 19 1 14 4 14 15 2 12 5!!!

A cipher—the simplest one. Easy enough to decode. "'We never went to Barnes and Noble,'" he translated.

"That's right," Sana said accusingly. Winter made a small sound, like a laugh or a snort. Tan set the paper down, feeling guilty. Sana was right. He'd said they'd go today.

"I promise we'll go before Mom and Dad get back," he said. "Crumbs, please?"

She lay out on the carpet, arms spread to either side like a snow angel, and closed her eyes.

"I'm tired," she said. "Mom said I need to nap."

Sana woke hungry a few hours later. This time, Tan was ready with a frozen pizza dinner, baked to perfection, thanks to Winter setting a timer. They popped popcorn and settled on the couch with the big glass bowl to binge-watch a few Disney movies.

Halfway through *Aladdin*, Sana finally fell asleep with her head pillowed on Tan's knee. His foot tingled, but he didn't dare move. Reaching over her body, he poked Winter gently on the shoulder. Winter's lashes fluttered as she pulled her attention from the screen.

"Should we wake her? Make her brush her teeth?" Winter whispered.

Mom and Dad would. But Sana was finally quiet. If they woke her, who knew how long it would take to get her to go back to bed?

"We can brush her twice in the morning," he finally decided.

Winter lifted Sana gently and carried her into her bedroom. Relieved for the brief break, Tan changed into pajamas. He brushed his teeth, although it was early to be getting ready for bed. But at least they were finally getting babysitting under control.

Back in the empty living room, he stabled Sana's ponies himself and shelved her box. Then he carried their empty glasses into the kitchen.

"You know, I remember my mom asking me to help," he said to Winter, who was wiping down the kitchen table. "Pick up my laundry, put my dishes in the sink. I said I was tired, and she did it for me, too." Not because she wanted to spoil him. But because she was busy, and it was easier.

"How old were you?" Winter rinsed her rag out in the sink.

"Fifteen?" he guessed, only half-joking. She snorted. "Sadly, it might be true." He started to unload the hot, clean dishes. "Rebecca used to say—"

He stopped. Winter's eyes turned a colder shade of amber. He hadn't meant to mention Rebecca, but she'd just popped to mind. And with Winter, Tan usually said what was on his mind—at least, before prom he did.

"What did Rebecca used to say?" she asked with an edge to her voice.

"Never mind," he said.

Winter sniffed and moved to the dining table, where her laptop was playing a Taylor Swift song. It was opened to a bunch of green designer purses, which wasn't really her thing. She didn't even carry one. Just her JanSport backpack. He followed her, resting his hands on the table beside her.

"I'm over her," he said quietly. "Really, Winter."

"Are you?" Her tone was disbelieving. "She disappeared on you for four months and never bothered to let you know she was okay. And you're still talking about her! Every few weeks."

"I ruined her life," Tan said. "She wanted to stay here in Palo Alto, remember?"

"But you didn't ruin her life," Winter said. "If anyone did, her parents did. They're the ones who made her go home."

Tan winced with the memory even now.

When Rebecca's parents visited town for winter break, Tan had assumed they'd want to meet the boyfriend. Wouldn't any parent? Tan was pretty open with his parents, and he'd assumed Rebecca was the same.

She'd hesitated. He didn't pick up on it. She'd insisted on buying him a $5,000 suit to wear when he met them, charging her credit card without batting an eye over his protests. But that dinner never got scheduled. So when he spotted her and her parents heading into a restaurant, he'd crashed it—in his usual worn jeans and T-shirt. He hadn't thought it was a big deal, and he'd seized the chance to meet them. Why not?

Turned out she knew her own parents better than he did.

"They didn't just make her go home," Tan said now.

"Because they thought they'd lost control of her. You know. Headstrong daughter with a secret boyfriend on the wrong side of the ocean. Springing you on them just confirmed they'd lost hold of her. It wasn't about you. It was about them and her."

"Maybe." He'd searched frantically for her until April—lost fifteen pounds, barely slept—until he'd finally tracked her down under her Chinese name, which he hadn't even known existed. She was snugly living at home in Shanghai and dating a college student with a British accent.

If he were honest, Tan was glad Rebecca was gone. As much as he had admired her, he knew she was trouble. Her world and his were too far apart. He had felt a huge sense of relief when he finally understood they were broken up.

"We don't have to talk about her," Tan suggested now.

"You brought her up." Winter returned to her laptop, her back stiff. "Honestly, when you were dating, you became a different person. Like . . . a doormat."

"A doormat?"

"Yeah, like you were in . . . a perpetual headlock—"

"What? I was not—"

"And sometimes, I still think you're in her headlock."

"I'm *not* in a headlock!"

So she thought he was a doormat. All this time. And she was probably annoyed by his inability to do basic things like show up to an internship fair or properly take care of Sana.

Tan watched her work. A suspicion dawned on him. What if, all this time, their landlord-tenant relationship really *had* just been an excuse? Winter's way of letting him down easily? After all, he'd been so clueless about Rebecca and how she really felt about him. He'd chased her all over the virtual map, convinced she was trying to find him . . . and he'd been dead wrong. Not Tan's finest hour.

And the lesson learned was: Tan had no idea how to read girls.

Maybe Winter's asking him to prom was just her standing by him. Making sure he didn't stay sunk in a bleak pit of depression, because she was a good friend like that. It was never meant to be.

He hung on to that. Better a certain shutting of the door in his heart, locking it tight, instead of losing himself as he did with Rebecca. He was safer this way. Everyone was better off.

He poured himself a glass of cold water, then found himself watching her scroll through more purses. For a play she was going to be in? For herself? With Winter, these days, everything felt encrypted, and he was tired of not knowing what was going on in her life.

"What are you doing?" he asked, wanting to decrypt at least one small mystery.

She paused, fingers hovering over the keys. "I'm looking for a graduation gift for my mom. I want something special, but I'm so bad at picking gifts, you know?"

It was like Winter to try anyway. And Tan wasn't bad at picking out gifts.

"What else does she like?" He joined her, setting his glass on a coaster.

"Food. Pretty things, like painted mugs and candles, although she doesn't like to ruin them by actually using them." She scanned the screen. "Something personal and meaningful, you know? My dad always wanted her to go to law school, but she didn't because she got pregnant with me and didn't want to miss my early years. This is a big deal."

"What about something to do with the scales of justice? She loves Greek mythology."

"Ooh, maybe a miniature she can put on her desk. She'd love that." Winter searched on a website, pulling up a few brass models. "You are sometimes, occasionally, the best."

"I try." The knuckles of her hand grazed his arm, startling the both of them. He was leaning in too close to her. Or maybe she was to him.

She pulled away, shifting her chair back. "Why don't we work on the science fair project after all?" she asked shakily.

"What do you have in mind?" His voice was shaky, too.

"We can just have a conversation. Here." She rose and got her iPhone and took her mom's usual seat, diagonally across the table from him. "I'll video us. We'll just talk about it. If we say anything good, we can edit those parts together."

"Sure," Tan said.

Winter's iPhone wore big mouse ears, unlike Tan's phone, which he'd sheathed in a plain black case. She propped it against her open laptop and turned on the camera. "All right-y, Mr. Tan Lee, you're here *live* from the Lee kitchen, and I'd love to ask you a few questions," she said with a heavy faux-British accent. "Are you game?"

Winter wasn't going to let this be a regular, boring, old presentation. No way.

"I'm game, Winter Woo," he said.

"Tell us about your beautiful mind," she said.

He choked on a sip of water. "Beautiful mind?"

"How does it work? How do you look at a code and just crack it like an egg?"

"I don't know what you mean," he said honestly.

"Tell us about your favorite puzzle."

He thought back to his favorite book of codes. "Ten thousand light bulbs are off. Ten thousand students come by. The first one flips them all on, counting one, two, three, four, etc. The second one flips every other one off—two, four, six, and so forth. The third one flips three, six, and nine—which means three goes off, six goes on, and it goes on like that until the ten thousandth student flips the ten thousandth light switch. Which way, on or off? You have ten minutes to figure it out."

Winter was laughing. "What? That's impossible."

"It's not."

"So was the ten thousandth light switched on or off?"

"You're not even trying," he chided. "If I tell you, it's like skipping to the last page of a book. You have to figure it out."

"Did *you* solve it? How old were you?"

"Yes, and ten."

"Did you switch every single light on and off all the way to ten thousand?"

"You can't in ten minutes. That's the point. There's a pattern."

"He says it so casually!" Winter moaned tragically. "But fails to realize not everyone has a brain like his. Okay. Moving on." She twitched her freckled nose at him, and he held back a laugh. "Now, with the entire universe of uncool science projects to apply your beautiful mind to—"

"Stop that!"

"—you picked—da da da *dum*—what topic?"

He was *really* having a hard time not laughing. "Encryption."

"Absolutely *fascinating*," she gushed. "What about it?"

"Well, we need it for privacy. Not just for bank stuff, but our daily lives. Like for example, my phone sort of knows everything about me. When I leave home for school, what classes I go to—"

"What time you go to the bathroom."

"Every single day. I mean, that's a lot of personal information, right?"

"TMI, for sure!"

"And over time, my phone"—he held his up—"could actually know me better than I know myself. The tech companies are always talking about how they protect your privacy, but *can we really know*? What about you, Winter Woo?" It was time to turn the tables. "Why did you agree to join my circus?"

"The honest truth is, I have always aspired to be a girl in STEM. Those girls are the *coolest*. But my dad was an English professor. My mom is a newly minted law school graduate. There isn't a mathematical bone in my body. So when my genius friend—that's you—mentioned his plans, I saw my chance. I could ride on his coattails. I could be that girl. I could, most of all, get enough extra credit to get a passing grade."

She stood and took a deep bow.

Tan applauded and whistled. He'd forgotten what a ham Winter could be. Then again, she was considering that program in London. "You're such a good actress," he said.

She ducked her head. "I'm thinking about auditioning for Eliza for the school musical next week. Hamilton's wife."

"I didn't know that. You totally should try out," he said.

"It's a huge role," she said dubiously.

"They'd be lucky to have you. And not just as an actor performing the role. Just by your being around. You have a knack for making everything fall into place."

She narrowed her eyes at him. "What do you want?"

He didn't laugh this time. "Nothing. It's just—I'm sorry I didn't know. That you were thinking of auditioning." He'd helped her practice for her last one. And they were supposed to be *friends*. That was the point of not getting together. "Do you want me to read lines for you?"

She smiled. "That would be great, actually."

Should he ask about the brochure? It wasn't his business, but he needed to know. "Was that why you were looking at that camp in London?"

"Oh, *that*." She dismissed it with a wave of her hand. "I picked up a pamphlet in the guidance counselor's office. But I've never been that far away from home. My mom won't say it, but I'm all she's got left, and . . ."

Winter reached to shut off her phone at the same time he did. Their fingers connected, setting his arm tingling. He heard her intake of breath.

And impulsively, he took her hand. It was warm. Her eyes dropped to their joined fingers, and she went still. His own eyes dropped to her mouth. The mouth that he'd felt like he would drown kissing. He *wanted* to drown in her and forget about the consequences. It had been her first kiss. For him, it had felt like the only kiss that mattered. Did she think about it even half as often as he did?

Ding-dong.

At the chime of the doorbell, he dropped her hand. They pulled apart, both blinking as if they were waking up.

"The neighbor?" Winter's cheeks were pink again. "Maybe your parents asked them to check on us."

Ding-dong.

"You get it," Winter said. She tugged on her nightgown. "I should put on, um, outdoor clothes." She slipped away, taking care not to touch him.

But he could feel her anyway.

Still dazed, Tan headed for the front door. It was one of Mom and Dad's favorite parts of this home. They'd found the slab of teakwood during their honeymoon in Bali, Indonesia, and custom-made it into this door, set with a single stained-glass panel.

Tan unlatched the lock. He took a few steadying breaths so he wasn't facing Mr. Keller so flushed and flustered. Then he swung the door open to the night.

A person stood on the doorstep, but not Mr. Keller. A girl. Drowning in an oversize black hoodie, her face barely visible inside its shadows. The lamplight lit her from behind. A girl he hadn't seen in months.

His ex, Rebecca Tseng.

Chapter 6

Rebecca was even more beautiful than Tan remembered. Thick black hair framed her smooth skin and dangling pearl earrings, along with her long lashes and cupid's bow lips. Her flawless beauty was part of the reason he'd always been so tongue-tied around her.

"What are you doing here?" he blurted.

She pushed inside past him, dropping her giant Prada purse onto the floor. Her familiar jasmine scent lingered in the air. The delicate blue dress she was wearing under her uncharacteristically casual hoodie probably cost thousands of dollars.

"Tan, who is it—oh!" Winter walked in, tugging her striped sweatshirt down over skinny jeans. She stopped abruptly at the sight of Rebecca. Her own lips turned down in a deep frown, and she combed a hand through her hair.

"I need a place to stay for a few days," Rebecca said stiffly.

She carried no suitcase. Nothing at all except her oversize leather purse. She spoke with a stronger British accent than Tan recalled her having. She'd always spoken with a slight lilt of a Chinese accent, but her command of the English language—her vocabulary especially—was better than most people, including Tan's. She'd been studying it since she was five as a kid in Shanghai. And while she was a student at Palo Alto, she'd done everything she could to embrace all things American, including adopting an American accent.

The British accent was probably because her new boyfriend was British Chinese. Tan had met him briefly over a Zoom with Rebecca while she was in Shanghai, once he'd finally tracked her down. Tan recalled lots of hard muscles and a cocky, possessive air. The new boyfriend had basically told Tan to stop stalking her. Which Tan had only been doing because he thought she was in danger.

Tan remembered his manners, finally. "Why don't you come in?" he said, although she was already inside. He closed the door and led her toward the living room. She didn't remove her beige pumps, which went against the Asian custom they all observed: keeping the outdoor dirt outside. Winter and he were always barefoot in the house.

Winter folded her arms over her chest as she followed. The irritated expression on her face told Tan she'd noticed, too.

Rebecca sank onto the couch with a sigh of relief. She leaned down to massage the back of her ankle. "I've been traveling for almost twenty-four hours. I've left home. For good."

Tan gaped at her. "You . . . ran away?"

"Did something happen?" Winter asked.

She fluttered a hand. "I needed to get away."

"From who? Your parents? Or . . . Albert?"

"Albert was a big mistake," Rebecca said grimly.

Winter was giving Tan a *look*. He tried to keep his voice down. Sana was sleeping, and the last thing they needed was for her to burst in and complicate an already complicated situation.

"Look, you can't stay here. My parents won't allow it." His parents had never said so, but he was pretty sure that was the rule for ex-girlfriends. And he was more than happy to obey. "You can crash for the night, but my parents are out and—"

"They don't have to know." She removed her hood and sank deeper into the cushions, as if she were trying to disappear into their folds. "I broke up with Albert. His fragile little ego couldn't take the blow." She touched her cheekbone with an unconscious gesture and winced slightly. "This is why I need a place to hide out. Until I figure out what to do next."

"Did he hit you?" Winter asked.

Rebecca gave her a sharp look. "Does it show?"

"No, but you—" Winter touched her own cheekbone.

"Why didn't you tell your parents what happened?" Tan was furious. Albert was twice Rebecca's weight. Twice her size. "Why are *you* on the run and he's still home?"

"I can't tell them." Rebecca shook her head, letting her black hair fall over her face. "I've tried bringing up Albert's problems before. But they think he's such a great match. They'll think it's all my fault. You've met them."

"Twice," Tan muttered. Twice was more than enough.

Her dad was a distinguished-looking man with salt-and-pepper hair and a regal bearing. At the dinner Tan crashed, Mr. Tseng had been wearing a $10,000 suit—fitting for a billionaire head of a pharmaceutical company. Her mom was youthful, more like an older sister. Despite their obvious wealth, they were what Tan's mom would have described as *delightful*—until they weren't.

Rebecca had announced they were dating, and her mother had hit her across the face—just like Albert. Bodyguards appeared out of nowhere and hustled her away. Frightened for her safety, Tan had intercepted her at the airport. His cousin Sean, a local cop, had asked Rebecca if she was leaving the country of her own free will. She'd raised her chin, looked Tan in the eye, and said yes. And they'd flown out.

"They want to send me to boarding school with Albert in the UK," Rebecca said now. "They've already planned it out." She shuddered, as if a gust of arctic wind had blasted through the living room. "You don't go from middle-class obscurity to a billionaire in your own lifetime without controlling everyone around you. Me included. Well, I'm done with them. I've blocked Albert's calls. I've blocked my parents' calls. I'm never speaking to any of them again."

"You've really left for good?" Winter asked.

"They don't know where I am. I came on a fake passport."

"What?" Tan yelped. "How'd you get that?"

"That part was easy," Rebecca said. "All it takes is money."

Tan shook his head. Rebecca had acted like everyone else at school. But she flew first-class around the world, and her parents dined with royalty. She'd always been surrounded by things he couldn't even begin to imagine or ever access. Enough money and the connections to buy a fake passport was sort of par for the course.

"If I'm lucky, my parents won't even know what country I'm in," she concluded.

"You lived here for almost five months," Winter said. "You had a boyfriend here—why wouldn't they look here?"

"I've traveled a lot," Rebecca said stiffly. "It's not like Palo Alto was my only other home, or that Tan was my only ex or even the one they knew the most about."

Tan had known she'd had other boyfriends. And in their pecking order, Tan was not that important, clearly. He'd gotten over it since. But hearing it still made him feel like gum on the sole of her shoe.

"How are you going to live?" Winter pressed. "You're still in high school."

"Can you use your credit cards?" Tan asked.

"No, I can't use them, or my father will trace me. I brought a few hundred US dollars. And I'm going to, um, sell these." From the pocket of her sweatshirt, she pulled out a red velvet pouch tied with a golden drawstring. She opened its mouth and spilled three gold coins onto her palm. Four Chinese characters surrounded a square hole in their centers. They were just a bit smaller than American quarters, the thickness of nickels and slightly misshapen, as though their edges had been worn down by different hands over the centuries.

"What are these?" Tan asked.

"Rare coins from the Tang dynasty. My father collects them. They're worth, um, about a hundred thousand dollars all together."

Tan whistled. Rebecca had always been careless with money. But stealing a hundred thousand dollars from her family—yes, it was chump change to her billionaire dad, but it was way more money than Tan had ever seen.

"It's enough to live on for the rest of the school year," Rebecca continued. "While I apply to college and figure out the rest of my life. In the meantime, I have to keep moving. So I need to sell these. As soon as possible. I've got a few contacts I can reach out to."

"Wait, why do you have to keep moving? Has your dad sent people after you?" Winter asked.

"Like security?" Tan asked sharply, remembering the bodyguards. They had been his first encounter with the Tseng empire that wasn't sugarcoated by Rebecca. He would never forget it—that moment in time when he'd realized just how vast the gulf was between her life and his, and how ignorant he'd been of it.

Rebecca lifted her chin. "All I need is a week to set myself up with a fake identity here. Then I'll head somewhere else. Los Angeles or New York maybe. Wherever I decide to go, it's probably best that you don't know." She helped herself to a buttery piece of popcorn on the coffee table. "I'm sorry to burden you, Tan. But there's nowhere else I can turn."

Tan shoved his hands into his pockets. Rebecca was the last person he wanted in his house. But he couldn't just turn her away at this late hour. Ex-girlfriend aside, hospitality was a religion to his parents, and they'd indoctrinated him, too. He could board her overnight. But in the morning, she'd have to be on her way.

"When's the last time you ate?" he asked.

She gave him a grateful look. "Yesterday, I think. I was too nervous on the flight."

"Come on, then." He headed for the kitchen. Winter frowned as he passed her. But she followed him to the kitchen and began pulling snacks from the cupboard.

"It's just food," Tan whispered to her, but her brow furrowed with a scowl.

"Famous last words," she whispered back.

"Um, where is the restroom?" Rebecca asked.

Tan realized Rebecca had never been to his home before. He'd invited her many times, but she always said no. That she wasn't ready to meet his parents. Her eyes swept the gingham curtains and the old dining table from Dad's bachelor days. It was a pretty far cry from her five-star apartment, he knew, but it was home.

"It's down the hallway," Tan answered, pointing, and Rebecca headed off.

"I can't believe she's back." Winter brushed by him as he pulled open the fridge and reached for a box of blueberries. She leaned against the counter. "I feel bad for what she's going through, but she treated you so badly, Tan. And now she just expects you to drop everything and take her in?"

"She's in trouble."

"I think she wants you back, Tan," Winter said seriously.

He scoffed. "We've been through that already. She realized what she wanted after dating me. She wanted Not-Tan."

"That was when things were great with Albert. Now that they're not—she's back."

He pulled out the leftover pizza, changed his mind, and put it away. "Rebecca was never one for leftovers."

"I know," Winter said. "She always commented whenever I brought them for yearbook lunch."

"Really?" He frowned. Rebecca's voice got edgy whenever Winter came up, and vice versa. He'd known Rebecca was on yearbook, which had been part of her experiencing Life In America. But he hadn't known their dynamic there. "You never mentioned."

"What would be the point?" Winter pulled out a can of tuna fish. "She needs help, Tan. A social worker. Counseling. There are shelters and services run by people who know how to deal with her situation. We can make some calls."

"Can you see Rebecca in a shelter?" He shook his head.

"We're not going to turn her out on the streets tonight, but, Tan, you were a wreck after she took off. You weren't even *here*, your head at least, and you didn't have room for anyone—not even Sana. I don't want to see you like that again."

He frowned. "Well, you won't!"

They were talking too loudly. He glanced in the direction Rebecca had vanished. Winter bit her lip as Tan found the rest of their bread.

"Look, don't you see?" Tan said in a quieter voice. "It's my fault she's in this situation."

"How do you figure that?"

"I got her sent home to Shanghai. If she weren't there, there would be no Albert in the picture."

Winter handed him the mustard, and he spread it on the bread for the sandwich. They both fell silent as he finished the sandwich and cut it into two triangles.

Rebecca wasn't back yet, so he opened his laptop. Maybe they could help her find a pawnshop nearby. He googled the Tang dynasty coins. Similar coins were selling, but he couldn't find anything worth more than a few hundred dollars. Not enough to live on for the next year. He hoped Rebecca knew what she was doing, or she'd find herself forced to use her dad's credit cards after all.

As he shut down his laptop, Rebecca stepped through the archway. To Tan's surprise, she'd changed out of her dress and into a pair of Tan's cotton boxers and his favorite *Mandalorian* T-shirt. Winter had gotten it for him last Christmas. Rebecca must have found it in his drawers.

"Are those . . . my clothes?" Tan asked.

Winter straightened, furious. "You can't just help yourself to whatever you want. This isn't your house."

Rebecca tugged Tan's shirt a bit tighter around herself. A flush crept into her cheeks, but she lifted her jaw and gave Winter a long, measuring look. "It isn't yours, either." Winter flinched. Rebecca's eyes narrowed, and she glanced between them. "Are you two dating?"

Winter and Tan looked at each other. "No," they chorused.

"Of course not," Winter added.

"Well, then." Rebecca looked to Tan. "Is that for me?"

Tan pushed the plate toward her, and Rebecca devoured the sandwich in about three bites. She drained the glass of milk he poured her.

"Um, that was so good," she sighed. "I haven't had a glass of milk in a year. It's not a thing in Shanghai."

Tan rinsed her glass and added it to the dishwasher.

"Your skin looks amazing," Rebecca said.

"Uh, thanks." Tan automatically touched his nose. His acne had flared pretty badly when he was dating Rebecca. He'd gotten on top of it since, thanks to the dermatologist, but he'd wondered if that was part of why her parents had disliked him on sight. Everything in Rebecca's world had been beautiful—and Tan, back then, was not.

Winter's face was set and tense, and Tan avoided her gaze. He could practically hear her telegraphing *Mayday*. He needed to figure out what to do with Rebecca. Winter was right. She couldn't stay here. At least, not for long. That was for sure.

"Can we talk now?" Tan asked.

"Yes, of course." Rebecca clasped her hands and moved back to the living room. Tan and Winter followed. Rebecca started to sit on the sofa but stopped abruptly and began to sift through the papers on the coffee table.

"My coins," she said, panicked.

"What?" Tan asked.

"I left them here—now they're gone!"

"Well, they must be here somewhere," Winter said. "Or did you bring them to the kitchen?"

"No, someone must have taken them!" She tossed pillows from the couch, searching wildly. She peered down the darkened hallway and out the window into the backyard. "My father's people. Maybe they're here. Maybe they came through while we were in the kitchen."

Rebecca had always been weirdly paranoid about her family, and for good reason as it turned out. But this was taking it to another level. Like a conspiracy theory.

"The doors are locked," Tan said, trying not to sound impatient. "We'd have heard them. There's no one here to—" Tan broke off. "Actually, there *is* one person around."

"Who?" Rebecca demanded, but Tan was already headed toward the bedrooms. He poked his head into Sana's darkened room. All was still.

"You're awake, aren't you?" he whispered.

No answer. He waited without making a sound. Then he heard a giggle.

"Sana!"

"I fooled you!"

"Did you happen to see some Chinese coins lying around?"

"I cleaned up," she added proudly.

And here it was. "Cleaned up what?"

"Pirates in Pink."

Tan flipped the light switch to the dimmest setting. Sana sat up in bed in her pink Baby Yoda nightgown, blinking in the sudden light. He crossed to her bookshelf and scanned the boxes of games.

"This one?" he asked, pulling it off the shelf. He peered inside.

Scattered on the bottom of the box was a handful of realistic-looking gold coins with square holes in their centers—along with Rebecca's. "Sana, these aren't yours! They're Rebecca's."

"They looked the same!" she huffed.

"They're very valuable!"

Her mattress squeaked as she crawled toward him and grabbed a coin. "See? It has a square hole in the middle, too."

Sure enough, they all did. They even had worn symbols surrounding the square holes, like Rebecca's. Games were so well made these days. Even he might not have known the difference.

But she'd freaked Rebecca out. His own heart was racing.

"You shouldn't have been out of bed," he said. "Cleaning up is an excuse."

"You're a booger," she shot back.

He shelved her box, turned off the lights, and headed back to the others.

"Mystery solved," he said, handing the coins over to Rebecca. She clutched them, and her eyes literally welled with tears. "My sister thought they were her game pieces."

"We're babysitting for the week," Winter explained.

Rebecca was confused. "Our nannies always lived with us. Babysitting was never an issue."

Yes, she had gobs more money than he did. Why did it feel like she was throwing it in his face? She'd never acted that way before.

"All right." Winter folded her arms. "You've got your coins. If you have dangerous people coming after you, you have to call the police. You're going to need protection."

"They're my father's people," Rebecca said. "I just need to stay off their radar."

"You were positive they'd tracked you here. Broken in, even." She looked to Tan for help.

"I took all the precautions I could coming here. Tan." She turned her gaze to him. "Look, I know we didn't end things on the best terms. But you're the only person I can trust. I can't go back home. I can't go to Albert. All I'm asking for is a few days to figure things out, and then I'll be out of your hair."

"You can't involve your family in this, Tan," Winter said. "Especially with your parents gone."

Tan didn't like feeling squeezed between the two of them. But Winter was right. They couldn't get tangled in a family feud. Especially not one involving *Rebecca's* family.

"If people are coming for you, Winter's right," Tan said. "You need help from law enforcement. And this time, you need to tell them you don't want to go home!"

Rebecca flinched. She reached for her purse and clutched it to her chest.

"There are things you can do. Like apply for asylum," Winter said. "They won't force you back into an abusive situation."

"You don't understand," Rebecca said.

Winter picked up her phone. "If you don't call them, I will."

"No!" Rebecca lunged at Winter, but Winter dodged with quick reflexes. Rebecca's amber eyes flared with incredulity. Winter punched in three numbers and hit the call button.

"Winter, wait a second," Tan said. "Rebecca's family is sort of above the law. We need to be strategic."

"Please," Rebecca begged. "Hang up. You'll ruin everything!"

"I'm sorry, but this is way out of our hands," Winter said. "If they're after you, your last residence is definitely the first place they'll look. We have Sana to take care of, not to mention our parents."

"911—what's your emergency?" A woman's voice was audible through Winter's phone.

"Hi, this is Winter Woo. A—friend—is in trouble here. With her family. She's hiding out with us, but we're worried they might be coming after her."

"Are you in a safe place now?"

"Yes, we're at home."

"Is anyone hurt?"

"No . . ." Her eyes strayed to Rebecca. "Nothing life-threatening."

"Is it going on right now?"

Winter grimaced. "No, but she had to run away from home."

"What is the address where I can send a dispatch?"

"88 Grove Avenue—"

Rebecca tackled Winter, sending her phone flying under the coffee table.

"Hey!" Winter said. Rebecca was scrambling under the table. Winter grabbed the back of Tan's *Mandalorian* shirt. A brief scuffle ensued, with Winter finally grabbing the phone. "Hello? I'm here!"

"Please stay put, and don't open the doors until the police arrive."

"They're coming?"

"Yes, they should be there in ten minutes."

Winter hung up, her face flushed.

"I asked you not to do that!" Rebecca cried. Both girls were breathing heavy, their chests rising and falling.

To be honest, Tan wasn't thrilled to have cops on the way, either. He was by nature suspicious of the police based on his parents' experiences getting pulled over and harassed while they were growing up, but Winter had made the call. It was done.

"We'll just talk to them when they come," Tan said. "If they're not helpful, we'll send them away."

A loud knock on the door made them all jump. "Police here! Open up!"

The three of them exchanged wide-eyed glances.

"That was . . . fast," Tan said. He moved toward the door and set his eye to the peephole. Two men in black uniforms stood just outside, with silver badges gleaming on their breast pockets.

"No!" Rebecca cried in a low whisper. "Please. Tell them I'm not here." She turned and raced back toward Tan's bedroom.

Tan gritted his teeth. Rebecca was like a grown Sana, playing hide-and-seek. The pounding continued. He backed quietly away from the door. "Coming!" he called. But now what? If he opened the door, wouldn't they insist on searching for the girl in trouble?

"Hi, what are you here for?" Tan stalled, making sure they identified themselves first.

"911 dispatch," they said.

"But . . . I just called," Winter said, mystified. She set her hand on the door, her arm brushing Tan's. She gazed up at him, her brow wrinkled.

"We're local, with the county. We were in the area. Are you the one who made the call, miss?"

"Yes," she answered.

"Are you hurt?"

"Um . . ." Winter took a step in the direction Rebecca had taken, but then turned back uncertainly.

Tan reached for the latch, but something was off. He couldn't

60

put his finger on it . . . He'd seen his cousin in uniform before. These officers didn't look the same. Their collars were strange. Tan's Spidey senses were tingling.

"Can I see ID?" he asked.

"You called us, kid." The cop sounded irritated. "Is Ms. Rebecca Tseng here?"

Winter sucked in a gasp of air. "I never said her name," she whispered.

There was no reason for them to have connected Winter's call to Rebecca.

"Rebecca?" Tan tried to sound like he barely knew who she was, let alone run into her. "She's in Shanghai, last I heard."

"We have reason to believe she's in California. Her father is very concerned. He's looking for her swift return."

Tan and Winter stared at each other, their eyes wide, dumbfounded. This was exactly what Rebecca said would happen. These men knew about her. They wanted to return her to her father. Maybe they worked for him.

In which case, no way was Tan opening the door. He needed to make these people leave.

"Is she in trouble?" he asked, feigning ignorance.

"That's between her and her father. Have you been in touch with her? Is it possible she's hiding here?"

They knew too much. Way too much. "We haven't been in touch in months," Tan said. "I really need to see ID."

"Fine."

Tan backed away and motioned for Winter to take his place at the peephole. He moved to the kitchen window. Thankfully, Winter had snapped off the lights earlier, so he could safely look outside without being seen. Their front yard was hidden behind the high stone wall that surrounded the house. So he couldn't see their police car, if there was one—but even more problematic, no one from the street could see the men on their doorstep.

They were tall, illuminated by the porch light over their heads. One pale blond with a hawklike nose, the other dark-haired and stout. They put Tan in mind of Robin Hood and his sidekick, Little John. As one shifted back, a gun glistened at his holster. Tan suddenly broke into a cold sweat.

"They're showing ID," Winter whispered. "I can't tell if they're legit or not."

"We're here to help Rebecca," called the blond man, less patiently this time. "If you won't open this door, we will."

Rebecca met Tan halfway through the living room. Her nails bit into his arm above his elbow. "Who are they?"

"They said your dad's worried about you," Tan whispered.

Rebecca's face went deathly pale. "How did they find me so fast?"

The front door thudded angrily under a heavy fist.

"I need to see a warrant," Tan yelled. He tugged Winter from the door.

Thump thump thump! "Open up!"

"Do they think we've kidnapped you or something?" Winter's eyes were wide.

"I told you." Rebecca's fists were tightly clenched. "My father won't hesitate to take me back by force."

Tan believed that. He'd seen it once already.

Bang!

To Tan's horror, the carved teakwood door splintered. A single vertical crack appeared right down its center. It had been built to welcome people, not withstand a frontal assault.

"Oh my gosh!" Winter choked.

Tan's heart had kicked into a higher gear. Rebecca was right. These guys weren't here to fold her into a friendly hug. Or to shake Tan's hand and thank him for his help.

They had guns. They were going to take Rebecca, and they didn't care what collateral damage they caused along the way.

"We need to get out of here," he said, already racing toward Sana. Judging by the crack in the door, they didn't have much time. "Go through the garden out back. Hurry, before they find it themselves."

He ran into Sana's room and shook her awake, throwing back her blankets. Her Baby Yoda nightgown was hiked up to her thighs. She sat up, brushing hair from her eyes.

"Sana, we've got to go. There are bad men trying to break in."

He sounded ridiculous. Maybe he was blowing this out of proportion. More likely the men were getting aggressive because Tan and Winter were acting suspicious. They'd called 911 and then refused to open the door. Maybe the men at the door were genuinely concerned with keeping her safe.

But his Spidey senses told him that more was going on.

And then he heard the front window shatter.

Chapter 7

Sana moved fast. She grabbed her Hello Kitty doll as Tan scooped her into his arms, closed her door to buy them a few seconds, and darted toward the back door on as silent feet as he could manage.

The men were coming into the house. He could hear glass fragments scattering, just on the other side of the hallway wall. Sana let out a small whimper and clutched his arm. He carried her out to the garden, sliding the patio door closed behind them, shoving his feet into his sneakers.

Winter and Rebecca were already beyond the garden at the back gate. He hoisted Sana higher into his arms and joined them. Winter's fingers were fast on the lock. She was wearing her favorite vintage faux leather shoes, with a keyboard printed over the curved top of each foot.

"They broke in," he said hoarsely.

"I don't have my wallet. My phone!" Winter whispered.

"Me neither." Tan felt a dig of anxiety in his stomach. His cell phone was like an extension of his hand. His *mind*. He never left home without it, and now they had no money, internet, or way of communicating with anyone. But they had no choice. "We have to go."

"Becca! Did you go away?" Sana asked. "Where have you been? You missed Tan's birthday."

Tan grimaced. Rebecca's eyes glittered in the dark.

"Shh!" Winter said. "You have to hush now."

Sana quieted. The wooden gate creaked as Winter pressed it open. Tan set Sana down and sent a prayer heavenward that the men inside couldn't hear them.

A sprinkler showering the Kellers' yard sprayed Tan in the ear as they crossed through. Sana gave a soft squeal. Her hand tightened around Tan's.

He wanted to pound on the Kellers' door, but from the direction of their home came the crashing sound of the Lees' splintered front door slamming open.

"Move it!" Tan tugged on Sana's hand and swung through the backyards, emerging onto a parallel street. The four of them ran down the sidewalk.

"My feet hurt," Sana cried.

Tan swore under his breath. Of course they did. She didn't have shoes.

"We have to keep moving," Rebecca urged.

Tan squatted beside Sana, offering her his back.

"Come on," he said. "Piggyback."

She wrapped her arms around his neck, and he grabbed her legs under their knees and hauled himself to his feet.

They pounded down the sidewalk. Sana weighed about forty pounds. Too heavy to carry for long. And they were exposed, with few places to go. Most of the homes on this street were guarded by high walls.

Behind them, Tan could hear feet pounding on the concrete.

He swerved around the next corner. His pulse raced in his throat.

Was all this just so Rebecca's father could get her back? It seemed so out of proportion. Something else must be going on. Something Rebecca wasn't telling them.

"We can't outrun them," Winter said.

"We have to hide!" Rebecca agreed. She darted toward the shelter of a large oak tree.

The good thing about fleeing in your own neighborhood was you knew the turf. Tan had played hide-and-seek often enough with Sana after they moved here.

"Too easy. They'll find us there," Tan and Sana said together.

"The trick shed!" Sana pointed ahead. Lamplight illuminated the cornice of a green wooden shed. The shed was always locked, its windows covered with curtains inside. The kids all called it the trick shed because, by dropping something near its door—like a hat or a book—you could make it look as if you were hiding inside, delaying your pursuers while you got away.

"Rebecca, do you have anything we can leave here?" he asked in a hurried whisper.

Her eyes widened, and she clutched her purse tightly. "I need everything in here."

"Here. My necklace." Winter grabbed the silver chain off her neck and hung it on a low-hanging branch before the door, where it caught the light as it swayed. It was a gift from her father. Tan's stomach clenched. He wanted to protest. But the footsteps were coming closer. He banged a hand on the shed door, making it sound as if it were slamming shut.

Then he veered left through a grove of trees that took them toward the shaded bike trail. Behind them, the footsteps paused in the vicinity of the shed. Its door rattled vigorously.

"It's working," Winter whispered.

"Caltrain," Tan whispered. He put on a burst of speed toward the train station. Sana was growing heavier on his back. The cool night air scraped in and out of his lungs.

"Here, let me take Sana a bit." Winter reached for her, and Tan gratefully transferred her weight to Winter's back.

"Scooters." Tan pointed to a pair of silver and green ones lying on a driveway down the street. They were similar to the rental scooters scattered around the city: metal plates shaped like a slanted L, with handlebars at the top and a wheel at each bottom corner. When Tan and Winter were running late to school, they sometimes grabbed the rentals to speed up their journey.

"I don't know how to ride," Rebecca said dubiously.

"You can ride with me," Winter said.

These scooters weren't rentals; they belonged to whoever lived at this house. They needed to return them—later. Tan righted one scooter, and Winter the other. Sana climbed on behind him and hung on to his waist, as she was used to.

But Rebecca's feet stayed planted on the sidewalk. "You're not strong enough for my weight," she protested.

"I've carried Tan," Winter snapped. "Get on, or I'm leaving you behind."

Rebecca gritted her teeth, grasping Winter around her waist. Tan pushed off with his right foot, and he and Winter cut across a pathway and emerged onto University Avenue, where Rebecca had once lived in an apartment.

"Train's coming." He pointed toward the street's end. In the distance, a whistle sounded. Growing louder. He glanced over his shoulder, but the thugs were no longer in sight.

The wind hummed in his ears as they sped down the avenue to the station. Abandoning the scooters at the base of the concrete stairs, they charged up to the platform.

Twin headlights pierced the darkness, bearing down the tracks toward them. The silver and red face of the train sped past with a whoosh of air and a rattling of wheels. The doors jerked open.

"Come on!" Tan said, and they hurled themselves inside. The floor rumbled under his feet, carrying them northward from the station toward San Francisco. A handful of night-shift workers spared them only a cursory glance.

Only then did Tan's legs collapse under him. Grasping the vinyl seat backs for support, he dropped down into the lower deck and chose four seats facing one another. He sank into the upholstery, and Winter took the one beside him, Sana in her lap.

"We need to tell Colin we took his scooter," Sana said.

Tan didn't know Colin. He didn't know any of the neighbors, but clearly Sana did.

"We'll tell them when we get back," he said.

But when would that be? And how?

Rebecca sank into the seat opposite them. "Sana, you got so big." It was such an ordinary thing to say, in the middle of chaos, that Tan almost laughed.

Sana's cheeks were flushed from the excitement. "Becca, are you back to marry Tan?"

"Shut up, Sana, of course not," Tan grated. He avoided looking at Winter, but he could feel her frowning.

And there were more pressing things to discuss.

"They got there so fast," Tan said. He still felt dazed by it.

One minute, he'd been talking to Winter in the kitchen. The next, Rebecca was there, and now they were here. *Everything* had happened so fast, but Robin Hood and Little John arriving had happened the fastest of all.

"Because Winter called 911!" Rebecca kicked off her shoes and massaged her feet. Her flesh was red.

"I didn't give them your name," Winter said. "Whoever showed up wasn't sent by 911." She peered closely at Rebecca's heel, which was bleeding. "You're hurt. We need to get that cleaned." She darted down the aisle to the bathroom, returning to thrust a roll of toilet paper into Rebecca's hand. "I gave 911 *my* name," Winter finished. "I called the *police*. Not a bunch of thugs."

"They must have intercepted your call. The point is, I told you I can't trust anyone." Rebecca dabbed furiously at her heel.

"Why is your dad sending thugs after you?" Winter asked. "Has he not heard of texting?"

"You're talking about someone who doesn't get crossed. By anyone." She touched her cheek, gingerly feeling her bruises. "Besides, I've blocked his number."

"But *how* did he get his people there so fast?" Tan asked. "Unless they knew where you were—" He broke off. Of course. It was the only explanation.

He held out his hand, panicked. "Rebecca, I need your phone."

Fear dawned in Winter's eyes. Even Rebecca blanched at the tone in his voice. She handed it over without a fight this time.

"What for?" she asked, fidgeting.

"Your family may be tracking it." Gold flecks from her phone cover came off on his fingers. It might even have been real gold. "Unlock it?" He held it out, and she typed in her password.

"I like your nails," Sana said.

Rebecca bit her lip. Her nails were pink and sparkly, with maybe more real gold.

"Thanks," she answered.

Tan dug into her phone's settings and inspected its apps. "Did you install this app?" He flipped her phone around to show her the gears turning.

She frowned. "No, but someone else sets up my—" She shot to her feet, her face pale. "They know we're on this train."

"We need to keep moving," Tan said.

"And leave her phone," Winter said.

"No, I can't!" Rebecca said. "It has all my information on it. My numbers. My bank cards."

"You can't use them to pay for things anyway!" Winter snapped. Rebecca's lips parted, but she remained silent.

The doors opened. They'd reached the Menlo Park stop. Across the platform, another train headed in the opposite direction was rolling to a stop. "Stay here and don't let this train leave without me," Tan said. He darted out the door with Rebecca's phone still in hand.

"Wait, Tan!" Winter called, but he was already headed across the platform. He rushed through the opposite train's doors and took a sharp left down its aisle, running southward between its rows of seats. Halfway to the next door, he powered off Rebecca's phone, ending its signal on board. He hoped the thugs would believe they'd transferred here and doubled back.

"Tan, hurry!" Winter called. She was standing in their train's doorway across the platform. The doors started to close but shuddered open when they hit her. A warning beep began. "Hurry!"

Tan sped toward her, squeezing in with her as the doors forced themselves closed. Only then did he allow himself to breathe.

"What were you doing?" Rebecca exclaimed as they returned to their seats. Sana was bouncing excitedly on her seat by the window, where she'd been watching Tan.

"I turned it off on the other train," Tan said shortly. Her phone was hot in his hands. He thrust it back at her. "Hopefully, they'll think we transferred."

"You should have left it," Winter said, eyeing Rebecca's phone as if it were a time bomb.

"We're okay as long as it's off," Tan said.

"So that stops them from tracking us?" Winter asked.

"Yes, the phone stops sending signals to cell towers," Tan answered. "That must be how they got to my house so fast. They were tracking your cell phone signal, Rebecca."

"But they still knew about *her* call," she said, jutting a thumb at Winter. "I wouldn't be surprised if my father has a mole in the police. They might have been monitoring the lines for any calls about me."

"Why don't we just get off at the next station?" Winter asked.

"Where will we go?" Rebecca asked. "It's past ten."

"Best bet is to get off at Millbrae and transfer lines," Tan said. He studied the train map printed on the wall. "That's in nine stops."

"We still need somewhere to stay." Rebecca looked at Tan. "That's why I came to *your* house." She narrowed her eyes at Winter.

Winter started to retort, but then her gaze strayed down the aisle. "Oh no."

A burly man in a Caltrain uniform and bristly brown beard was coming toward them. He stopped at Tan's seat.

"Tickets, please," he said.

Tan swore under his breath.

Chapter 8

The fine for fare evasion was steep—he'd heard about it from classmates—but it would be worse if they were kicked off before they figured out a safe place to land for the night.

"I don't need a ticket," Sana said from Winter's lap.

"Is she four?" the conductor asked Winter.

"No, I'm five!" Sana said.

"Then all of you needed tickets before you boarded the train."

Sana's mouth formed a small O.

"We can pay now," Rebecca said, opening her purse. "I have money."

"Too late for that. The policy is to prevent people from buying tickets only if they get checked. Just like this." His uniform was crisply ironed at the sleeves. A no-nonsense guy who wasn't going to let them get away with cheating the system.

"We have student passes," Tan said. It was on an app he and Winter had. "But we don't have our phones on us."

"Do you have ID proving you're under nineteen?"

"Um, we don't have our wallets."

"No IDs." He was skeptical. "You'll have to step off at the next station with me and wait until the police can verify your identities."

"No!" Rebecca clutched her purse tighter to herself. She had

ID. Fake ones, which would be even more problematic if they were checked by the cops against their database.

Tan counted the gray seats to the door. Could they risk making a run for it at the next stop? Or would that just land them in worse trouble?

"You can't sic the police on us," Winter blurted. "We're in danger."

Rebecca gave a startled yelp. "Don't!"

Winter lifted her chin. "Please, just let me speak!" She was trembling slightly. She looked back up at the man. "We're cousins. Our uncle has custody over us, but he drinks too much. He was drunk and super-angry tonight, and we had to leave in a rush. That's why we don't have anything. That's why they're in pajamas." Winter indicated Tan and Sana, whose eyes had grown round with Winter's tale. Which Winter was making so unbelievable it was believable.

"We're going to our aunt's house in San Francisco," Winter continued. "But if the police get involved, they'll send us back." She shuddered. "So, please, we—we can't stop. We just need to get to our aunt's."

The conductor tugged on his sleeve. Tan held his breath and tried to look as bedraggled as he felt. "It's past curfew for that little one." The conductor indicated Sana. Then he headed off. "Tickets please," he said to the next passengers.

"Wow," Tan whispered. "Major improv skills."

Winter gave him a half smile. "I've heard too many stories like that, sadly." He wanted to ask where, but she was intently watching the conductor head into the next car.

"Now what?" she asked when he was out of earshot. "Do we dare go back?"

"I don't know." Tan wanted his bed back, and he felt the weight of responsibility for 88 Grove Avenue. "Those thugs could be emptying the house out right now."

"They're not thieves," Rebecca said. "They're after *me*. They won't be carting off your dishes."

"Well, you're obviously not there," Winter said. "So maybe they're gone."

"I'm not there . . . But then why would you guys run off?"

"Wait." Tan's seat squeaked as he leaned forward. "You're saying we should have stayed? That we confirmed you were there because we ran?"

"No, they might have hurt you to get to me. So we were right to leave, and you can't go back. Not yet. You could be walking into a trap."

"I don't believe this!" Winter said.

"We can't just abandon our house forever!" Tan said. "Our parents are coming back in a week. We have to call the cops at some point."

"Call them when I'm gone!" Rebecca flared. She exhaled sharply. "Look, tomorrow I'll get these coins cashed in. I'll fly to New York and buy a few things on my credit card to make them think I'm there, then I'll fly somewhere else."

"So you're just going to run the rest of your life?" Winter asked.

She gripped her purse's handle. "Once I've got my money, I'll have what I need to keep myself safe."

"A hundred grand doesn't last that long," Tan said. Not to mention those coins were not as valuable as she believed.

"There's more where it came from," she answered vaguely.

"Fine. So that's the plan," Tan said, irritated. "You sell the coins, you fly to New York, as soon as you're gone, Winter and I can call the cops and go home, and if anyone shows up, we can honestly tell them we have no idea where you are."

"That's fine. But we need to split up now," Winter said.

Rebecca's head came up sharply. "What? No! You can't leave me alone. My father has people *everywhere*. You saw it already. You have no idea what I'm up against!"

"As long as we're with you, we're all in danger," Winter said. She shifted Sana into a more comfortable position on her lap. "I'm sorry you're having issues with your family, but this really isn't *our* problem."

"Of course it's your problem! You're the one who got me in this trouble!"

Winter bit her lip. Tan hated to admit it, but Rebecca wasn't entirely wrong.

"Your father must really want you back," he said to Rebecca. "Why is he so—"

"Insane?" Winter asked.

"Hell-bent?" Tan finished. "I mean, *they broke down our door*."

Two spots of color appeared high on Rebecca's cheeks. "I'm his only child. His heir." There was a note—not quite pride, but close—in her voice. She was wanted, if not beloved. "I know it seems desperate—"

"Just a bit!" Winter said.

"But if something happened to me, his whole empire, everything he built over his lifetime, would go to his younger sister."

"But he trusts you," Tan said.

Rebecca's lips tightened, and she lifted her chin. "Well, he's not getting me back. I'll be eighteen in less than two days. I'm almost an adult."

"Happy birthday," Sana said. "Will you have a cake?"

Rebecca looked out her window at the sleeping town they were passing through. And didn't answer.

Into the silence, Sana whispered, "I need to go potty."

At the Millbrae station, Winter gave shoeless Sana a piggyback ride to the restroom, then they transferred lines to the BART. This time, Rebecca bought them four tickets *before* they boarded the train. Then they rode another thirty minutes to San Francisco.

Tan felt safer as soon as they emerged into foot traffic near Oracle Park, the Giants' stadium in SoMa, and blended into the crowds. Car horns honked and rock music pulsed from someone's speaker. It was eleven o'clock, but the heart of San Francisco never slept. Thank God for that.

"We need to find somewhere to stay for the night," Tan said. "A hotel. Motel. But we don't have money."

"I have cash," Rebecca said.

"Most hotels require a credit card," Winter said. Rebecca pointed to a pizzeria, its windows glowing in neon lights and framed by red-and-white-checked curtains. "Let's get some food while we figure out next steps."

"Pizza!" Sana's face lit up.

Tan normally didn't like other people paying for him, although in this case, food sounded like a very good idea.

Rebecca caught Tan's eye. "It's the least I can do," she said.

"All right," Tan said.

Inside, the restaurant was warm with cozy vinyl booths filling a dark, wood-paneled space. The air smelled of slightly charred pepperoni.

"Can I help you?" A guy in a checked uniform gave them all an odd stare. Tan had to admit they looked pretty disheveled, even for a pizzeria: all of them sweaty, with Rebecca in boxers and carrying a Prada purse, and Tan and Sana still in pajamas.

Sana plucked at her Baby Yoda nightgown and explained, "We had to run away from home while I was sleeping."

Tan shushed her, but the host had already raised a brow.

"Table for four," Winter said, and the host led them to a booth.

"Sana, we can't share what happened to us," Tan said after the host had left.

Her eyes opened wide with incredulity. "You want me to *lie*?"

"No," Tan started to say, but checked himself. "We just can't tell anyone who we are. It's not safe."

"Whatever," Sana said, and opened her menu. Tan exchanged an exasperated glance with Winter over Sana's head. This was a game to Sana. He didn't want to scare her with the whole ugly truth. But he *did* need to make sure she kept quiet.

Sana wanted to order one of each kind of pizza, even though she had devoured several slices for dinner. Rebecca insisted on ordering drinks: root beer for Tan, coffee for Winter, and lemonade for Sana. It was a treat for Sana, and another difference between Rebecca's and Tan's families. The Lees never ordered drinks at restaurants because they were so much more expensive than buying them at the grocery store. But Rebecca always did.

"We could go to my cousin for help," Tan said after their waiter left. "I trust him, even if I don't trust the general police force."

"We can't." Rebecca nervously drummed her fingers on the table top. "He'll have to report us, and if we're logged into a police report, someone somewhere is going to track us. We don't know who we can trust. And I'm sorry, but I've met your cousin. He'd get eaten for lunch by my father's men."

It was probably true. Tan's cousin was young—just five years older—and the most mild-mannered guy Tan knew. Tan didn't want to put a target on his back, too.

"We could stay with Stephanie," Winter said. Her friend from yearbook. "We could call our parents from there. Hopefully, we can figure all this out tomorrow, but if not, at least Sana could go to school Monday. She'd be safe there."

"We have guards," Sana said. "For shooters."

Winter sighed. "Pretty messed up."

"You really don't get it, do you?" Rebecca said. "These people know everything about you now. Your address, personal information. They know where Sana goes to school!"

Tan felt a cold dread wash over him as he imagined Robin Hood and Little John pawing through his parents' office, their file cabinets. And the Palo Alto Schools calendar hung on the wall.

"Are you saying they'd hurt Sana?" he asked.

"I'm saying you can't underestimate what my father will do to get me back."

"Your mom's emergency list and contacts are on the fridge, too," Winter said soberly. "All their hotel and Airbnb information. And the conference, although that doesn't start until Thursday."

Tan swore. Would the thugs try to call his parents, too, and pump them for information? He didn't know how widely they'd cast their net for Rebecca. Only that it was tightening around them, cutting off all escape. He needed to call his parents before they did. And the most important thing was to keep Sana safe. She depended on him.

Tan met Winter's gaze across the table. She was frowning. It was her bad luck she lived in his house, and definitely not her fault he'd once dated Rebecca.

"Winter, you could go stay with Stephanie," Tan said.

Winter considered, pursing her lips. "You need me. To help look after Sana." She handed Sana a napkin to wipe tomato sauce from her chin. "Your parents asked the both of us to babysit. And you said it yourself. Sana isn't a one-man job."

Tan was secretly grateful. That was the truth. And who knew when Sana might out them to the wrong people?

"Besides," Winter added, "Stephanie would have questions, and I don't want to get her tangled up with us."

"Then I'll get us a hotel tonight," Rebecca said. "Someone is always willing to take cash if there's a little more of it."

"I'm going to ignore you talking about bribing people," Winter said.

Rebecca drew herself up sharply.

"Okay. Let me call my parents," Tan said before they started another argument. "They might still be awake in Hawaii." He automatically reached for his phone, but of course his pajamas pocket was empty. "Damn. No phones."

"Is there a pay phone around?" Winter asked, craning her neck to look.

"Do those even exist?" Rebecca asked. "There are only a few left in Shanghai for nostalgic reasons. New York City did away with almost all of theirs."

"Well, they still exist here," Winter said. She pointed to the back. Tan tipped back against his seat and spotted a red phone booth by the restrooms. It blended perfectly with the 1970s decor. "Although probably a lot fewer than before."

"Um, do you have a quarter, Rebecca?" Tan asked. She handed him a dollar. "Winter, my parents can let your mom know what's going on."

Tan exchanged the dollar for quarters with the cashier, then headed to the phone booth. It was quaint, with a wooden frame and frosted glass walls. The pay phone itself was a metal rectangle with an elongated C-shaped handset hanging from a cradle, hiding a keypad from view.

But as Tan lifted the heavy handset, another problem struck him: He didn't know his parents' numbers. They had always just been on speed dial on his phone. One soft button each, labeled MOM and DAD.

He walked back to their table, lost.

"Did you reach them?" Winter asked.

"I can't remember their numbers," he admitted.

Winter looked stumped. "I speed-dial my mom from my phone, too," she admitted.

"I know their numbers," Sana said.

"You do?"

"We memorized them in kindergarten," Sana said proudly.

"Wow," Tan said, blinking. He hadn't realized Sana was learning anything at all really.

"That's awesome, Sana," Winter said.

Sana smiled and went with him to the phone, reciting the numbers while he dialed. But his call went straight to Dad's cheerful voice mail. They were probably in a dead zone climbing a cliff in Hawaii's tropical rainforest.

"Hi, Mom and Dad; hi, Aunt Fannie," he said to voice mail. "Um, something came up, and we aren't home. Everything's fine, and I'll call you when I can. Don't answer calls from any strangers. Hope you're having fun!"

He hung up and grimaced. He'd meant to reassure his parents, but that message would only alarm them. His mom especially—she presented so strong and competent, but an anxiety attack could leave her struggling for weeks. Besides, he wasn't sure what his parents could do to help from Hawaii.

They'd call the cops. They'd cut their vacation short. Neither of those would help.

If he could just get Rebecca on her way tomorrow, the thugs would also be on their way, and Tan and Winter could set everything else right at home . . . But he didn't love the idea of sending Rebecca off to face the wolves alone, either. That felt wrong, even if, as Winter said, this wasn't their problem.

At the table, Winter was wiping Sana's face with a napkin. Rebecca was at the counter.

"I left them a voice mail," Tan said. "I think they're on their hike."

"Should we try their hotel?"

"Do you remember which one is today's?"

"No. Did they email it to us? We could get on a terminal at a library tomorrow."

"No, the list is only on the fridge. I'll have to call again later."

Winter blew out a breath. "I can't believe this is happening."

"We didn't exactly have a choice, did we?" Tan asked.

"Didn't we?" She crumpled the napkin and dropped it.

Rebecca returned, tucking green bills into her wallet. "Tan, how about the St. Regis? We know the manager. My parents stayed in the presidential suite for a few weeks when they were setting me up here. I don't think they'll mind the cash, and if they do, I can pay double in advance. It's one of my favorite hotels."

It was also fancy and conspicuous, and if he were looking for a runaway princess in San Francisco, the St. Regis owned by family friends was exactly where he'd go first. Winter made a small snorting sound.

Rebecca's eyes narrowed. "Do you have a better idea?"

"My dad stayed in a youth shelter in Oakland when his parents died," Winter said. "It's still operating. In a cathedral. I used to volunteer there with him."

"A shelter?" Rebecca asked blankly. "Like for homeless people?"

"For youth," Winter said.

It was an idea. Tan hadn't known there was a shelter in Winter's father's past. "Would it be open at this hour?" he asked.

"I don't know," Winter admitted. "But life problems don't fit neatly into business hours. And the BART stops at midnight, so if we're going to go, we need to get moving."

The three of them looked at one another. A youth shelter seemed exactly what they needed.

"It saves money," Tan said.

"I'm getting my cash tomorrow anyway." Rebecca pulled a folded sheet of paper from her purse. "I need a specialist. To help me with the coins." She showed them a short list of names and addresses printed in her loopy handwriting: San Francisco, Daly City, San Jose . . .

"Coin dealers?" Tan guessed.

"Sort of. This one is in Oakland, too." Rebecca tapped the last one. "Same city as the shelter. So that could work."

"Where are we going?" Sana plinked her finger against her empty water glass.

They couldn't risk Sana blurting out the wrong things. And he didn't want to scare her.

"We're going to see if we can stay at a place where Winter's dad grew up," Tan said.

"Are those robbers staying in our house?" she asked.

"They better not be," Tan answered grimly.

"If they've put their feet up on the coffee table, I will personally cut them off at the ankles," Winter said. "Like in *The Princess Bride*."

Tan almost laughed. Sana did, and even Rebecca smiled.

"On that note," Tan said, "let's go."

Chapter 9

They rode the BART to Oakland. Winter led them down cracked sidewalks deep into the heart of a neighborhood where scattered streetlights illuminated graffiti-covered brick walls and a boarded-up adult club. Tan piggybacked Sana and watched the road behind them over his shoulder. He was fairly sure Rebecca's phone couldn't be tracked while off, but Dad always told him it was important to know what he didn't know. Maybe he should have listened to Winter and left it behind after all.

Winter turned onto Berkeley Avenue, which was lined with two-story Victorian houses with gaunt shapes, triangular roofs and an occasional turret. Most of them had multiple mailboxes overflowing with neglected newsletters and ads.

"All renters here," Rebecca observed.

"Nothing wrong with that," Winter answered.

"I didn't say there was," Rebecca said coolly.

Winter shook her head. "I can't remember the exact address, but it's on this street. Oh, over there!" She pointed toward the next block. "Those domes are it." She picked up her pace, only slowing when they reached a high stone wall. Tan set Sana down and stretched out his back.

"I haven't been here in years," Winter said.

"Wow, your dad lived in a church!" Sana said. "Was he a pastor?"

Winter laughed. "No, he was just a kid. Like my age."

Rebecca's hands tightened on her purse as she took in the graffiti on a lamppost. She'd probably never been to a neighborhood like this. Tan couldn't tell if she was more afraid for her safety here or back at home with the thugs on their heels.

The night air was chilly. The stone wall surrounded the entire property, but its metal gate stood wide open, welcoming people even at this late hour. A plaque on the stone wall featured a row of silver numbers, the address. Beyond the gate rose a modest cathedral of white stucco and orange trim, with two rounded domes that gleamed in the moonlight.

Winter started forward. "Come on."

Then Sana let out a shriek behind Tan.

He spun around. Sana was on her hands and knees on the concrete, beside a large cinder block that must have tripped her up. She rolled sideways to a sitting position. Below the hem of her Baby Yoda nightgown, her knees were a bloody mess. So were her palms.

"Sana, are you okay?" Tan knelt beside her, taking hold of her ankle. Bright red blood was swelling up through breaks in her skin. He swore under his breath. He never should have set her down in the middle of a strange place, and in the dark.

At the sight of her own blood, she let out an ear-piercing wail of fear.

A couple farther ahead on the sidewalk turned. The hairs on the back of Tan's neck prickled. They were drawing attention. A guy and a little girl in pajamas, close to midnight, loitering with two other teenagers. But they couldn't afford to be noticed, anything that could get back to the men after Rebecca, through whatever channels they had access to.

"We need to get her cleaned up," Winter said. "She might need stitches."

"No stitches!" Sana shrieked.

"Come on." Tan hoisted Sana, still wailing, into his arms and charged through the gate.

The cathedral was named for St. Mary Magdalene. A statue of a praying woman in a long veil stood watch among the shrubbery. The stone walls were graffitied in bright blue colors, but the entranceway was tidy and swept clean. The courtyard was slightly overgrown but homey. An inviting jungle gym stood in the side yard, and a pair of wooden swings swayed from a tree limb.

"It's unlocked!" Winter said. She swung the heavy door open to reveal a vestibule with dark-paneled walls.

Inside the dimly lit space, a young nun in a black habit lifted her head from her work at a wooden desk. She appeared to be just a few years older than them, with smooth skin and bright blue eyes. Under her black veil, a white head-covering neatly concealed her neck and hair, though a rebellious black curl peeked out.

She took one look at the wailing Sana and rose from her seat.

"I'm Sister Ava," she said briskly. "Come with me."

She snapped on a light, and Tan followed her through a hallway lined with two dozen hooks hung with jean and letterman jackets, the kind he'd see at Palo Alto High School, with sneakers and sandals stacked in cubbies. It looked like the messroom for a schoolhouse. The hallway opened into a cozy common area, with a green and a beige sofa surrounded by sturdy beanbag chairs, a double row of photos on the walls, and a stack of board games on a worn coffee table. Winter took in the space with bright, appraising eyes.

"Look, Sana," Tan said, trying to distract her. "A fireplace. A real one." An old-fashioned wood-burning one was set into the wall. Even unlit, it made the room feel cozier.

"Cathedrals don't usually have fireplaces," Winter remarked. "My dad told me this one was added while he was here. It hasn't changed much since I last saw it."

A girl with long dark hair flowing over her shoulders was lying on one of the couches under a colorful patchwork blanket, reading a paperback edition of *A Wrinkle in Time*. She looked about twelve. At the sight of a strange girl, Sana reined in her sniffles.

"Ready to try to get some sleep, Lucia?" asked Sister Ava.

Lucia nodded miserably, rubbing at her inflamed nose. She closed her book over her thumb to hold the page. Tan's eyes roamed the room. Other personal items were strewn around. Hoodies. Backpacks. Pages of math homework. A foosball table. Not the sort of room Tan would have expected inside a church.

"I'm Sana," Sana said. "I fell down."

"I have strep throat," Lucia croaked.

"A cold," Sister Ava corrected.

Lucia sneezed. "That's why I'm here. My parents work night shifts."

"Lucia," Sister Ava said chidingly.

"Also, I know I look young, but I'm fifteen."

"Yes, that's true," Sister Ava said.

"Wow, that's really old," Sana said. Tan couldn't tell if Sister Ava meant everything else Lucia had said wasn't true, but he was focused on keeping up with her speed-breaking stride.

The nun swept past a bulletin board covered in artwork, to a sink and cabinet. She pulled out a first aid kit and gauze bandages.

Rebecca had wrapped her arms around herself, taking care not to touch anything, as though she were afraid of getting germs on her exposed skin. Tan was annoyed. This place was threadbare, yes, but it was clean. Of course, Rebecca was used to living in a museum. A palace museum.

"Set her on this chair here, and let's have a look. You're siblings, right?" The nun's eyes darted between Tan and Sana.

"Yeah," Tan said.

Sister Ava examined Sana's knees, hissing a bit. "This was quite a fall," she congratulated Sana, who swelled with pride. Sister Ava was good at this. Tan caught Winter's eye, noting the relief there. He started to smile.

But then Winter dropped his gaze. Tan felt his smile turn wistful. It was instinctual for him to turn to her, always. But now that they were on the run with Rebecca, that wall between them felt taller and thicker than ever.

Tan turned back to Sana, who rubbed her cheeks, drying off her tears. "Will she need stitches?" Tan asked anxiously. He was worried for Sana, and if they had to go to a hospital, their electronic records could be traced.

"I don't want stitches," Sana said.

"Well, let's clean you up and find out if we need to worry about it," Sister Ava said, running the water. With a gauze pad, she cleaned Sana's knees and palms. Tan hovered, feeling utterly useless. He was supposed to be the big brother watching out for Sana. Not this.

Almost as if Sana could hear him thinking, she reached out her less-injured hand to him.

"Hold my hand, Tan." It was that simple for her.

He took it gently. "You're so brave."

Her hand was like a hot little thermos in his. Maybe Winter was right. He'd gotten so caught up in his own life—dating Rebecca, finding her after she went missing, getting over her—that he hadn't had any room left for Sana. But he didn't want it to be that way anymore. She was counting on him to look after her, even if she didn't say that in so many words, and he would never forgive himself if he let her down.

In no time, both Sana's knees and her palms were cleaned with antiseptic and bandaged. "No stitches needed, fortunately, but we should change the bandages every few hours," Sister Ava said. "I can help with that."

"Thank you," Tan said. "Can we check her feet, too?"

Sana lifted both bare legs and flexed her toes. The bottoms were dirty, with a nasty cut still bleeding. Sana hadn't even complained. Sister Ava patched her foot up, too.

"So you people live here?" Rebecca asked.

"I run a shelter for youth here," Sister Ava said. "Would you like something to eat? A glass of warm milk?"

Tan started to automatically decline. Adrenaline was still coursing through his body. He needed to run. Sitting down right now would only make him more nervous.

But both Sana and Rebecca chimed, "Yes."

There really wasn't any good reason to refuse. Tan picked up Sana again, and they followed Sister Ava into a large mess hall. Rows of tables ran its length, and a buffet line waited with a stack of trays. One table was covered with cardboard boxes full of educational donations: used books and science lab equipment—microscopes, beakers, test tubes.

Sister Ava opened the biggest fridge Tan had ever seen and

pulled out a gallon of milk. A vine tattoo on her arm peeked out from under her black sleeve. Tan hadn't known nuns were allowed tattoos.

"We're called Cornerstone of St. Magdalene but the kids just call it the Cove. I have a few beds left, and I'm happy to let you stay in exchange for several hours of volunteer work per night."

They hadn't even asked yet. The surprise must have shown on Tan's face, because Sister Ava added, "Most of my charges come here for space and a roof."

So she was accustomed to runaways. Although probably not on the global scale of someone like Rebecca. Her blue eyes were calm, but Tan had a feeling she didn't miss much. Rebecca must have felt it, too—her fingers went automatically to her cheek.

"What kind of volunteer work?" Rebecca asked. She looked like she was trying hard not to wrinkle her nose.

"I've just received a generous donation, and I'd love your help setting them up in our library," she said, tapping one of the boxes. "We're also building a tree house in the back."

"We have a tree house, too!" Sana declared.

That they did. Transplanted to their backyard from Tan's childhood home. He still went there to think, and before prom, he'd had some of his best talks with Winter there, both of them lying flat on their backs and gazing into the thick green leaves overhead.

He caught Winter looking at him. This time, she gave him a tentative smile, which he returned.

"Well, you're experts, then," Sister Ava said. "We're laying boards tomorrow afternoon, and I'd love your help."

"That would be perfect," Tan said. "We only need to stay overnight." In the morning, Rebecca could unload her coins and be on her way, and hopefully, after helping out here, Sana, Winter, and Tan could head home.

But then again, how long would it take to sell $100,000 worth of antique coins? It wasn't exactly like running into the store for milk. And even after Rebecca got her money from the pawnshop, she'd have to make enough noise leaving a false trail for her father's thugs to follow her and leave the Lee home alone. But did he even dare go back with Sana and Winter until their parents returned? And once the thugs realized they'd lost Rebecca . . . would they return?

"What's a tree house?" Rebecca asked now, shaking him from his thoughts.

"You don't know what a tree house is?" Lucia gaped at her. "You're older than me."

"We all know different things, Lucia," Sister Ava said. "It's like a little clubhouse. Built into a tree instead of on the ground."

"Don't you have tree houses in China?" asked Sana.

Rebecca flushed. "I'm sure people do," she said. "I live in a city. We barely have trees except in the parks. Not usually big enough to hold a whole house."

A knock sounded on the door. Tan startled and Rebecca dropped her metal cup, which clattered onto the floor and rolled under a table. Sana scrambled after it.

"That's a delivery of medicines I was waiting on," Sister Ava said. Her eyes were kind, but she took in Rebecca's shaky hands.

"So late at night?" Rebecca asked. She accepted the mug Sana handed back to her.

"We have a network of neighborhood volunteers who help us with errands and such, but yes, it does mean odd hours. Excuse me a minute. Help yourselves, please." She slipped out toward the front doors.

Tan let out a breath. "I guess we're all jumpy."

"Well, the Cove is exactly what we need," Winter said. She poured herself another glass of milk. "A sanctuary. No questions asked."

"I've never stayed in a place like this," Rebecca said.

"Well, we do need a safe place till we can sort things out," Tan said.

"I'll stay here with Sana in the morning while you guys take care of the coins," Winter said. "It's, uh, my day." She gave him a lopsided smile.

"It's actually my day," he said. "But this wasn't exactly the arrangement we'd planned," he added wryly.

"Yeah, well, all bets are off now. Besides, I want to look around here." She raised her glass toward the sanctuary. "I was just a kid when I came with my dad. I wonder if there are photos of him anywhere."

He wanted to ask her why her dad had been at this shelter. That man had shaped and was such a big part of Winter, but of course, Tan had never met him. He'd died so young. In his early forties. Winter had been fifteen going on sixteen. And Tan was sorry to hear her dad's parents had died young as well. But he didn't want to ask all these personal questions in front of Rebecca.

"The pawnshop can't be far, right?" Winter asked.

"I saw a computer in the common room," Rebecca said. "I can look it up there."

Sana suddenly cried out, "Where's Hello Kitty?"

"Oh no," Tan said. He hadn't seen Hello Kitty since he scooped

Sana out of her bed. "Wait here." Tan quickly retraced their steps. Hello Kitty had been Sana's since she was born. Tan had picked her out at the store, in fact. He searched the common room, the hallway of coats, the vestibule. He went all the way back to the spot on the sidewalk where Sana had tripped. No Hello Kitty.

When he returned empty-handed to the dining hall, Sana was sobbing inconsolably.

"Did we leave her on the train?" Tan asked. "At the pizzeria?"

"I don't remember!" Sana cried fresh tears. She seemed much more upset about Hello Kitty's loss than anything else that had happened tonight.

But maybe this wasn't really about Hello Kitty at all. Tan felt as bad as Sana looked.

Then Lucia entered the room, moving gingerly. "You can borrow my bunny if you need to sleep." Lucia held out a very well-loved stuffed animal by its long ear. "Everyone says I'm too old for one, but—" She shrugged.

Sana put her finger to her lip, considering. Tan was worried Sana was about to rudely refuse, but she said, "Thank you. That's very kind of you." She used words Winter's mom often said, but Tan knew she meant them. He'd forgotten this side of her existed. It had sort of vanished with the start of kindergarten.

Sana cradled Bunny with expert tenderness while Lucia squeezed an orange stress ball shaped like a basketball. Sana pointed to it. "I go to the same school Jeremy Lin went to," she bragged.

Tan swore quietly under his breath. "Sana," he said.

"Who is Jeremy Lin?" Lucia asked.

"Only the greatest basketball player in the world!"

"Do you live here permanently?" Rebecca asked Lucia curiously.

"I do now." Lucia stretched out her legs. "I got suspended from my school last year, and my foster-mom-of-the-month kicked me out. I've been here ever since."

"Suspended for what?"

Lucia flashed an angelic smile. "Pickpocketing."

Rebecca's hand went immediately to her purse. Lucia's smile widened, and she handed Rebecca's wallet back. "I wasn't going to keep it," she reassured her. Rebecca looked frazzled and a little skittish as she scooted away. Likely reconsidering the wisdom of staying here at all.

"You really *are* fifteen, aren't you?" Winter asked.

Lucia looked offended. "Why would I lie about *that*?"

"Do you want to learn how to write in code?" Sana asked. "I can teach you. We can write each other secret messages!"

Tan pressed Sana's hand. "Sana, can I talk to you for a second?" He carried Sana toward the far windows, just out of Lucia's earshot. "Remember what I said? We shouldn't share where we're from."

Sana's eyes opened wide. "I didn't say!"

"Jeremy Lin only went to kindergarten in one school. Just like you. People can figure it out if you give them details like that."

"So you *do* want me to lie," she said in a carrying whisper. Lucia eyed them curiously.

Great. He was corrupting a little kid. And in a cathedral of all places. "Sometimes we have to hide the truth to protect ourselves." The word gave him an analogy. "Like in hide-and-seek. You're not going to tell anyone where you're hiding, right?"

"No," Sana scoffed.

"Same thing here. Think of us like playing hide-and-seek from those guys who broke down our door."

"Are they still seeking us?"

"I think so," he answered. "So just in case, we don't want to give them any clues where we are. Okay?"

She frowned. "Lucia isn't going to tell them."

Honestly, she was probably right. He was being paranoid, but still, the fewer people who knew about them, the safer they were.

Tan led Sana back to the table, where she handed Bunny back to Lucia. "I feel better." She gave Tan the stink eye, daring him to challenge her. "That wasn't *a lie*."

Tan gave up. Sister Ava returned and handed a bottle of nasal spray and allergy pills to Lucia. Tan noticed Sister Ava wore black tennis shoes with a white Nike checkmark logo. He'd never before thought of what shoes a nun might wear. It made her feel very ordinary, in a good way. Whatever was coming tomorrow, for tonight at least, they'd made the right choice.

As if the universe wanted to underscore the point, Sister Ava clasped her hands then. "May I show you to your beds now?"

Chapter 10

Sister Ava gave them each a toiletries packet, including a tooth-brush, toothpaste, bar of soap, and face towel. She showed them a closet on the second floor, full of shelves of clean clothes in all sizes. Rebecca chose a worn T-shirt and held up a pair of jeans like she wasn't sure what they were. Tan was pretty sure she'd never worn anything used, except for his *Mandalorian* shirt.

Winter helped Sana find jeans and held out a plain navy shirt to Tan.

"This should fit you," she said. "It's wide enough in the shoulders."

"Thanks." He caught Rebecca's gaze and dropped them. Winter knowing his shirt size wasn't a big deal, and yet, somehow, it felt like one. To him, and to Rebecca. He pulled a plush towel off the shelf and asked Sister Ava, "Can we find a pair of shoes for Sana, too?"

"Of course," Sister Ava said. "I've got a collection downstairs. We can go through it in the morning. I can find you a pair as well, Rebecca."

Rebecca glanced at her pumps but didn't answer.

Sister Ava led them along a moonlit hallway of floorboards that creaked underfoot. Tan gave Sana another piggyback, and they passed an antique grandfather clock with a sun and moon face, paintings of biblical scenes, and rows of well-watered potted plants.

Tan couldn't help thinking that Dad would be impressed by their care.

"This is so fun!" Sana bounced slightly. Her clasped hands dug into his Adam's apple, but he didn't mind. He was glad to have her close after what they'd just gone through.

"Why did your dad live in a church if he wasn't a pastor?" Sana asked Winter, who was walking beside him with her arms around all their clothing.

"His mom and dad passed away," she answered. "He didn't have any relatives to stay with."

"That's sad."

"Shh, people are sleeping," Winter whispered. "It was sad at the time. But even when he was passing away himself, he said we have to make the most of the time we have."

Sana sniffed. Tan almost stepped on Winter's foot. He was shifting too close, trying hard to catch her hushed words. But her story explained so much about her. Winter was so grounded and solid. She'd come through a lot, and so had her father before her. Her sights were set on what mattered.

"There it is!" Sana's finger scraped Tan's cheek as she pointed ahead.

They'd reached the darkened girls' room, a large one full of beds covered in comforters in all colors, spaced out in a grid. A number of girls lay sleeping. Tan counted twelve beds as Rebecca crept inside.

Sana's eyes opened wide. "Do we get to sleep in there?" she asked in a whisper.

"You bet," Tan said, lowering her to the floor.

She moved inside with an exaggerated tiptoe. Winter handed

Tan his stash of borrowed items and caught up to Sana, taking her hand.

Sister Ava showed Tan to the boys' room next. He took bed number eleven, close to the door. Each bed came with a little nightstand and a single drawer underneath. There was no privacy, but the bed was firm and the cotton comforter warm.

Still, even knowing that Sana was sleeping peacefully down the hallway, Tan slept poorly himself. Silvery moonlight streamed through the row of windows and threw unfamiliar patterns across his eyes. His dreams were punctuated by his parents' worried faces, which clashed with the colorful leis around their necks.

"Sana? Tan?" they kept calling. He waved, trying to catch their attention, but he seemed to be invisible, because they turned away, still crying out their names.

Tan woke a few hours later, sandy-eyed and surly. A pale morning light was streaming through the windows, but the other boys were still asleep. His neighbor was a large redhead with his freckled face in his pillow and long legs sticking out from under his blue covers. A round clock on the wall told him it was only seven. It was Sunday, so maybe all the kids would sleep in.

Rising, he quietly pulled his borrowed jeans over his legs and yanked the cotton shirt on. It would be easier to slip out without meeting new faces and fielding questions. And the sooner he took care of the coins with Rebecca, the sooner they could get their lives back.

After washing up in the bathroom, he found Winter, Sana, Lucia, and Rebecca downstairs in the dining hall. Rebecca was on a computer, her back to them. Winter was digging into a box of corn flakes. She met his gaze as he approached. The weight of his dream, which he didn't even realize he was carrying, ebbed slightly.

"Couldn't sleep, either?" Winter asked. She handed him a bowl.

"The bed's fine," he said.

"Mine is diagonal from Lucia!" Sana said, bouncing in her seat.

Lucia picked up a flat box, decorated with glitter glue, stickers, and actor headshots. She was smirking.

"Want to see my collection?" she asked as Tan took a seat opposite her.

"Sure." He reached for a spoon. "Collection of what?"

"My loot." She lifted the box top, offering him a glimpse of a stash of Magic: The Gathering cards, a Swiss Army knife, even a cell phone with a Captain America case, before snapping it shut again.

Winter pretended to shudder. "I'm not sure I'm safe sleeping next to you."

"I got it all from the boys' room. Girls are safe," Lucia reassured her.

Winter laughed. "Boys are human, too," she said. "I hope they get their stuff back eventually."

Lucia shrugged. "Finders keepers."

On the computer, Rebecca pulled up Google Maps. She'd changed back into her blue dress, which she must have stashed in her big Prada bag. There was no sign of the jeans and T-shirt from Sister Ava.

"The Oakland contact is a shop downtown. It opens in half an hour," she said, swiveling on the squeaky seat toward them. She refolded her page of addresses in half. "We can take a cab there. It takes about twenty minutes."

"At least this will all be over soon," Winter said.

"We have show-and-tell Friday," Sana said. "Mrs. Peterson always brings cookies."

"If we're lucky, we won't even miss a day of school," Winter said. "And this is as good a place as any to spend our Sunday."

"Yes, this place worked out well," Rebecca said, looking around at the brightly lit room. "These are good people here, and I'm practically an orphan myself."

"Oh my God, you're *not* an orphan," Winter said heatedly. "You have two parents sending people chasing you all over the world. You have the resources to set yourself up with a cushy life. These kids are here because they don't have alternatives."

Rebecca jerked back, as if Winter had whaled her with a pillow. "What is wrong with me trying to relate?"

"Because you can't," Winter said flatly.

"You have no idea what you're talking about."

"I know what my dad went through to land here himself," Winter said.

"You know nothing about *my* life!"

"Then why don't you try telling us? We're roped into this mess with you now. The least you can do is explain."

"What do you mean all over the world?" Lucia asked, popping a corn flake into her mouth. "Where are you all from anyway?"

Winter and Tan exchanged glances. They were on the same page. Tread carefully.

"Sana and I grew up here in the Bay Area," Tan replied.

"I was born in Sacramento," Winter said.

"Right. But where are you *really* from?" Lucia gestured at her own narrow face. "Your face is more like mine."

101

"You're not supposed to ask that," Sana chided, something she might have learned in kindergarten. "We're Americans. We're from *here*."

"You mean our ethnicity?" Winter asked.

"Yes. Ethnicity." The answer clearly mattered to Lucia, personally, not with the underlying you-don't-belong-here assumption that often came with that question, that Sana was responding to. Tan wasn't sure what ethnicity Lucia was. She could be part Italian, Indian, Chinese, Spanish, Latino. It was a safe enough question, on several fronts.

"Our family came from China originally, but we've been in the States for three generations and over fifty years," Tan said. "What about your family?"

Lucia was wistful. "Maybe I'm part Asian, like you."

Sana looked puzzled. "Wouldn't you know?"

Lucia turned to Winter. "What about you?"

"My dad was from Hong Kong, but he passed away two summers ago. I still have my mom, though. She's half German, half Taiwanese."

"Do you miss him?" Lucia asked.

Winter set down her spoon, startled. "Yes, I still miss him. But my mom and I make it work. Every day, something good happened that kept us going. Like meeting Tan's family. We're incredibly lucky."

On the run from thugs, but lucky. That was Winter.

"We're lucky, too," Tan said, and Winter smiled.

Rebecca and Tan rode a cab to a quaint, redbrick house with shingles missing from its roof. It stood in the middle of a commercial district. Big red letters spelled PAWNSHOP, and a dozen smaller signs

screamed WE BUY GOLD AND SILVER, PAID IN CASH!, and no QUES-
TIONS ASKED! The overall effect was jarring.

Rebecca handed the cabdriver a crisp, fifty-dollar bill. "Keep the change," she said, which was generous. She'd always been that way, not just with friends but with strangers. Tan remembered now that it was a quality he'd appreciated about her. One she and Winter had in common.

Tan and Rebecca started up the sidewalk toward the shop. Tan ducked a low-hanging wire that threatened to lop off his head.

"Does anyone ever *want* to sell anything to a pawnshop?" Tan asked. "I mean, it's a last resort, isn't it?"

"Maybe." Rebecca stepped around a handwritten billboard, *BUY-SELL-LOAN*.

"They might as well add a sign, 'We aren't doing anything illegal! Honest!'"

"My coins are small potatoes compared to the stuff I've seen some of these people handle," Rebecca said. But her face was set and still as she opened the door. A bell chimed overhead.

Tan had never been inside a pawnshop before, and this one was dizzyingly full. The walls were covered with cardboard prints from old Spanish movies he'd never heard of. Ukuleles, fishing poles, wooden masks, and even a hunting rifle hung on the wall. A glass counter held an odd assortment of jewels, watches, and even gold coins, although none like Rebecca's. Tan idly picked up a small lamp. The place smelled of machine oil, steel, and dry wood.

Behind the counter appeared a heavyset man in a too-small California Bear Republic T-shirt. His heavy brown hair stuck out around his head as if he'd been electrocuted recently. His arms were covered in tattoos.

"It's a treasure hunt in here," he said, gesturing magnanimously. "You never know what you'll find. Our inventory is always changing."

"We'll take the lamp," Rebecca said, pointing to it in Tan's hand. Before Tan could protest, she handed over a ten-dollar bill.

It was a gesture, Rebecca-style. Letting the man know to take them seriously. Tan wasn't sure it would help. The man's laptop was the most modern thing in the room, sleek with a neon geometric screen saver floating in darkness. But the rest of this place didn't look like it had twenty bucks to lend someone, let alone hand over $100,000 in cash. Not to mention there was no evidence this shop had any expertise in antique coins, especially not ones from China.

"I got a referral to you." Rebecca set her purse on the counter. "Are you Marlon?"

"That's me." Marlon gave Rebecca a harder look. "That a real Prada?"

"I heard you buy antique coins," Rebecca said, ignoring the question.

Marlon's expression grew cautious. "You got any ID?"

Tan shifted closer. That was odd. Why would he need her ID to buy her coins? Did they need to be eighteen to sell stuff?

Rebecca handed over a red passport stamped with gold lettering. Marlon opened it, and Tan caught a glimpse of Rebecca's photo and the name SARAH MOON before he closed it.

"Whaddaya got for me?" Marlon slapped it against his palm.

"Discretion is important."

"Of course. That's why you were referred to me."

Rebecca pulled the pouch from her purse. The coins made a tinkling sound as she emptied it into her palm. She held them out.

Marlon plucked one and grabbed a magnifying glass. He held

it over the coin, turning it over. "'*Kāi yuán tōng bǎo.*'" He read the four characters surrounding the square hole in the center. "That was the name of the Tang emperor at the time. Late six hundreds to seven hundreds AD. Not bad." So he knew how to read Chinese. That was unexpected.

Marlon set down his glass and opened a black velvet case to reveal a silver monocular loupe. "People used to wear these coins like amulets to ward off evil energy."

"Yes, I've heard the stories," Rebecca said.

Marlon set the loupe to his eye and studied the coin. He went over to his laptop and began to enter numbers, returning to squint at the coin with every few keystrokes. As though he were reading something there.

What exactly was he doing? Validating their authenticity? Tan saw the anticipation fade from Marlon's expression, replaced by what looked like fear. His eyes shifted rapidly, as if he were deciding what to do.

"Something wrong?" Rebecca asked nervously. She rubbed her hand against her side.

Marlon set the coin down.

"I'm sorry to be the bearer of bad news," he said. "But these are encrypted. I can't access the digital keys."

"Encrypted?" Tan asked sharply. Digital keys? Digital keys unlocked digital locks, but these were *gold coins*. Pieces of malleable metal forged in a fire fifteen hundred years ago. Not exactly high tech . . . but Marlon wasn't joking. Clearly, more was going on than met the eye.

And judging by Rebecca's tight expression, she wasn't one bit surprised.

"Can't you unlock them?" Rebecca asked.

"Can't help you, I'm afraid. I'm not familiar with these security features." Marlon deposited the coin back into Rebecca's hand, where it clinked against the other two.

"I mean, that's why I came to you."

"It's outside my expertise. Next customer please." He beckoned to a man dragging in a heavy black garbage bag. Marlon's warm weight was suddenly against Tan as he herded them outside and firmly shut the door behind them.

"The lamp," Tan said, turning. But the door was now locked. "What the hell?"

"Just leave it," Rebecca said, and started down the sidewalk.

"What's going on?" Tan hurried to catch up. "What was he saying about encryption and digital keys?"

Rebecca took a deep breath. "Tan, I'm going to need your help. Those coins—they're actually, um . . . more like USB drives. They hold data."

"What kind of data?" Tan asked.

"Keys to my father's cryptocurrencies."

"What?" Tan felt slow in the head. "I thought you were here to pawn off *coins*?"

"That man was supposed to help me access the funds. But seems like the wallet's locked. Encrypted." She frowned. "I suspected my father might have extra protections. I was hoping Marlon could deal with them."

"So those coins . . . are fake?"

"In a way. But that doesn't matter. They're even more valuable than if they were the real thing."

Tan shook his head. "Why would your dad store his money on

fake gold coins?" She pursed her lips, unwilling to say. Tan was all too familiar with this side of her. "Rebecca! You're asking me for help," he snapped. "I'm not helping if I don't know what I'm getting myself into. If you're doing something illegal, like money laundering or smuggling—"

"I'm not!" she flared. "Why would you think that?"

"Maybe the fake passport? The thugs after you? You tell me!"

"Keep your voice down!" She grabbed his hand and tugged him around the block, creating a safe buffer between them and the few people there. "Okay, I'll explain everything." She bent her head closer so that her hair brushed his jaw. "Those coins are storing my family's getaway stash. Like, doesn't your family have an emergency bag in case of an earthquake or something?"

"Yeah. We have a big camper's backpack of food and stuff." Dried foods, water, an astronaut blanket, and even duct tape, in case they needed to seal off a room against toxic air. He wasn't sure which of his parents had added that touch. Probably both of them, since they'd lived in Manhattan during 9/11. "And an envelope with a thousand dollars in cash."

"Exactly! Because if there's a disaster, banks could get shut down, credit cards might not work, and cash is king. And if you were going to flee the country, you'd want to bring enough with you so you could survive for a while."

"But what does this have to do with those coins?"

"My father's the CEO of a major pharmaceutical company in Shanghai. He's influential, but if he crossed the wrong person, the government could seize all his assets and lock his accounts. So he stores his wealth in different places—Swiss banks, Singaporean banks, and . . ."

"Cryptocurrencies. Because governments can't regulate them," Tan said.

"Which you know more about than me, but it's all about the digital keys, right?"

"Right, private keys." For cryptocurrencies, digital keys were long strings of code made of hundreds of letters and numbers. They were the only way to access the cryptocurrencies they were designed to protect.

"If my father ever had to flee across a border, his laptop, his phone, even a USB drive would all be inspected. They'd find his accounts and digital wallets.

"But no one would bother him for old coins. So . . ." She opened her hand. The three coins gleamed on her palm. "He stored his digital keys here."

Things were becoming clearer. Why Rebecca said these coins were valuable even though real Tang coins sold for so little. Her caginess.

"So you're smuggling money across borders—is that why Marlon freaked out?"

She frowned. "Maybe. Cryptocurrencies are banned in China. But I'm not in China anymore—I'm here and so is he. And I need to access the digital keys and convert the cryptocurrencies into cash. So I, um, need your help."

"You need my help." He could barely keep his tone civil. He shook her hand off and continued down the sidewalk. She caught up.

"Your parents work for a digital-currency exchange. You used to talk about the technology. You know exactly how it works."

"This is why you came to my house." He folded his arms and glared at her. "It had nothing to do with feeling safe." She was using him, and using information he'd shared with her while they were dating. "I was your backup plan if you couldn't find someone else to cash in your crypto." And he was a fool.

"No! That's not it."

"It's pretty clear it is. And you couldn't be bothered to tell me the truth when you showed up on my doorstep. And put all of us in jeopardy. You—you used me."

"I wasn't *using* you." Rebecca grabbed his arm before he could stalk away again. "I came to you because . . ." She ran nervous fingers through her hair. "I told you. I *trust* you. I didn't know if I'd need to ask you for help like this. I hoped I wouldn't." She said the words stiffly, softly. She wasn't an actor like Winter, and he could tell that hadn't been easy for her to say. It was her vulnerability that convinced him she was at least partly sincere. "I didn't want to get you in trouble or anything."

"Well, you have! And my sister. And Winter."

"I never expected them to chase me down like *that*."

"I'm not helping you rob your dad!"

"This is his spare money! He doesn't *need* it. I do."

"Look, you need to call your dad and tell him to call off your thugs."

"I can't! He'll come get me. All I'm asking is that you help me get the money. Then I'll be gone"—she gulped—"and they'll have no reason to bother you. Look, I'll even share the money with you. I'll give you a cut. That's only fair."

"I don't need a *cut*. I just need to make sure Sana and Winter are safe!"

"Please, Tan. I wish I didn't need your help. But I do."

Tan gritted his teeth. He could practically hear Winter's voice.

Why are you stuck solving her problems? That had been the story of their relationship, from that first English assignment he'd helped her finish to navigating her Wi-Fi issues in her apartment to those months trying to rescue her from a kidnapping he'd conjured up. But this was different. If he didn't help her get on her way, he was stuck with her father's thugs.

"I need to take a closer look. I'll need a loupe like he had." He held his finger and thumb in a ring against his eye.

"A jeweler? We could go to Tiffany's and borrow theirs," Rebecca suggested. "There are several in San Francisco."

"That's an hour away by BART."

"We could take a cab."

He wasn't sure how much money she had left on her. "I wouldn't spend all your cash so fast. Who knows how long it will take to break the encryption on the coins?"

She bit her lip. A clock struck the hour, the sound of the bells ringing gently over the street. The cathedral wasn't visible from here. But maybe one of the Cove kids was pulling on a rope below it.

Then he thought of Sister Ava's big box of donated lab equipment.

He *really* hoped he wasn't going to regret this.

"Let's start with the Cove," he said, and headed down the sidewalk.

Chapter 11

Inside the cathedral, Tan hurried past the rows of hooks and cubbies with Rebecca on his heels. The jackets all still hung on their hooks, but the shoes had largely disappeared. The Cove had woken up. Two teenagers Tan's age were playing foosball in the common room, where they'd met Lucia last night. A third person was juggling apples. There was no Sana or Winter, but no signs of any trouble, either.

"Hey, I'm Guy," said a big freckled redhead. His black Magic: The Gathering shirt was pulled taut over his barrel-like chest. Tan remembered the Magic: The Gathering cards stashed in Lucia's box. Guy was probably a victim of Lucia's pickpocketing. "You looking for Sister Ava?" Guy's meaty hand idly rolled the soccer goalie pole. He was a pro.

"Yeah, I'm Tan, and this is Rebecca. We came in last night." He didn't try to explain. Their reason was beyond believable. But by their understanding glances, he got the feeling people here accepted you as you were and didn't ask too many questions.

"I'm Perry," said the juggler, curly blond hair bouncing as their eyes followed the apples. They bit into one and kept going.

"Jaxon," said the other foosball player. "Your friends are in the yard, working on the tree house. We'll be out in a bit. After I destroy this guy."

"Ahem. It's the other way around, bro," said Guy.

"They who do not deign to play lose least," Perry declared.

Jaxon snorted. He gave Tan and Rebecca a shrug under his striped jersey: *What can you say?*

Tan couldn't help smiling. They were clearly a close-knit group, but somehow in a way that felt open, not exclusive. Out the window, Tan spotted Sana and Winter carrying buckets of paint deeper into the yard. They were accompanied by a group of Cove kids. So they were safe. Good. He wanted to join them, but—the coins.

"We need to borrow some of Sister Ava's science equipment," Tan said.

"It's all in the dining hall." Guy glanced up from his game. "But good luck getting it away from the girls."

The foosball thunked into Guy's net. "Score!" Jaxon yelled gleefully.

"Oh *man*," Guy said.

"Sorry, Guy," Tan said ruefully.

In the dining hall, two girls around Tan's age had emptied the boxes of donated lab equipment and spread it out like a smorgasbord over a long table. They had flipped open an experiment manual and were trying out various beakers, test tubes, and microscopes.

"Um, hi," Tan said. "Mind if we share?"

The older girl met his gaze and blushed a bright red that matched the ribbon tied around her brown braid. Tan had to refrain from turning around to check if one of the other guys was coming in behind him. None were.

"Go right ahead." The second girl pushed the box toward them.

She was also dressed for church, which Tan realized must have just taken place. It was Sunday, after all, and they were in a cathedral. "I'm Ilene. This is Christine. Help yourselves."

"I'm Rebecca. This is Tan," Rebecca said. He dug through glass test tubes, plastic racks, and metal tools, searching for an eyepiece similar to Marlon's. He came up empty-handed. Now what? He was about to ask Ilene when he spotted a loupe held to her eye. She was inspecting a glittering rock.

Rebecca followed his gaze. "That's actually what we're looking for," Rebecca said.

"I'm using it. We wait our turns here, usually," Ilene said, like she was explaining a different culture, instead of calling them out on bad manners.

"It's sort of an emergency," Tan said apologetically. "Would you mind?"

Ilene frowned, but she handed it over. Tan and Rebecca moved to one of the far tables, where he fitted the loupe to his eye and looked at one of Rebecca's coins.

The coin looked like a coin. The characters were worn, with indentations that made it look like they'd been clacking against other coins in a pouch for centuries. Tan turned it over in the light, impressed with its realism. Rebecca's dad must have anticipated they'd be examined like this, too. He could see the planner behind them: a man who left no room for contingencies. Except for his daughter.

"Could you shine a lamp on it?" he asked Rebecca. She aimed a headlamp at his hands, leaning in so that her jasmine perfume tickled his nose.

Tan studied the coin more closely, identifying a slight texture to the gold surface. Like a matrix. No, more like a grid with alternating stripes. It reminded him of the magnified hard drive he'd seen in one of his computer programming classes. Which made sense. This was a hard drive for storing digital data. He rubbed his fingers against the coin. It wasn't gold, but it was still made of metal.

He scrutinized each of the other coins and found the identical image.

"Can you see the digital keys?" Rebecca asked anxiously.

He handed her the eyepiece. "See those lines? Those are bits. They represent about six letters of text. You can fit hundreds across a human hair. Those are the digital keys. But we'll need much stronger magnification to read them. And Marlon said they were encrypted, so we'll need to decode them, too."

Rebecca returned to the main table and handed the eyepiece back to Ilene. Christine gazed at the coin in Tan's hand, her brown eyes widening. "Is that an original?"

Tan closed his hand over it, hiding it from view. He didn't want word of Tang coins spreading any further than it needed to.

"No, just a replica. Thanks for letting us crash."

"Crash again. Anytime." Christine smiled.

Rebecca frowned slightly. "We're only here temporarily." She took Tan's arm and headed outside and back into sunlight.

In the backyard, pine needles crunched underfoot. Their spicy scent lingered pleasantly in the air. Tan and Rebecca found Sana and Lucia carrying a short wooden board between them. Winter walked beside them, balancing a stack of boxes. Her shiny black hair was pulled back from her face and bound into a practical ponytail.

Winter's eyes lit up with relief when she spotted him. "You're back!"

She'd been worried for him. It was all there in her face. Tan wanted to gather her and his sister into a hug on the spot, but their arms were full. He settled for taking one of Winter's boxes and walking beside her.

"Something wrong?" Her expression grew cautious. She glanced back and forth between Tan and Rebecca. "Did you sell the coins?"

"Look at my new shoes!" Sana interrupted. She held up her foot, showing off a pink gel sandal. "I got to choose!"

"We have a surprising lot of shoes in all sizes here," Sister Ava explained, moving swiftly by toward the cathedral with an empty platter in her hands. "I'll be right back with more snacks. Take a look around!"

"Thank you," Tan said as she vanished around a corner. Rebecca paused as a few girls stopped her to compliment her dress. To Winter, Tan said, "There've been some new developments."

"What? Really?" They reached the giant tree, where kids were climbing over the massive limbs. The tree house was more of a tree fort, with landing points built at every branch. Winter dropped her boxes with a heavy thud and reached for a can of green paint. "I was ready to go home tonight."

The yard was crowded with kids ranging in age from Sana's to Tan's and Winter's. Too many who could overhear. Including Sana, who thrust the plastic handle of a paintbrush into his hand. "I'll explain in a bit."

Winter's brow furrowed.

"Where did all these kids come from?" Tan asked.

"There was a Mass in the sanctuary," Winter said. "You missed it. A bunch of kids came to hang out afterward. I guess this yard is pretty popular."

"I can see why." Kids were playing tag and swinging from long ropes and tire swings hanging from the tall trees. A table was loaded with apples and cookies. The surrounding high walls gave the whole place a secret-garden vibe.

"During the week, Sister Ava runs a day care for younger kids while the older Cove kids are at school. It's to help out the working parents in the neighborhood."

"She makes really good use of this place," Tan said.

"I was thinking the same thing."

"So this is the tree house," Rebecca said, rejoining them. "I can see why it's such a hit."

"Yes! Everyone here helped make it." Sana beamed as though she were the owner herself.

"We've been painting," Winter said, pointing to a row of drying green boards.

Sister Ava returned carrying a tray with two big pitchers of lemonade swimming with strawberry slices. She was followed by two helpers. A child came over to hug her, and, after she set down the tray, she handed him an apple. Sister Ava clapped her hands, catching everyone's attention. "Kids, we have some special guests joining us for a few days. You've already met Sana and Winter. Let's give Tan and Rebecca a warm Cove welcome, too."

"That's my brother!" Sana said.

From around the yard and up in the tree limbs rang applause and cheers. Tan couldn't help smiling. Clearly, Sana and Winter had been a hit. These kids barely knew them. Even Rebecca looked touched.

Tan squeezed Sana's hand. "Thanks for making friends for us all."

"This is Jaxon, Guy, and Perry," Sana introduced them as they emerged from the cathedral's side door. "My brother, Tan, and Rebecca, who isn't marrying my brother—"

"Sana," Tan admonished.

"And I forgot to tell you Winter lives with us because she doesn't have a dad," Sana finished.

"Sana!"

"It's okay," Winter said. She smiled at the Cove kids. "My dad lived here, too, years ago."

"No way," said Guy. "So what happened to him after he left here?"

She smiled. "He became a professor of English literature. He fell in love with my mom." Her smile turned wistful. "He'd survived a lot, and he was strong because of it."

"Sounds like me," Jaxon said. "I'm strong. Roar!" He made a bear face for Sana, complete with claws. Sana raised her own claws and roared back. Tan couldn't help laughing. She'd won them all over in such a short time.

"Rebecca?" Sister Ava offered her a glass of lemonade, then one to Tan. "You two are just in time to help paint, if you'd like."

Rebecca looked to Tan, inquiring silently. That was their deal after all, a safe place to stay in exchange for volunteering. And he planned to make good on it. But they had to figure out these coins. And soon.

He gave Rebecca a slight nod, then caught Winter looking at them. She ducked her head and busied herself with her paint can. But as Sister Ava led them toward a pile of long roller brushes and other supplies, Winter grasped Tan's arm. "Tan, I considered using

Sister Ava's landline to try to reach our parents in Honolulu, but I figured it would be better not to."

"Good call. Better not to link the Cove to them."

Sana had skipped off. Rebecca had moved ahead with Sister Ava. No one else was listening, so he quietly relayed what had happened at the pawnshop. "Her coins are fakes. They're actually data-storage devices with digital keys to cryptocurrencies."

"Fakes?" Winter's brows rose into her forehead.

"Sana was on the right track. She confused them with her game coins, right?" The memory made Tan want to laugh. Among them all, Sana had the clearest head. Maybe because she had fewer worries to muddle what was in plain sight.

"But Rebecca knew? All along?"

"Yeah. She came to me in the first place because she figured she might need help cashing them in."

"Can you do it?"

"Yes, I think so. But I'll need to get past some encryption first."

"Tan! This is *a lot* for Rebecca to ask from you. Won't this get you into trouble?"

"Winter . . ." Tan spread his hands helplessly. "I'm doing this so we can get back to our house. In one piece," he added, thinking of their splintered door.

Winter scowled. "Seriously, Tan. This headlock she's got you in—"

"Please stop saying that!" he groaned.

"But it's true! Tan, look. You're brilliant."

He rubbed his brush bristles against his palm. "No, I'm just—"

"Tan, stop. You have knowledge most people don't. Talents some of us can only dream of. Like, remember that time Mr. Heinz gave us that encrypted test as a gag, and you were halfway done before he sprang the truth on us? No one else could read a word."

"I forgot about that," Tan admitted. "But this is more complicated."

"And you're a genius at codes and ciphers. That's why Rebecca came straight to you. But she doesn't own you. And just because there's a problem to solve doesn't mean you need to be the one to do it."

"It's not like that," he said.

"Do you know what she reminds me of? That line from *The Great Gatsby* about the rich people who didn't even notice they were smashing up lives and letting other people clean up after them. 'They were careless people.' *Rebecca* is a careless person."

Winter had a point. "I'm not defending her, but . . ." His voice trailed off. Her expression was shuttered. And he couldn't think of anything to say that wasn't repeating what he'd already said.

Winter heaved a breath, steadying herself. She moved to a partially painted bench, opened her can of paint, and drew her brush across its surface before speaking again.

"Okay. So we're stuck with—those coins. Why not coins, I guess. Refugees get their money out of their country in all kinds of ways. Like people swallow diamonds or smuggle expensive silk rugs." Her brush paused mid-stroke. "Are we helping her steal from her dad?"

We. That was Winter. She didn't agree with him, but she wouldn't abandon him. She was going to help him figure this out. He felt humbled and grateful.

"She figures the money belongs to her," Tan said.

"Yeah, well that clears it all up!" Winter said sarcastically. The brush swept on. He dipped his own brush into the pungent green paint in her can. Then he tackled the bench's back, which allowed him to face her.

"Look, I couldn't care less if Rebecca swipes her father's secret stash of cash. He doesn't need it. And it means she'll be free from him and her creep ex-boyfriend. I just need to find someone who can help with the encryption part of this."

"You're asking me, Winter Woo, the aspiring actor, for help with that?"

"I'm asking Winter Woo, the girl with her head on straight, for any ideas."

He got a smile that time. "I only seem that way because *your* head is on backward."

He laughed. "Probably true."

She tapped her finger to her lip. "Well, what about that grad student at Berkeley who spoke at our school last year? You liked her. Maybe we could ask her for help."

Tan tried to remember back. Palo Alto High often invited speakers from the community. Some were hit or miss, but that talk had been really good. "What was her name? Maria."

"Maria Orslo. She specialized in quantum cryptography, which I didn't know anything about, but I remember she said encryption is in a race against quantum computers, which sounded like it should be the plot of a movie someday."

"You can star in it." He laughed. "I'd watch." She always managed to make him laugh, no matter how dire his situation felt. And now they were getting somewhere. "That's a *really* great idea. Let's try Maria."

They finished the bench, then Winter led Tan back inside. The foosball players had left the common room surprisingly tidied up. Even the pillows on the couches were straightened.

Winter sat at an ancient computer terminal in the corner. Tan pulled up a wooden chair as she searched online for Maria and found her contact page. Tan recognized the researcher's photo from her visit. But only her email address and the general Berkeley campus address were available.

"We could email her . . . ," Winter said.

"No, we shouldn't risk it. Gmail logs your location when you log in. It's more an issue for Rebecca than us, but still. Anyway, it could be days before she answers. If she answers. I should just go find her."

"It's a huge campus," Winter said dubiously. She scrolled farther down Maria's web page. Tan was leaning in against the desk. Her arm tickled his, warm from the sun, and he found he didn't want to move away and she didn't ask him to.

"She teaches a section for CS 2230." Winter searched for the course. "No days or times or location information though." Her fingers flew over the keys, searching for *Maria Orslo, Berkeley*. "Hey, look. She's a residential adviser in the International House. So she lives there. Maybe that's where you can track her down."

"Amazing." Berkeley was only fifteen minutes away. "I could go now and be back in an hour or two." He noticed the six-digit number doodled on the back of Winter's hand and touched it gently. "Maybe I can ask her about accessing your dad's iPhone photos," he suggested.

Winter covered the numbers on her hand, then released them ruefully. "I've been thinking about him more now that we're here." She pointed to the row of framed pictures on the wall. "I found his photo up there."

"So he's here?" Tan rose and moved closer to inspect them. They were blown-up eight-by-tens, landscape shots taken in the cathedral yard, each featuring between five and maybe twenty kids, with the group changing incrementally year by year.

"Yes, there weren't that many Asian Americans here back then. It was pretty easy to find him."

Tan moved down the line of photos, which were taken annually. The group expanded and contracted through the decades of fashion. "Why did his parents pass away so young, too?"

"Same cancer," she said. "It's genetic."

He whirled to face her. "Winter . . . do you . . . ?"

He didn't realize how his throat had tightened or how he'd stiffened until she put a calming hand on his arm. "It's okay," she said. "I was tested. I don't have the gene."

He let out a huge breath, embarrassed by how strongly he'd reacted. She was the one who'd had to live through it. Not him. But he couldn't help wrapping his hand over hers, holding its steadying warmth to his arm.

"It's not fair how some people get the short end of the stick," he said.

"Well, he tried to live life to the fullest." She frowned, as if something about that didn't sit right with her. Then she tugged her hand free.

"How long was he here?" He returned to his search for her dad, but now he couldn't distinguish any faces. Holding her hand had rattled him.

"Just his last two years of high school."

He recognized Jaxon, Guy, and Lucia in the photo before him. He was in the wrong section altogether. Tan moved down the line, his footsteps muted by the soft rug. "How long ago?"

"He was our age. So almost thirty years ago. See? Right here. He looks so young."

She straightened a photo near the center of the row, featuring a slim Asian guy their age. Handsome, with a distinctively retro flair to his hair and clothes. Tan had seen only a few photos of Winter's dad, closer to his parents' age today. The caption included his name: NOAH BARTHOLOMEW WOO. He had his arms slung around the shoulders of two guys, and he was smiling Winter's smile.

"He could have been an actor, too," Tan commented.

"You think? It was pretty special to find this. I remember him saying once that coming here was a fresh start for him after his parents passed away. He was an only child, too, so it was a bit like Mom and me moving to Palo Alto, I guess. He loved Father Luiz—who was the Sister Ava of his day." Winter pointed to a priest with a lined face and warm hazel eyes. "The Cove became his family. He didn't have close relatives."

Family. That was how the Woos felt to him. Even her dad, whom he'd never met. He studied Winter's father more closely. A pair of long fingers made bunny ears behind his head, courtesy of his smirking friend beside him, for all posterity. Tan smiled. He wished he'd had a chance to meet him.

"He looks nerdy. Like me," Tan said. "Even though he was good-looking."

"He wasn't nerdy." She batted his arm gently. "And neither are you."

"Sure I am," he said, turning to her. She was closer than he realized. Just inches away, with her face right there at his shoulder and her lashes framing dark, serious eyes looking up at him.

He meant to pull back. Except that his feet stayed in the same place.

And then he leaned into her.

And then she rose on her toes and pressed her lips to his. Her mouth was as warm and soft as he'd dreamed. But then she pulled away, eyes stricken. "Tan, I'm sorry—"

He grabbed her by the shoulders and kissed her back. He felt starved for her. Her mouth parted under his, and he found himself tasting her sweetness, lemonade and mint leaves, drinking her in—

"Oi!" Rebecca said behind them, her British accent more pronounced than ever.

They broke apart.

Rebecca stood in the doorway. She was still wearing her dress but had changed into a pair of more practical Keds, which Sister Ava must have provided.

"I'll be outside," she said stiffly, and walked out.

When Tan looked back, Winter had retreated to the far wall, her back pressed to it, hanging on for support.

"I'm sorry," she said again. "I didn't mean to do that."

His heart was pounding. Her eyes widened—without realizing it, he was moving closer to her. Closing the gap between them. He stopped just before her and set his hands to the wall on either side of her so that their noses were six inches apart.

"Is that really true?" he asked, looking into her eyes. She was like a deer in headlights, which was maybe cliché but also exactly the right metaphor. He wanted nothing more than to close these last inches between them and pick up where they'd been interrupted.

She tucked a lock of black hair behind her ear and looked away, at the computer. "Uh, this whole situation is just getting to me. Us.

I mean, kissing—it's not the same as wanting to be *together*. I know that."

Ouch. She was right in theory. But was that true for them? A silence fell while he debated whether to blurt out all the pent-up feelings churning inside him and to let the chips fall where they fell.

Then she ducked under his arm and walked to the computer.

"I'll stay here with Sana again." She turned her back to him, pulling up Maria's web page. "Someone has to, and it's not going to be *her*." She gestured at the door through which Rebecca had just vanished. "And you need to go because you're the only one who will know what Maria's talking about. Sana and I will do the work we owe Sister Ava."

Winter's kiss was still tingling on his lips. He didn't like leaving her and Sana here. But Winter was one of the few people in the world he'd trust with Sana. He trusted her love for Sana, and she was the most capable and practical and levelheaded person he knew.

Maybe he just needed to accept the good and the disappointing that came with that.

He started to go, but Winter spoke. "Tan, her section starts in a half hour. I don't know where it is, but you better hurry."

Fifteen minutes to campus. "Thanks," Tan said, and raced out the door.

Chapter 12

Rebecca held herself stiffly in the seat beside him on the bus trip to the University of California, Berkeley. Tan gazed out the window at the passing campus buildings, willing the bus to move faster. His chest was a tangle of emotions: frustration, confusion, longing. One kiss, and all the magic and heartache of prom was back. He needed answers, and not just about encryption.

But he was on a mission here. To find Maria.

As the bus stopped with a hiss of breaks, just outside the Greek Theater, Rebecca said, "You know, I always suspected something might happen with the two of you. It's natural with two teenagers living together."

Ugh. The kiss was none of her business. He hopped off the bus and headed down the sidewalk in search of a campus map, but Rebecca kept pace with him, continuing.

"It happened with Albert and me when he was staying with my family," Rebecca said. "I only realized months later that my parents invited him with that in mind."

Tan could only imagine what they'd been thinking. Invite the anointed chosen boy in to wipe away the stain of the guy from the wrong side of the tracks.

"It doesn't mean it's love," Rebecca concluded.

"We are not discussing my personal life." Tan studied the concrete buildings. A few cars whooshed by. He was lost. He wasn't used to going anywhere without the maps app on his iPhone. "There must be a campus map somewhere," he said, turning down the sidewalk. Rebecca followed.

But was Rebecca right? Were he and Winter just a side effect of living in the same house? Winter had been clear. She was attracted to him but didn't actually want to date him.

His parents had always said attraction—chemistry—was important. But, of course, it wasn't everything. He wasn't sure what it was between him and Winter. He was drawn to her. But the past few days of simply getting to be friends again, the easy way they worked together to take care of Sana and triage this situation—what they *did* have was too precious to mess up any more than he already had.

Just past a café, he found a large map sketched on a wooden board. He touched the star marking their location. He didn't know where Maria's section was being taught, but maybe he could ask someone at the International House, where she lived. With his finger, he traced the path there. Fortunately, it was close.

"This way," he said, heading off. A blur of movement on wheels sped past him—a student on a skateboard. Behind him, Rebecca cursed in Mandarin.

"Tan!"

He spun around. Rebecca's purse had spilled onto the sidewalk. She herself was crouched down, peering anxiously through the metal grate of a storm drain.

"What's wrong?" He knelt beside her.

"My coins!"

The drain's bottom was full of dried pine needles about two feet below the grate. The red velvet pouch peeked out, half-buried under a large leaf.

"I dodged that skateboarder, and they just—" She gestured at the pouch.

Tan peered anxiously into the shadowy space. A half-inch nudge in the wrong direction, and the coins could disappear down a pipe forever. Tan tried to reach into the grate, but his hand jammed at the base of his thumb. "You try," he said, pulling back. "We need to hurry. Or we'll miss her."

Rebecca grimaced. She gingerly slipped a manicured hand into the grate. "Gross," she said, sounding like Sana. Her arm went through to her elbow before it got stuck. "I can't reach it, either."

Tan ran his fingertips along the grate's rough edges. "It comes off. We'll have to lift it. Come on." He repositioned himself and grasped the metal grate. It was too heavy for one person. Rebecca came around beside him. Between the two of them, heaving and shoving, they yanked it aside far enough for Tan to reach in and snag the pouch's golden strings with the tips of his fingers. He tossed it to Rebecca and shoved the grate back in place.

"Come on," he said, panting slightly. They hadn't even gotten to Maria's dorm, and things were going wrong already. "Let's go."

The International House spread across an entire block: a large Spanish-style building of white stucco walls and a bright orange-tiled roof. The front doors were locked, accessible only by keycard. Which they didn't have.

"Now what?" Rebecca pressed her face to the glass door and looked inside. There didn't appear to be anyone there.

"Everyone's probably out on a Sunday."

"Should we wait for her to come back?"

"That could be hours. We could check for a back door." Tan turned. A girl in shorts and a sports bra, about five years older, was jogging up the walkway.

"Um, hi," Tan said as she reached them, dripping in sweat. "I'm looking for Maria Orslo. She's a residential adviser here, right?"

"Yes, she's not here." The girl swiped her keycard, earning a soft click of the door.

"Do you know where she could be?"

"I think she's teaching a makeup section."

"Where would that be?"

"All the sections are in Cory Hall." She was in a rush. "It probably ends in ten minutes. Good luck catching her!" The door swung shut behind her.

Tan looked at Rebecca. "Cory Hall. Let's hurry."

Several precious minutes ticked by as Tan found another campus map and pinpointed Cory Hall. It was a ten-minute walk. "We better run." He broke into a jog, weaving in and out among the students populating the sidewalks.

They reached Cory Hall just as a large class or presentation let out. The hall smelled lemony. College and grad students, dressed casually in jeans and shorts, headed outside, chatting about clubs, problem sets, dinner plans. Rebecca was the most dressed-up by far, drawing a few curious eyes.

Tan scanned the many faces for Maria.

"How are we going to find her?" Rebecca asked, dismayed.

"Start asking people," he said tersely.

Rebecca gulped. She flagged down a passing guy, clearly out

of her element. "Um, excuse me. I'm looking for the CS 2230 section . . ."

Tan continued searching for Maria's face. He spotted a woman in a black dress whose curly brown hair bore a slight resemblance to Maria's. But as he neared her, she turned a stranger's eyes onto him. She wasn't Maria. He passed her by. What if Maria's hair was done differently? Would he even recognize her?

Rebecca was still asking people, gesturing at the hallways. He rejoined her, still scanning faces of the people now pouring out of the building. Had they missed her?

The girl Rebecca was speaking to pointed down the hallway. "I think it's that way."

Rebecca dashed to the door at the far end. "Tan! She's here!"

Maria was in animated conversation with a horde of students gathered around her. A colorful floral scarf held back her brunette hair and matched her velvet jacket.

Lucky for them, Maria was popular, or she might have already left the building. Tan waited with growing impatience as her students mobbed her with questions well into the next hour. A roller bag topped by a sun hat waited nearby.

Maria caught his gaze. Recognition dawned in her brown eyes. Tan took a half step forward. She lifted a delicate finger, acknowledging them, then returned to the student before her. When the last student took her leave, Maria stepped toward Tan and shook his hand.

"We met at Palo Alto High School," she said, pleased. "You asked great questions."

He was surprised she remembered him. "I'm Tan Lee, and this is Rebecca Tseng," he said. "Do you have, like, ten minutes for an encryption question?"

"Hello, Rebecca. And yes, I always love a good puzzle." She lifted her wrist, checking her Apple watch. "I need to take an Uber to the airport, but I can spare a few minutes. What can I do to help?"

Rebecca handed over a coin. "These belong to my family back in Shanghai," Rebecca said. "They're like USB drives. Pretty old school, though. My father set them up years ago. I need to access the data on them. Tan thought you might be able to help decrypt them for me."

"Fun." Maria turned the coin over, inspecting it. Her expression reminded Tan of himself when he was trying to crack a delightfully complex code. "I've seen data stored in some strange places but not yet on an ancient gold coin. Let me take a closer look in the lab."

Maria grabbed her roller bag and led them down the hallway to a lab laid out with large white machines. Cone-shaped robots with long, mechanical arms sorted items into bins. She reached a desk decorated with a row of red and gold nesting dolls and put the coin under a large scanning machine. She opened her laptop and displayed her view on a large screen on the wall. Then she zoomed in on the gold coin with its square hole until they were looking at the grid lines Tan had observed earlier.

"How remarkable. Such cleverly disguised digital storage." Maria adjusted her view on the screen, zooming in further.

"Can you access the information?" Tan asked.

"I can download the data, but after that . . ." Maria moved the coin into a silver rectangular device that she connected to her laptop with a cable. Her fingers flew over her keyboard. "It will depend on whether my quantum computer is stronger than—"

"Your/our cryptographer," Tan finished with her.

"Exactly." She smiled, still gazing intently at her screen. A light blinked red, and Rebecca snapped a pencil she was holding, startling herself.

"Sorry," she muttered, setting it back on Maria's desk.

Maria pulled up long sequences of gibberish words, numbers, and letters.

"A code? Passwords? I can't make sense of them," she said.

At least they were large enough to read now. And now that Tan could see them, *he* could make sense of them. Their form and shape were as familiar to him as the pages of his favorite book. Which made sense since his parents' work often spilled into their home life.

"They're digital keys," Tan said. "But they're scrambled. Encrypted."

"They must contain very sensitive information for your family to go through the trouble of hiding them so carefully," Maria remarked. Her fingers flew over her keyboard, producing a soft, rapid clacking. "It's almost like they're designed for smuggling."

"Um." Rebecca rubbed her arm. "My family likes technology."

Funny how the same sentence could be used to describe Tan's family, but it meant something totally different. For Rebecca's family, it was about making investments. For Tan, it was mental gymnastics and family bonding time around the coffee table.

Maria was running her computer against the encrypted keys. Numbers and letters flashed on her laptop.

"It's not looking promising," she admitted.

Because she was going about it in the wrong way. Not her fault, because his parents' digital keys came with a few extra security protections that even an experienced cryptocurrency broker might not know how to navigate. But she had the tools to do it.

Tan moved closer. "May I?"

"Sure." She pushed her laptop toward him. He was clumsy, but he knew this stuff, and that boosted his confidence. Tan remembered how Dad had ruffled Tan's hair after a particularly challenging game.

Young minds see things more clearly, Dad had said fondly.

Tan's *mind sees things more clearly*, Mom had corrected him.

Tan hadn't let it get to his head. All those puzzles and the pathways to solving them were part of his schema. How his mind worked. It didn't feel difficult to him. It just was.

In a few minutes, rows of digital keys began to appear on Maria's screen in their unencrypted form. The first five were twelve-word phrases. Those gave access to cold wallets, which held digital currencies but weren't connected to the internet.

Then rows of sixteen to twenty alphanumeric codes began to appear, one after another in a growing list.

"Is it working?" Rebecca asked.

The nearness of her voice startled him. He lifted his head. She was leaning in, gazing intently at the screen. He had the impression she'd been talking while he was lost in the work.

"Yes, there are five wallets here, which probably correspond to five kinds of currencies. And these are the digital keys." He pointed to the alphanumeric codes.

"So we can access them now?" Rebecca asked. "Could I take them back to Marlon?"

"Once we unencrypt them. Then we can sell them on the open market to get actual cash into your hands. That part's straightforward."

Rebecca shuddered. "Straightforward to you, maybe."

The list kept growing on Maria's screen. Tan scrolled through line after line of alphanumeric sequences. It felt endless. Much more than he was expecting.

"There are a lot here," he said. "Are you sure these are just—" Tan zoomed out to view the lines at an aggregate level. Multiple wallets. Many multiples actually. If he were to guess, it looked more like . . . millions of dollars. No wonder Mr. Tseng had blanketed these coins with double-duty security features. If her dad really ever did need to flee his home country, he'd hidden away enough money to rebuild his empire. "These are—"

The desk phone rang. Maria startled, then leaned over to pick up the receiver. "Hello, Berkeley AI. This is Maria."

Her eyes narrowed, changing from curious to guarded. She punched the speaker button and turned to Tan. "They're calling . . . for you."

"Me?" Tan felt a wrench of fear in his gut.

Rebecca's brow furrowed. He leaned over the phone and motioned for Rebecca to listen in. "Hello?"

"Hello, Tan Lee," said a metallic-sounding voice. It grated on Tan's ears.

"Who is this?" he asked.

"You can call me Crane. Like the bird. Tell your Berkeley friend she can either break her computer now or we will break her neck."

The words were discernible, but mangled, probably with an AI voice distorter.

"What the hell?" Tan's gaze darted to Maria. Her brown eyes had widened with fright.

"Go to the Palace of Fine Arts tonight at ten. There is a bench between the theater building and the rotunda. It's dedicated to the memory of a deep-pocketed donor named Bill Chan. Under that bench is a stone. I want you to leave the coins under the stone and walk away."

"What?" Rebecca cried. "Why would I do that?"

"How did you find us?" Tan demanded. "And who are you?" The person sounded like a native English speaker, an adult, but if he or she had a British accent like Rebecca's parents, Tan couldn't tell.

"These are *my* coins," Rebecca said.

"Are they?" Crane's voice was tinted with sarcasm. "Why don't you tell that to your father? I don't think the Guójiā Ānquán Bù will take kindly to discovering their model citizen Tseng has been hiding his pocket change from them."

Maria's hands were white on her desk. Tan hit the mute button. "What's that?" he asked Rebecca. "What's he talking about?"

"Guójiā Ānquán Bù—that's the Chinese Ministry of State Security," she whispered. Tan hit the unmute button. "Who are you?" Rebecca repeated, louder.

"That doesn't matter. What matters is that I get those coins. So let me be clear: Tonight, Tan Lee, you drop them off as instructed."

Why was he calling Tan out specifically?

"This isn't any of my business," Tan said. The music of an ice cream truck sounded in Crane's background.

"It just became your business. If you do as you're told, you all live. If not, we kill you. If you try to run, we will find you, and there is no place in your country or on earth that you and your friends can hide."

Tan's mouth went dry. His mind leaped to Sana, hidden in the Cove.

"Who are you?" he demanded.

But the line went dead. Crane was gone.

Chapter 13

"Who the hell was that?" Rebecca yelped.

"He knew me!" Tan said. His mind spun. "Could he be your dad?"

Rebecca's dark eyes widened. "No!" she said. "My father wouldn't threaten to report *himself* to the Chinese government. And definitely not to kill me!"

"He threatened to kill us all!"

"My father's controlling. But he's not a murderer. He'd have told me to come home."

"Or maybe he just wants his coins back," Tan said. "There are millions of dollars on those coins."

"Millions!" Rebecca gasped. Maria made a choking sound.

"Yes, and no wonder your dad's men are chasing you!"

"He has no idea I have the coins," Rebecca said. "They've always just sat in his vault. It's his spare money."

Tan could practically hear Winter's explosion. *Spare millions of dollars!* Was Rebecca really this out of touch?

He expelled an angry breath. "Well, *someone* clearly knows you have them!"

She rubbed the back of her neck. "I was really careful," she said in a smaller voice. "I—I didn't know I'd taken so much money."

"How is that careful?!"

"How did this—Crane—even know we were here?"

A wrench clattered to the floor. Maria was searching through a toolbox, frazzled. Her scarf had fallen off and her curly brown hair tumbled in her face.

"I'm so sorry," Tan said. "We never intended to involve you in any trouble."

All the light had gone from her eyes. "I'm on a foreign student visa from Ukraine. I can't afford to get accused of anything illegal. I could get sent back!"

"Cryptocurrencies aren't illegal in the US," Rebecca said.

"He said something about a ministry!"

"That's in China," Rebecca said. "These are my family's coins. Crane, whoever he is—he's a thief."

"I can't get involved." She flipped her laptop over and removed the hard drive. To Tan's surprise, she took a small hammer to it: *BAM! BAM! BAM!* Metal pieces scattered across her desk and dents appeared on its wooden surface.

"No, wait!" Rebecca cried.

Completely unnecessary, but Maria had done exactly what Crane asked her to do. "If he calls you again, tell him there's nothing left. I don't have any of what was on those coins. Now, please leave. I need to catch my plane."

Tan's stomach knotted. Maria had transformed. Her frizzy hair had fallen free of her scarf and her face was lined. She was terrified. And this wasn't fair to her.

"We need to get help," Tan said. "If not the police, maybe the FBI—"

"No!" Rebecca and Maria chorused together.

"I don't want to get entangled with your authorities," Maria said.

"None of us have done anything wrong," Tan said. "We just need to get this guy put away."

"Can I just get the digital keys?" Rebecca begged. "We're so close."

"I don't have them anymore, so please leave!" Maria cried.

"I need his number." Tan grabbed Maria's desk phone and a pen and jotted Crane's number onto his arm. Maria made a frantic shooing gesture, forcing them from the lab. Then she shut the door firmly after them.

In the hallway, Tan could still feel Maria's fear radiating through the walls.

"I was *so close*!" Rebecca groaned.

"I exposed her." Tan felt terrible. "We can't let this Crane guy hurt her, either."

"How did he even find us? And so fast?"

"We must have triggered some security alert when we started to access the digital keys."

"So they know where the coins are?" Rebecca checked the hallway before they stepped out the double doors into sunlight.

"They know we're here now. But he wouldn't be forcing us to drop the coins off after dark in a deserted place if he could track them. He was scared we were about to unencrypt the digital keys. And he must be too far away to reach us." At the moment, at least. Tan picked up the pace. He wanted to get back to his sister and Winter and put as much distance between them and Maria's lab as he could.

Rebecca hurried to keep up. "Where are you going?"

"I need to get back to the Cove."

"You can't leave me to deal with this alone!" She grabbed a handful of his shirt, stopping him. "You're involved, like it or not."

He wrenched free. "I did my best to help you get the cash, but now we don't have the equipment *or* the time."

"Crane wants *you* to drop them off. Didn't you hear?"

"Why me? These aren't *my* coins."

"I mean, he knows where you live now," Rebecca said.

"*What?*" Tan rocked back on his heels, bumping into a passerby. "Are you saying he's after me because my family doesn't have bodyguards to protect them?"

"I don't know," she admitted.

He started furiously down the sidewalk, and Rebecca fell into step beside him. Tan hadn't been to the Palace of Fine Arts in a few years, but he remembered tall stone columns, a lake, and a windy pathway. Plenty of places for thugs to hide.

"We need to figure out who he is," Tan snapped. "He said 'your country' to me, so he's probably not American."

"Probably not," she agreed. "Cranes are a Chinese bird. They represent longevity, immortality, wisdom."

"He knows about your dad's private stash. Who knows high-level shit like that?"

She rubbed the back of her neck. "A few employees. His executive assistant. His chief of staff. His general counsel. His bodyguard. But they've worked for him for twenty years. People would kill to get their jobs. They wouldn't try something like this. It would blow up their lives! They'd lose everything!"

Rebecca knew her own world better than he did, of course, but he wasn't so sure she understood *people*. She assumed everyone wanted to take care of her.

"So who would have gotten the alert when we accessed the keys?"

"Staff would probably see it first." Rebecca's eyes narrowed. "My father would get it, too, eventually, unless they intercept it."

"So it has to be someone on the staff, trying to steal your dad's coins. Maybe this person's got big debts to pay off or something. If he's close to your dad, he knows you've run away. And now he's taking advantage of the fact that you got those coins out of your dad's vault. So you need to call your dad. Warn him someone on his staff has gone rogue. Get his help."

"My father? He's the reason I left—to get away from him!"

"And we're in over our heads!" Tan said. "Look, all we can do is exactly what Crane's told us to do. Drop off the coins tonight. Let your dad handle the rest—he's the only one with the resources to deal with Crane."

She grabbed his arm again, her expression fierce. "I'm not crawling back to him, and I'm not letting some traitor walk away with my money! I need it to start a new life. I'm down to fifty bucks."

"And *I* need to keep my family safe!"

"Then help me! Because if anything goes wrong for any reason, Crane could pin us for money laundering and disappear, just like that."

"What?" He shook her hand off. "How is that even possible?"

"I've seen it done before," she said stiffly.

Yeah, she'd probably seen a lot more that he couldn't even begin to imagine. He, Rebecca, and even Maria could get implicated. Rebecca didn't seem to have anyone looking out for her, and Maria was an international student without any of the rights he took for granted as a citizen. He didn't know the ins and outs of foreign student visas, but Maria was probably right to worry about putting a toe out of line.

"You're naive to think it all just ends here." Rebecca crossed her arms, her face set and tense.

Tan wiped his sweaty palms on his pants. He'd always been able to think his way out of any puzzle. This shouldn't be any different. But something felt off. There were more straightforward ways to force Rebecca to turn over the coins than threatening Tan.

"Maybe we need to take a chance on the cops," he said. "Even if your dad has a mole there, they'll want to stop Crane, too, right? We tell them to watch that bench. When Crane shows up, they nab him."

"Crane may not even be in the States," she said.

"He's in San Francisco."

She frowned. "How can you possibly know that?"

"The ice cream truck singing in his call."

Her brow rose. But that didn't mean Crane would show up himself . . . If he could only reach his parents, they would know what to do.

They took a circuitous route through campus until Tan was certain no one was following them. By the time they reached a BART station, Rebecca was out of breath. The next train was five minutes away, headed for San Francisco, not Oakland and the Cove, which was what they needed to throw off any pursuers.

Tan spotted a pay phone booth in the back corner and made a beeline for it.

The call to his dad went straight to voice mail. Damn. Was he still in the wilderness? Or maybe he forgot to take his charger, which the whole Lee family tended to do. In that case, he might not even have gotten Tan's voice mail yet.

"Hi, Mom, Dad, um, I'm going to try you later, so leave your ringers on, okay?" Should he ask them to come home? Would that put them in more danger?

But he couldn't explain everything in a voice mail. He hung up. He'd have to try again later. He wished he could check his own voice mails, but he didn't know how without his actual phone.

He held the handset out to Rebecca. "Try your dad."

She didn't take it. "He won't answer a call from a strange number. In fact, he doesn't usually answer most calls or voice mails. Just from a few people. His staff handles the rest—and if Crane gets wind we're trying to reach him, he might interfere. No, we have to time calling my father carefully."

Mr. Tseng felt like an explosive with its trigger on the other side of the planet. He could help end this. But she was right. They needed to set him off at the right time and place, or they'd risk blowing themselves up instead.

"Fine, we'll call him from your phone when we drop the coins off. They'll know where we are at that point anyway." He returned the handset to its cradle with a clatter. "Let's get back to Sana and Winter."

The attack came just before their train reached the next stop.

A new influx of passengers drove him and Rebecca apart. As the doors shut again, Tan found himself standing behind a man in a beige coat, hanging on to the plastic loop overhead.

Then, without warning, the beige coat backed hard against Tan, pressing him against the glass windows. Two tall men hemmed him in, all still facing forward, moving so smoothly and subtly that no one would even know Tan was buried and fighting back behind them.

"Get off me," Tan snarled. He called on all his afternoons on the tae kwon do mat as he struggled to break free.

But their hands were relentless. They seized Tan's wrists. They dug into his pockets. Tan planted his foot on a back and shoved hard. Across the aisle, Rebecca had also been hemmed in by two buff men in flannel shirts. Tan saw her frightened, furious face flash between their shoulders.

Tan ripped himself free, but the aisle was too crowded for him to reach her.

"Need help, sonny?" An elderly man rose shakily to his feet.

"Call 911!" Tan's eyes fell on an emergency exit hatch in the roof of the train. Kicking off his attackers, Tan leaped for the cord and yanked hard. A ladder unfolded, leading up to the sky. He heaved himself up. A blast of wind rushed over his face as his head cleared the ceiling, giving him a view across the entire metal top of the train. But as it jerked to a stop, hands grabbed his legs, yanking him back down. The automatic doors opened onto a deserted platform.

Before Tan could react, the man and his partners lifted him by his elbows off his feet. They hauled him smoothly off the car—he didn't even look like he was being carried.

"Let go of me!" Tan yelled. A few passengers were gaping after them, confused, as though they weren't quite sure what was happening.

Opposite him, Rebecca was being carried out the second set of doors between the two beefy guys. The train pulled away, leaving Tan and Rebecca struggling alone with the five men.

The thug in Tan's face was older, in his mid-twenties. And built like a Marine. Tan could only hope someone had called the cops—and that a cop who wasn't in Crane's pocket would respond.

"Where are the coins?" The guy's voice grated in Tan's ear.

"I—don't—have them!" he snarled back. Once again his feet left the floor. They began carrying him toward the station's exit. Tan flared his elbows, breaking their holds and landing on his feet. He dropped into a crouch, backing away from them. He needed to fend them off until another train or reinforcements came.

But from behind, powerful hands closed around Tan's neck, compressing his windpipe.

"Tell me where they are!" grated the Marine guy before him.

Gripping the hands, Tan did a chin-up, kicking both legs outward. His feet made contact with a hard vest, earning only a minor grunt from the Marine. These guys were pros. He dug hard into the gap between his neck and his captor's sweaty arm, trying to break his hold.

"Careful," warned one of the men holding Rebecca. "We need him alive." Tan turned his head as far as he could. Just a few feet away, Rebecca stood immobilized with her hands locked at her sides.

The ground vibrated. With relief, Tan spotted another train rumbling into the station. Startled faces pressed against the windows, watching them. A few cell phones rose into the air, snapping videos and photos. The thug holding Tan swore. He shoved Tan at Rebecca, and the men took off.

As passengers began to disembark, Tan gasped for breath. Sweet oxygen filled his lungs. His throat felt bruised and achy. Rebecca held a hand to her heaving chest. There was a scratch on her cheek. Blood covered her hands. She was pissed.

"Is something going on?" asked an elderly woman.

Rebecca paled. "No. No, we're fine."

"You're bleeding quite a bit. You should go to a hospital." The woman's companions murmured in agreement. One handed her a handkerchief.

"It's his blood, not mine." She mopped blood from her arm, steadying her voice with an obvious effort. "I scratched him. A lot."

Tan stumbled aboard. Rebecca followed. He didn't know where this train was headed, but it didn't matter.

"Did they get the coins?" he asked.

Rebecca reached down the front of her dress and pulled the red pouch out. "I still have them."

She'd protected the coins. That was something. Tan wasn't sure he'd have been as successful. He massaged his aching throat. "Those guys meant business," he said. He'd felt their purposefulness as those hands had closed around his windpipe.

"They weren't going to hurt us," Rebecca said. "Whoever sicced them on us told them not to hurt us."

"They told them not to *kill* us." But yes, the man had said they needed Tan alive. It had made the difference. But why? And why had it felt like they were trying to haul him off somewhere, instead of just trying to take the coins?

Taking a seat, he glanced out the window. "I was almost positive no one was following us from Maria's lab. But they found us anyway."

He checked all their pockets and clothes for AirTags or other tracking devices that might have been slipped in somewhere. They found nothing. Tan's mind whirled as they transferred to a bus headed for Oakland, and then finally disembarked a block from the Cove.

"The only thing we did between Maria's and that attack was call my parents," Tan finally concluded as they neared the cathedral's gate. That was it. He turned to Rebecca. "They're tapping my parents' phones."

She grabbed his hand and held it tightly. "Tan, if we could get access to equipment like Maria's, you could finish the job, right? You know how to decrypt the digital keys and convert them all the way into cash, don't you?"

"Well, yes . . ."

"So why don't you before we turn them over? I'll still give you a cut. Fifty-fifty. And now that we know what they're worth . . ." She gave him a probing look. "That kind of money is life-changing, Tan. I know it would be for you."

Tan's head spun. It *was* life-changing. There was no denying it. He could afford any college he wanted. Winter, too. They could afford that and so much more.

But all that was beside the point. They were being so reckless, all for Rebecca to get her hands on a big pile of money.

"We *don't* have the equipment." Tan ran his hands through his hair, and turned into the cathedral, heading for its heavy front door. "And it could take me days to figure it out. We only have a few hours, and don't you think this Crane guy might be a little pissed if we dipped into his pot before we turned it over?"

"It's not his pot!"

"Well, he seems to think it is, so maybe it is somehow!"

"It's *not*." Rebecca glowered. "I think I know who Crane is."

Chapter 14

The Cove buzzed with energy, its vaulted halls echoing with voices. There was nowhere to talk privately about Crane. In the dining hall, people their age were bent over homework together. They dug into ceramic bowls full of popcorn, which gave off a buttery scent. Sunlight through the stained glass windows threw colored patterns on the floor, giving the whole place an idyllic atmosphere that felt blissfully removed from the attack.

Tan popped his head into the common room, needing to see for himself that Winter and Sana were safe. But the common room was vacant, the couches emptied of lounging kids.

Rebecca tugged him by the arm toward the shared computer. "Let me show you him."

She took a seat and pulled up a Chinese-language online article. A photo at the top featured her dad, a distinguished man in his forties, with salt-and-pepper hair and posture Master Kwon would die for. According to the caption, he was shaking hands with the British ambassador to China.

Rebecca pointed to a thin, balding man in the background, hovering respectfully at her father's elbow. He almost blended into the wallpaper and wasn't named in the caption.

"That's Liping," she said. "He's my father's chief of staff. He oversees everything. His personal security. His finances. Even the housekeeping staff. I call him Uncle Li. His full name is Chen Liping."

Liping was close in age to Rebecca's dad. Late forties. His crisp blazer hugged a white button-down shirt, and his hair was neatly cut, but somehow, next to Rebecca's immaculately groomed father, he still looked a little frumpish.

Was this Crane? Standing elbow to elbow with power, but unhappy with his spot? A knot tightened in Tan's middle.

"He knows about the coins," Rebecca said. "He probably set them up for my father in the first place. He's also one of the few people who would have gotten an alert. He has access to everything. My father must have told him I'd taken off. He's the one who would have sent those guards to your house."

"So he was supposed to come after you, but instead he's going rogue. Would he really try to steal from your family? Threaten you? I mean, he looks pretty cozy with your dad."

She spread her hands. "If you'd asked me last month, I'd have said Liping was a meek, mild-mannered man and there was no way he would cross my father. He even courted my aunt years ago—my father's younger sister. My father didn't approve of the match—he broke it off quickly."

"Did he make your aunt leave the country, too?" A bitter taste rose in Tan's mouth.

Rebecca flushed. "I always thought . . . Liping accepted it. I mean, he was a scholarship student at Peking University. He didn't have a penny of his own. Of course they could never be together."

"But if he'd married your aunt, he'd have had plenty of pennies, wouldn't he? Your dad thought he was good enough to be his right-hand man but not good enough to marry his sister."

"He *wasn't* good enough," Rebecca said. "I mean, he *works for my family*. My aunt is a princess."

In her voice, Tan could hear everything Liping meant and didn't mean to the Tseng empire. And Tan, too. Tan's family could work for Rebecca's. In fact, wasn't that sort of what Rebecca was expecting of him now as well? Tan was good enough to work for Rebecca, but he would never be good enough to be in a relationship with her. He'd sensed that while they were dating. Very few people were good enough for the Tsengs.

But that wasn't what mattered now. "Who would take over if your dad was out of the picture?"

"There would be a search for a successor to run the day-to-day operations," she said, studying the photo. "But Liping would run it in the meantime."

"I wish there were a way to confirm it's him," Tan mused. "If it's him, you need to warn your dad."

Rebecca was studying the photo on the screen. "My father looks fancy, doesn't he?" she said. "He's been in the papers my whole life. Everything so glossy and perfect."

"He looks like a regular person," Tan snapped. He was, frankly, tired of Rebecca building up her family into demigods. "A regular guy with the same problems as everyone else." Like runaway kids and controlling dysfunctional parents and people whose loyalties he couldn't count on.

She gave him an uncomprehending gaze. "That's what I meant. It came out wrong."

"Fine." He crossed to the back door. Winter and Sana were probably still working on the tree house. He needed Winter's take on all this—the ultimatum from Crane, Rebecca's theory about her dad's right-hand man. How they were going to end this nightmare.

Tan's hand was on the doorknob. But a sixth sense made him look back. Rebecca was still at the computer—logging into her email account.

"Rebecca, don't!" Tan dived for her, batting her hand away. But it was too late. She'd logged in, and her email account would mark her location.

Tan shoved her aside and took over her browser. Five unread messages stood out in bold font at the top of her inbox. He clicked into her settings and dug into her profile history. As he'd feared, her location sharing was turned on, with the latest login marked: *Oakland, CA*. Time-stamped *4:04p Pacific Time*—right now.

Rebecca gasped. "I didn't know—"

"Liping might be able to see this." Tan shut off the tracker, deleted the Oakland stamp, then logged her out.

She made no move to stop him. She backed away, knocking into a lamp that crashed to the floor. She still didn't move, and Tan righted it.

"Are you okay?" he asked. Her face was white.

"The location isn't that precise," Tan said, trying to reassure her. "At least Oakland's big enough he can't know exactly where we are. Just—" *Don't do it again*, he wanted to say. But she knew that. It wasn't her fault her dad's thugs were hawking after them. He was playing Whac-A-Mole against them.

But the location tracker gave Tan an idea. "If we could confirm Liping is in San Francisco or even at Berkeley, would that be surprising?"

"Well, yes," Rebecca said. "He never comes to the States. All his work for my father is done out of Shanghai." She frowned. "Can you track *Liping's* location?"

"Do you know his email address?"

"Of course."

Tan pulled the keyboard back toward him and began to create a new email account. "I can send him a tracker email. If he opens it, I'll be able to identify his city location. Whose email would he open right away? Not like a work email he could ignore for a while."

"My aunt," she said grimly. "Her name is Luli. Luli Tseng."

Tan's hands paused over the keys. "Not her. What about you? He'd read your email, right?"

"Especially now!"

"Let's create a new account for you. You're on the run. You'd do that." He pushed the keyboard toward her, and she created one using her middle initial and the year. "Okay, now send him an email. About anything. We don't want him to know you suspect him. I just need him to open it."

"I'll write that I need help," Rebecca said. "I do that all the time."

She addressed the email to Liping, then switched the keys and typed in Chinese characters. "I'm telling him I want to go shopping in Paris next week and need my credit card limit extended." She grimaced. "That's pretty much in character, as far as he understands me."

He added the tracker to her email and hit Send. Then he shut off the account. They wouldn't need it again.

"If he opens the email, I'll be able to check his location remotely. I'll check in an hour." He rose. "Let's go find Winter and Sana."

Rebecca didn't move, like she hadn't even heard him again.

"Rebecca?" he asked sharply. "What's wrong?"

Her eyes fluttered. "It was all spam," she said, almost to herself.

"Spam?"

She gave a wooden jerk of her head. "Let's go," she said.

Tan spotted Winter beside a massive tree, vigorously brushing brown paint onto boards for the tree house roof. A plastic smock tied at the back accentuated her waist. The scent of paint mingled with the aroma of pine needles as Tan hurried past a group of kids on stepladders painting the frames around the sanctuary windows.

Winter sensed him before he even reached her. She turned her head and caught his gaze, and her cheeks flushed with relief. She lowered her brush. "There you are."

"Rebecca, join us," Sister Ava said, extending an apron to Rebecca. Tan expected Rebecca to refuse, but she was still in that trance. She accepted the apron and moved toward a partially whitewashed fence. Deeper in the yard, Sana was splashing through a sprinkler with a group of older kids.

"Tan!" Sana veered toward him and enveloped him in a paint-spattered hug. "Guess what! Me and Lucia are best friends now, even though she's older than me. The boys here are stinky"—Lucia's influence—"and Jaxon keeps saying 'Hi, Sana' whenever he walks by. Why does he do that?"

"Because he has no imagination!" Lucia said, eliciting a giggle from Sana.

The yard was busy in motion, with kids sawing boards, kids hammering high in the trees—beats bouncing off the cathedral walls—and kids sweeping the clearing. Tan liked how everyone had a job. Sister Ava's doing, clearly. If only they could stay here and rest assured nothing bad would happen until their parents came home.

But Crane had made that impossible.

"Let's go paint the window," he suggested to Winter, pointing to the farthest unpainted frame of the cathedral. Winter wordlessly threaded a roll of blue painter's tape onto her arm and picked up a fresh can of paint. He grabbed a rusty stepladder, and they headed over the fragrant carpet of pine needles together.

"Can't believe we've only been here a day," Winter said. "It feels like weeks."

Their shoulders brushed. "I feel about a hundred years old."

"What happened?" She levered a screwdriver into the can of paint, popping the lid open.

He set their stepladder just below the window frame. "Complications. Turns out the coins are storing the digital keys to millions of dollars of cryptocurrencies."

She whistled. "All Rebecca's dad's?"

"Yep. It's money he's hiding from the Chinese government. Probably only part of it. Those thugs came after us at Berkeley, too. We had to lose them."

"Really? Is *that* why you were gone so long?" At his nod, Winter sucked in a breath, her eyes dark with worry. He filled her in while she laid wide strips of the blue painter's tape around the edges of the frame. She was a pro at it.

"Rebecca thinks Crane is her dad's right-hand man," Tan concluded. "He gave us an ultimatum. Tonight, he wants the coins delivered to the Palace of Fine Arts and left under a rock."

Her eyes widened. "She has to go there?"

"He wants *me* to do it, actually."

"Why you?"

"I don't know," Tan admitted. "Rebecca thinks it's because he can count on me to do what she won't do. Like, we're more vulnerable." More willing to cave in? Honestly, her explanation didn't fully do it for him. Especially now that they suspected it was Liping, who knew Rebecca personally.

"Maybe Crane already figures Rebecca won't do it. I mean, he'd be right. We want to turn them over. She doesn't."

"He said if we don't, he'll find us." All around the cheerful yard, kids were hard at work. Oblivious. "We can't risk the Cove. But once he has the coins, I'm hoping he stops coming after us. That would only expose him more."

Winter frowned. "Feels like every time we tug on one stray thread, a whole sweater unravels."

"Which is why we need Rebecca's dad to step in. It's his man." Tan frowned. "Rebecca offered me a cut, by the way. Half would go to you." He should at least let her know.

Winter shook her head. "It's one thing for her to take her dad's money. Completely different for us to take it."

"I figured you'd see it that way." He was relieved. "I wasn't able to ask about your dad's iPhone. I'm sorry."

"I didn't think she could help anyway." Winter ripped open a pouch containing a plastic drop cloth and shook it out over the ground like a picnic blanket. "Well, no way are you and Rebecca going alone. I'm coming this time."

Tan frowned. "What about Sana? She's the priority."

"She's like a sister to me, and she's perfectly safe here. I can't say the same for you. Or why not drop off the coins now? We can be gone before they arrive. And during daylight."

"Too many tourists," Tan said. "Someone else could find them. But we could go the hour before, after the crowds thin out. If they're planning an ambush, we can avoid them."

"If I come, that's a decoy. They're expecting two of you, not three."

"They know you from the 911 dispatch," Tan reminded her.

"Then let's go in disguise."

"Disguise?"

"I'll show you. Let's finish this first." She climbed onto the step-ladder and held out her hand. Confused, Tan automatically took it. She let out a low laugh and squeezed his fingers in her warm ones, then pointed over his shoulder. "I meant, can you hand me the tape?"

When the window frame shone a bright brown all around, Winter capped their paint can. She and Tan carried their equipment back to the group, where Rebecca was wiping paint from her hands onto a turpentine rag.

"Tan filled me in about tonight," Winter said. "I have some ideas."

Tan expected Rebecca to protest—after all, she hadn't agreed to turn over the coins yet. But she just said, "Like what?"

She followed Winter, surprisingly willingly. Winter led them into the common room, where she pulled a tote bag from the shelves. "They have costumes for cosplay." From the bag she pulled out wigs, hats, and glasses without lenses. "They're high-quality.

And we might as well make it harder for them to recognize us." She finger-combed out a blond wig and handed it to Rebecca.

"You want me to wear *this*?" Rebecca asked.

"Yes." Winter handed Tan a short, sandy-haired wig and pulled a matching guy's wig onto her own hair.

"We look like twins," Tan said, amused. He fit the wig over his hair, and Winter smoothed its curls over his forehead. "It itches," he complained.

"Don't be such a baby." Winter smiled. She opened the cabinet to reveal their reflection. Amazing. The wigs were so well designed, Tan couldn't tell they were wearing them. The three of them together looked like a slightly shaggy pair of brothers and a girl.

Then Winter's smile faded in the mirror, and she turned back to Tan and Rebecca. "What's to stop these people from kidnapping you for ransom?" she asked soberly.

"That would be a death sentence," Rebecca said. "Kidnapping a Tseng. Even if my parents don't care about me, my father wouldn't tolerate something like that against his family. Liping—if it's him—will do the minimum to get what he wants."

"So you've decided?" Tan asked. "To turn over the coins?"

"Like you said. We don't have much of a choice."

It wasn't the answer Tan expected. Rebecca was so dead set against it before. He'd expected a fight. What had changed? But if she was on board, he wasn't going to do anything to jeopardize this fragile victory.

Tan pulled off his own wig with some relief. His head was already sweaty. "Let me check if Liping's opened that email yet."

He moved to the computer terminal and logged in to the tracker system. Rebecca and Winter hovered over his shoulders. A notification indicated Liping had opened the email fourteen minutes ago. Tan clicked on it, and there was Liping's location: San Francisco.

"So he's here." Rebecca sat heavily on a chair. "He must be Crane. There's no other reason for him to be on this side of the Pacific Ocean."

"I'm sorry," Tan said. "We should leave early so you can call your dad from San Francisco. Warn him to take care of himself."

"And get our families out of this mess," Winter added. She dropped her wig into a spare tote bag and extended it toward Rebecca. "Tell him a five-year-old is involved, if you have to."

Rebecca dropped her wig into the bag. "I'm not calling him."

"We agreed to that!" Tan said, adding his wig to the pile. "You have to!"

She lifted her chin. "I said I'd turn over the coins to Liping. I never agreed I'd call my father."

"We need his help," Tan said. "Besides, it's his money. He doesn't deserve to have it stolen from him."

"He deserves to lose every cent he has," she said with a quiet finality to her voice.

This was a new twist. "Am I missing something?" Tan asked.

Rebecca ran her fingers tenderly over her cheek. Then she said, stiffly, "He hasn't even bothered to come after me."

"What? I thought—" Tan's mind spun. "They *broke down* my door."

Mr. Tseng had sent Robin Hood and Little John to get her back, hadn't he? Because even if he was blind to what had gone down with Albert, she was so important to him and his empire, his only child . . . That's what they'd all believed . . .

"Those guys who broke down your door?" Rebecca repeated softly. "They weren't sent by my family to try to get me back. They were sent by Liping."

"We know that already. Liping's acting on your dad's orders to find you, and that's how he figured out you had the coins."

"No, Liping sent them . . . to get the coins. *Not* on my father's orders. Because why hasn't my father called me? Why hasn't he emailed me?"

"I thought you blocked his calls," Winter began. But her voice trailed off.

"I unblocked his number at Berkeley. After we got that call from Liping. But he hasn't left any voice mails. And right before I flew out from Shanghai, I sent him and my mom a long email about Albert and why I was taking off. But I just checked my emails—Tan saw them—and nothing." She gestured at the computer. "No reply. Not from him. Not from my mom."

It was true: Only five new emails had appeared in her inbox since the date she left home. No flood of frantic emails begging her to come home or at least let them know she was safe.

"I left *days* ago," Rebecca said. "Turns out he *didn't* send anyone after me. To him, this is probably just a tantrum. I don't matter to him half as much as the crypto matters to a bunch of traitors and criminals." She spat that last part out.

So criminals after the coins had battered down their door. After the *coins*. Not the wayward, priceless Tseng daughter. Her running away was a complete nonissue for her family. She'd expected an apology, anger, being called a foolish girl by her dad—but nothing at all?

"Maybe he sent Liping to get you, not knowing Liping was after the coins," Winter said, but her voice was doubtful.

"Then why didn't they reply? Why haven't they called?" She hugged her purse to her chest.

"They didn't want to scare you away?"

She snorted. "That kind of delicacy isn't his mode of operation. Not with me, at least."

"He must not know about Liping, then," Winter said. "At the minimum, his pride wouldn't let Liping get away with this. You said it yourself—you're a Tseng. And someone's threatening you, stealing from him—it would be embarrassing, at the very least."

Rebecca gave a short laugh. "Well, I'm definitely not begging for his attention just because his pride's at stake." She turned to go, but Tan grabbed her arm. Her gaze, as she turned it on him, was wounded. He'd never seen her so defeated.

"Look, I get you don't want to talk to your parents because they've abandoned you," he said. "I'm sorry about that. I really am. I've hated the way they've treated you from the very beginning." He meant it.

She cast her gaze down at the floorboards. "I know," she said softly.

"But we need your dad's help. Winter and Sana and I can't go home until we're sure those thugs aren't going to come after us."

Rebecca broke free of Tan's grip and headed deeper into the cathedral. Tan started after her, but Winter lay a steadying hand on his shoulder.

"Give her some time," Winter said as he turned back to her. "It's a big shock for her. I mean, I can't help feeling sorry for her."

"Yeah. I can't believe they don't even care. But we need her dad."

"We'll get him. Nothing we can do until we leave the Cove tonight anyway. Come on."

"I'm still not sure about you coming," Tan said.

"I'm not letting you go off by yourself to face a guy who had you strangled in broad daylight." Her fingers rose to his neck, gently touching the bruise that had formed there. "Not if your only backup is Rebecca." She pulled away, leaving a burning sensation there that had nothing to do with the choke hold. "Also, they're expecting a guy and a girl, not two guys and a blond girl. And I don't want her screwing you over somehow."

Tan wanted to protest that Rebecca wouldn't do that. But her unpredictability was one of the qualities that had attracted him to her. And now look where they'd ended up.

Winter was looking into his face. He had the uncomfortable feeling she was reading into him a lot more than he wanted her to.

"Come on," she said. Then she took his hand and led him back to the yard.

At a long table near the tree house, Sister Ava was pouring lemonade into glasses. Slices of strawberries swam in her pitcher.

Sister Ava was bombarded by Cove kids and guests showing her a flower, a homework assignment, a note from a secret admirer. Sister Ava was delighted, sympathetic, charmed. Caring for Sana helped Tan appreciate the patience that went into caring for two dozen homeless teens. Sana asked for so much attention, and she had three adults and two teenagers to provide it. She was incredibly lucky. They all were. But Sister Ava was her own force of nature, catalyzing creative projects like making benches from spare lumber and moving tasks along like clockwork, while somehow making everyone around her feel comfortable.

"Sister Ava," Winter said. Winter pushed back a glass precariously close to the table edge. "We might need another night after all."

"You're welcome to stay as long as you need," Sister Ava said.

"Something came up tonight that we need to take care of," Winter continued. "Would it be okay if Sana stayed here with you? We'll be out past her bedtime."

"That means you guys will be out past curfew yourselves," she answered. "We usually lock the gates and doors after dark, unless we're expecting deliveries like last night."

Tan wasn't sure how effective locked gates and doors would be against a man with unlimited resources. Their best protection was that Liping didn't know about the Cove. Above all, they needed to keep it that way.

"Could we borrow a key?" Winter asked.

"I can get you a spare." She pursed her lips, as if deciding how much she wanted to challenge them. "I prefer my charges to abide by curfew while they are here, but I'd also rather they stay than leave because the rules don't work for them."

"Thank you," Tan said. His throat ached with gratitude. The worst things somehow also brought out the best things, and Sister Ava was one of them. But should he stay behind with his sister? That didn't feel right, either. How could he let Winter and Rebecca go off to face Liping by themselves?

"We will take good care of Sana," the nun added, as if reading his mind. Tan reached for the pitcher and accidentally knocked over the empty glass Winter had moved earlier. "Oh no!" He braced for the shatter of glass on the concrete, but Sister Ava grabbed it out of the air with a dexterity that surprised them all. She set it back on his tray without so much as a ruffled hair.

"You'd be surprised how often that happens." She smiled.

"Wow, good reflexes," Winter said.

Jaxon, Guy, and Perry appeared around the corner, coming toward them. Guy was dusting flour off a pair of oversize pants. Perry was juggling oranges instead of apples this time. Jaxon waved a piece of paper. Rebecca appeared just behind them, carrying the rest of the oranges in a bowl.

"Hey, Sana." Jaxon brandished the paper, which was covered in numbers and letters and Sana's larger handwriting in the center. "We cracked your code."

"That was a hard one," Perry said. "Can't believe a four-year-old schooled us."

"Five!" Sana insisted, running up to take the paper.

"Right! Five!" Perry said, pretending to be surprised. It was clearly a running joke.

"You did it!" Sana said, pleased. She revealed the paper to the code and its translation: *I WANT A COOKIE.*

"I grabbed you one from the kitchen." Guy handed over a large chocolate chunk cookie and bit into a second one. Sana bit into hers with a gusty sigh of delight.

"How many of those have you had?" Tan asked suspiciously.

"Five." Sana glowed.

"Tan, Winter, wanna give me a hand with this ladder?" Jaxon asked.

"Sure," Tan said. He and Winter braced short boards horizontally against the trunk while Jaxon hammered long nails into them.

"Why aren't we using a rope ladder?" Jaxon asked Sister Ava, who was bringing them a refill of nails. "Then we could pull it up behind us. Make it a real fort."

"The tree house is meant to be shared by everyone," Sister Ava said.

"My parents are busy building a *real* house for me to live in," Lucia said from her seat on a log. She was twining a long blade of grass through her nimble fingers. "That's why I'm here, waiting for them."

"Lucia," Sister Ava chided gently. "Our stories are our stories. The Lord gave them to us. We have nothing to be ashamed of."

"I *hate* living in a shelter." Her voice was fierce and low.

"We all live in one," said Jaxon. "So stop dogging on it all the time."

"I don't really have a home, either." Rebecca came to Lucia's rescue. She set her bowl of oranges on the snacks table.

Lucia gazed up at her, surprised. "Really? But your clothes are so nice."

Rebecca wrinkled a fold of her dress. "I mean, I have parents who have money. But I was raised mostly by people who weren't my parents. Now I . . ." She searched for the right words. "Don't have anywhere I belong."

"Then you fit right in," Guy said.

Rebecca's brow furrowed. "Really?"

"I've never met my birth parents," Lucia admitted.

Sana's eyes widened. "But you said they were working—"

"I know what I said." Lucia's voice rose slightly. "I don't know anything about my family. I just wish I did so much, sometimes it comes out that way."

"Oh," Sana said.

"Where are you from, Rebecca?" Lucia asked. "You never said."

Rebecca still seemed thrown by Guy's comment. She collected herself before answering. "I was born in Shanghai, and so were my parents, and my grandparents before them. My grandparents on both sides knew each other before my parents met and got married."

"Was it an arranged marriage?" Winter asked.

"No, but they were introduced with that hope in mind." She grimaced. "Their families wanted them to marry in the same circle. Same for me."

"The same *rich* circle, you mean," Winter clarified.

"Not like your dad's sister and Liping," Tan said. Rebecca's frown deepened.

Guy, Jaxon, and Perry began to clean up paint cans and brushes. Winter and Tan pitched in.

"Now that we've joined the Cove, we need cubbies, too," Sana said. "I spelled my name out in gumdrops on my bed table so everyone knows it's mine. Jaxon, why did *you* join the Cove?"

"Sana," Tan admonished. There was probably a code of respect for privacy here. Not to mention the Cove wasn't exactly a club to be joined . . . Although he could see why it felt that way.

"All good," Jaxon said easily, wadding up a sheet of plastic film.

"He says it's *all good*," Sana told Tan pointedly. "How old are you, Jaxon?"

"Seventeen." Jaxon laughed. "I came here two years ago to escape my mom's asshole boyfriend—pardon my French, Sana—and I stayed on as a volunteer. I live here full-time, like my pals here."

"Your turn, Guy," Sana declared, sounding exactly like her kindergarten teacher. "Start with your age, like Jaxon."

Sana persuaded Guy to share his story as they moved among the trees, collecting stray paint cans, brushes, and empty tape rolls. Guy was eighteen. A gentle giant with a single mom, who relinquished him to the foster system when he was four.

"*Four?*" Sana gawked. "Younger than me."

Guy tweaked her nose.

Like Lucia, Guy had gone from one family to another, until he finally landed on Sister Ava's doorstep last year. He'd found a clerical job at a doctor's office down the street. "I've been paying my own rent here for two months now," he said, low. "It's subsidized, but still. It's a first for me. For anyone in my family."

"Amazing," Winter said.

"Now you, Perry," Sana ordered.

"I just got here last month," Perry answered, pulling a napkin-wrapped cookie from their pocket. "I'm the newest. My family lives outside Sacramento. They found out I'm nonbinary and kicked me out." The Cove had been divided into boys and girls for its entire forty years of existence. But when Perry arrived, Sister Ava had given Perry their own room next to hers.

"Wasn't what I expected from a *nun*," Perry said around a mouthful of cookie. "But she said there were eight genders in ancient Jewish texts and even rules about how to know which rules applied to you if you weren't sure what gender you were. She really walks the talk. There aren't many human beings like her."

Tan sat back, letting their conversation wash over him. The evening plans still weighed heavily on him. And he had to persuade Rebecca to call her dad. But it was cathartic to listen in and work hard with his hands on a goal that had nothing to do with Liping or the coins or getting their lives back. And to see Sana make some new friends, which she apparently had a superpower for. Tan was also fascinated by their stories, and so was Winter, although surprisingly, it was Rebecca who inched closest to listen.

"Rebecca, did you paint this mural?" Sister Ava exclaimed as they returned to the tree house.

The newly constructed fence around the tree's base was covered in green and blue swirls that, together, made up a forest. Tan didn't know Rebecca could paint like that.

"I've never built a tree house before," Rebecca said in a low voice. "I thought this blended in nicely."

Sister Ava touched a frosted cluster of grapes. "These are stunning."

Rebecca gulped. "There was a Greek painter, Zeuxis, who painted grapes so real that they attracted birds. That's the true test, I always thought. If you can fool animals into believing your painting, then you're a master. I'm not there yet, but I'd like to be. One day."

"That's a beautiful thought," Sister Ava said. The other kids around them snapped their fingers to show their agreement. Even Sana, although her tiny fingers made no sound. Tan could almost forget they had an appointment set by Liping tonight. Almost, but not quite.

As for Rebecca, she did something Tan had never seen her do before. She blushed.

Chapter 15

It was only six o'clock. They planned to leave at eight, giving them time to get to the Palace of Fine Arts by nine, well before the appointed meeting time.

Meanwhile, Sister Ava showed them to a room with a high ceiling and large windows looking out on a massive oak tree. Empty shelves lined the walls, surrounding four tables stacked high with books of all sizes.

"Our old library was a tiny closet," she said. "Fortunately, we received this wonderful donation, so we set this room up just a few weeks ago. It's a work in progress."

Organizing the library was surprisingly fun. Tan recognized many familiar titles from his childhood. *The Chronicles of Narnia. The Little Prince.* A children's Bible with colorful pictures. There were also new books unfamiliar to Tan. *Too Many Tamales.* ("Oh, love that one!" Winter said.) Tan flipped through them as he cataloged them on an ancient computer.

Sister Ava gave Sana a stack of ten picture books. "Why don't you sort these for me?" she said. "Put them in alphabetical order by the authors' last names." She pointed to the last name on the cover with a slim finger. "By the first letter."

"Picture books?" Sana opened her eyes wide with surprise. "But everyone here is *old*."

Sister Ava laughed. "No one is too old for picture books. I find some of the greatest truths in them."

It was a good task for Sana, who had learned her alphabet in pre-school and exercised it through ciphers and codes now. Mom would approve; this was babysitting to the exponential power. From Sana's perspective, this week so far had been one long field trip . . . Except they couldn't exactly tell their parents about it.

Rebecca opted to paint the walls in the hallway, a difficult task that meant she'd be on her feet the whole time, but she seemed to like wielding her long roller brush. She caught Winter's surprised glance.

"What?" she said sharply.

"I'm just—nothing," Winter said, and Rebecca headed out the door.

Tan and Winter set up a cozy reading nook by the window, with a pile of pillows for kids to sprawl in any position, and plenty of natural light shining on their pages. Sana promptly laid herself down. Her stack of picture books toppled in a landslide.

"My dad and I used to read together under that tree out there." Winter's gaze was slightly haunted as she gazed out the window. "It was his favorite spot when he lived here."

"Have you figured out new things about him while we've been here?"

She flashed him a smile. "Thanks for asking. He always had a special interest in refugees. In a way, I guess he was one himself. And this community mattered. It kept him safe. It kept him going." She tied back the brocade curtains with their golden tassels.

"I wish I could have met him," Tan said.

Her eyes grew fierce. "He was the best dad. He knew me so well.

He made it his business to know me. And he and my mom, they really loved each other." She skimmed her fingertips over the gilded cover of a book of fairy tales they'd propped onto a book stand to entice readers. Her hand fell. "In the real world, why don't the good guys win?"

"The story isn't over," Tan said. "There's still you."

She locked gazes with him.

He meant it. Winter had so much strength, and so much to give. There was no way a person like her could not end up winning in the end.

The door swung open, startling them both. Lucia entered with a tray of cookies and milk. Tan was surprised to find his heart racing. He needed space. It was too hard to breathe when he and Winter were sharing the same air molecules.

"Hungry?" Lucia asked, setting the tray on one of the tables.

"How can we be? We are literally getting fed nonstop," Winter said fondly, joining Lucia at the table.

"That's the Cove for you. The apostles were always eating fish and bread, or something like that." Lucia shrugged. "I'm on dinner crew. Curry. Do you guys like spicy or nonspicy?"

"Wow, that's fancy," Winter said. "Spicy for me."

"Non for me," Tan said.

"Me too," Sana said, and Lucia headed out again.

Winter handed Sana a glass of milk and then one to Tan. "Should we take a break?"

The moment between them was over, and he was relieved.

"Sure," he said.

Winter bit into a sugar cookie. "Mm, *so good.*" She held it out to him. "Want a bite?"

He bit into the warm cookie, still in her hand, without thinking. Their eyes met over it. Then Winter dropped the cookie hastily and Tan caught it and backed away. A bit flustered, he touched the corkboard hung on the wall, pinned with old-fashioned Polaroid pictures of the current Cove kids.

Winter sat down at the table. "I can't believe Sister Ava looks after all these kids twenty-four seven," she said in a voice that told him she was determined to keep things normal.

"Right? One kid for a week is almost more than I can handle." Tan tweaked Sana's nose, also determined. "What? No eye roll?" He pretended to be astonished.

Sana smirked. "Lucia says rolling your eyes is only for little kids."

"And you are definitely a big kid," Tan said. Her palms were scored red from her fall, but she didn't let them get in her way. She even wore her knee bandages, which Winter had changed twice today, without a peep of complaint. But joking around with Sana only underscored the reality of how badly he was doing at keeping her safe.

He sat with Winter at the table, and Sana climbed onto his lap. "This is fun," Sana said. She threaded string through her fingers for a game of cat's cradle. "It's like a snow day."

"How do you know what a snow day is?" Tan asked. "It doesn't snow here."

"Lucia told me about them. She lived in Canada before. Your dad was so lucky he lived here, Winter. Winter! That's when it snows in Canada."

"At long last, we've opened the box of Winter-related jokes," Tan said.

Winter smiled. "I don't mind. I visited Canada with my mom and dad, and I got them nonstop. Those are some of the photos on my dad's phone." Winter touched the six-digit numbers on her hand. When Tan's gaze fell on it, she covered it.

"I'm not going to figure it out," she said. "I just have to accept it."

The quiet resignation in her voice tugged at Tan. He didn't want her to have to accept it. But it seemed that she'd have to.

Sana held out her string-laced fingers to Winter. "Play."

Winter took hold of the string for cat's cradle. Tan held Sana around her waist while the two of them played. Winter's gaze was intently focused on the shifting lines and shapes between her fingers and Sana's. It gave Tan an excuse to study her face. The mischievous tilt to her nose. Her quick smile, which she gave generously to match Sana's energy.

He felt as though he could study Winter for years and still not know enough of her. Silly small things like how many freckles she had and big things like what legacy she wanted to leave. He wanted to make it his business to know everything there was and ever would be about her.

And he also wanted to kiss her, every freckle, everywhere.

But was it wrong to feel this way about Winter, whom he respected so much? Tan felt a pang in his chest. Rising, he set Sana on her feet, still maneuvering the string with Winter, and went back to work on the shelves.

"Whew. I'm wiped out," Winter said when the last book was finally shelved. She settled into the newly created book nook. The sky outside was dark, and the streetlamps beyond the wall had turned on. They had a little more than an hour left before they had to leave.

"These won't stay shelved for long," Tan said. "Not if this library is doing its job." He spotted a copy of his childhood *Book of Codes* tucked between two fat books on a shelf. He pulled the copy free. "Case in point." He made it dance before Winter, who smiled.

"You are ridiculously obsessed with that book," she said.

He set it onto a book stand for display. "Just glad the kids here get exposed to this, too."

"Was the ten thousandth light switched on or off?"

He smiled. "Here, I'll show you." He pulled out a sheet of paper and pencil, sat at a table, and drew twenty cubes in a long row. "Here are your light bulbs. Here goes Student One." He marked them all *on* with a circle beneath. "Student Two." He marked every other one off with an *x* beneath. "Student Three. So, to recap: Student One flips every switch, Student Two flips every other switch . . ."

She joined him at the table. Their heads bent together as he filled in the first ten rows of the chart:

1	2	3	4	5	6	7	8	9	10	11	12	13	14	15	16	17	18	19	20
o	o	o	o	o	o	o	o	o	o	o	o	o	o	o	o	o	o	o	o
	x		x		x		x		x		x		x		x		x		x
		x			o			x			o			x			o		
			o				o				x				o				o
				x					o					o					x
					x						o						x		
						x							o						
							x								x				
								o									o		
									x										o

"So the early bulbs will never be touched again, since the next student will skip over them. So that pattern is set. Do you see it?"

She stared at the boxes. "No," she admitted. "Do you?"

"I've done this before, remember?"

"Yes, but at what number student did you realize the pattern?"

"Eight."

"See what I mean?" She stared at the grid again. "I don't see a pattern. I thought, maybe prime numbers? One, two, three, five, seven . . . but they're mostly off."

"Read the numbers of the ones that are switched on."

"Um, yeah. Okay. One. Four. Nine."

She paused. He waited.

"I give up!"

"They're perfect squares," he said. "One times one. Two times two. Three times three."

"No way!" She blinked at the chart. Then took his pencil and quickly filled in the chart until Student Sixteen flipped on the sixteenth bulb—the next perfect square. "Four times four!"

"And if you sketch it out"—he added five columns to the right—"bulb twenty-five doesn't get touched again—not by Students Seventeen, Eighteen, Nineteen, Twenty . . . until Student Twenty-Five turns it on."

"So the ten thousandth light is one hundred times one hundred—is on?"

"Yep."

She stared at his work. "Brilliant. Seriously."

He laughed. "It's just for fun." He could do this. He could be just-friends with Winter.

The bell chimed the hour. Seven o'clock. One hour to go.

They'd made good use of their time. He was proud of the library. The shelves were full of neatly organized books. The file cabinet was updated and color-coordinated. A few books with bent covers or missing spines had been lovingly re-covered and repaired.

"I found out from one of the girls what this room used to be," Winter said. "It was designated as the living quarters for the head of the shelter. Sister Ava gave it up. I mean, she didn't have to do that."

"She really loves these kids, doesn't she?" Tan said.

"Their life here is so different from ours," Winter commented.

"Right? All these kids."

"Lucia was talking about wanting to get adopted. It made me think how we all want to belong to a family. You guys sort of adopted my mom and me," Winter pointed out, smiling wistfully.

"Yeah, we did, didn't we? Or maybe it was the other way around."

A pregnant pause. Tan wondered if Winter was thinking the same thing: that it was a blessing and a curse. Because that adopted-family status made anything Tan-and-Winter impossible.

Or did it?

His fingers were inching toward hers of their own accord. He'd spoken too soon, to himself at least, about being just-friends. But these past few days had been jammed full of impossible things already.

What was one more?

The door opened. Rebecca came back in, covered in paint. Her blue dress, despite her apron, was a wreck.

"Why didn't you change?" Winter asked without any bite. "Do you need help cleaning off?"

Rebecca gave her an uncomprehending look. "I didn't think of changing." She plucked at the skirt of her dress. "My father's secretary bought me this. I guess I should have been more careful."

With a towel, Winter tried to wipe off some of the larger stains, but the dress was ruined.

"It's okay," Rebecca said.

Then Sister Ava entered, tucking a rebellious strand of curly black hair back into her wimple.

"How are things in here?" asked Sister Ava.

"We're just about done," Tan answered.

Sister Ava admired the orderly shelves of books, the cozy reading corners, the new vase on one of the tables. She dashed her hand against her eyes. "It looks fantastic." She handed a large brass key to Winter.

"Thank you," Winter said. "And we'll give you our—" Winter hesitated. "Our parents' contact info. They're, um, on vacation."

"I see," Sister Ava said gravely. She waited a beat, but none of them volunteered more information. It was too wild a story, even for Sister Ava, who seemed to have seen more than her share of sticky situations. She clasped her hands. "Ready to make dinner?"

After the curry dinner and an assembly line of cleanup, the dining tables became a study hall, with kids sitting with books and papers, and signing up to use the computer in the common room. Winter and Rebecca moved among the younger ones, correcting grammar and explaining math facts.

"I like your unicorn," Rebecca said to Lucia, pointing out a silver charm at her throat.

"I nicked it at a department store that went out of business," Lucia said cheerfully. "So I couldn't return it when I tried." She smiled at Tan. "Did you like my present?"

"Present?"

"In your pocket."

Surprised, he put his hand into his shorts and pulled out her Swiss Army knife. "How did you do that? I never even felt it."

"Exactly." She smirked.

"This doesn't belong to someone at the Cove, does it?"

"Oh, no." She waved that away. "I nicked it way before I got here."

"Tan, could you help me serve these mangoes?" Sister Ava asked. He joined her. Dessert was a whole yellow mango for each child, carefully washed and sliced vertically into three planes: two oblong bowls and the oval containing the large, flat pit.

"My dad taught me how to cut these . . ." With a knife, Tan scored each mango bowl into a grid and inverted them into easily accessible cubes.

"Like a hedgehog," Sana said. He handed a plate to her to pass out, which she did with a skip in her step that threatened the mango.

After the mangoes were all consumed, the kids migrated to the bathrooms to ready themselves for bed. Tan changed the bandages on Sana's knees. Then he helped her brush her teeth in the communal sink, reminding her to spit out the toothpaste. He rubbed at a slight layer of grime on her cheeks, leftover stickiness, which had attracted other things. Dang. He hadn't once washed her face since his parents left. And her hair was full of snarls and tangles. He combed it out with his fingers, feeling guilty. This was not what taking care of his little sister was supposed to look like.

"Why aren't you putting on your pajamas?" Sana asked.

Tan knelt before her, searching for the best way to convey what was happening tonight. "I'm working on getting us back home. Rebecca and Winter are coming with me."

"So we can fix the door?" Sana asked.

Among other things. "Exactly."

"I want to come," Sana said. "See, I have shoes now." She lifted a foot, displaying her pink gel sandals again.

Going with them was out of the question, but was leaving her here by herself wrong, no matter how much he trusted Sister Ava? He didn't really have a choice.

"I need you to help with the volunteer work, okay? That's paying for us to stay here. But since I'm not here the whole time, I need your help with my share. Is that okay?"

Sana's chest rose. "I've got you, Tan." He smiled. Sister Ava had found her a slightly too large nightgown, but it was pink and soft, so Sana was happy. That was something.

"Can I sleep in Rebecca's bed? Hers is right next to Lucia's."

He squeezed her tiny shoulders, glad she'd made a good friend here already. She wouldn't miss him at all. She'd be having fun, safe in her bed. He wished he could say the same for Winter, Rebecca, and himself.

"Rebecca might not mind trading for the night," he concluded.

"I'll go ask her!" Sana darted off.

Tan caught up with her in the common room, where she was headed for Rebecca. Winter was building a fire in the fireplace against the chill night air, poking a wad of kindling in among some logs. A few Cove kids were gathered around, enjoying the toasty warmth.

"Impressive," Tan said.

"My dad taught me how to build a fire here," Winter said.

"This is sweet," Guy said. "We should have used this ages ago."

Winter smiled and backed up to stand with Sister Ava. "You just won yourself some fans," Sister Ava said.

"Thank you, and everyone, for letting us stay. Especially Sana," Winter said.

"The kids enjoy having someone younger around," Sister Ava said. "Many of them have left and lost siblings. Jaxon and Guy both have sisters her age."

"No wonder they're so fond of her," Winter said.

"In a perfect world, we wouldn't need homes like this one," Sister Ava said. "But the world isn't perfect."

"No, but at least there are people trying to make it better," Winter said, and Sister Ava smiled and touched her cheek. "How did you end up in charge of the Cove?"

She pointed to the photo of Father Luiz on the wall. "My mentor. He advocated for me to take over after him. I'm the first nun to head it up after a long line of priests." She smiled. "The chapter was a little nervous, but I think the fact that I've come through my own shelter journey gave them confidence that I had what it took."

"For sure," Winter said. Her eyes strayed to Tan's.

He crossed to her. "Is anyone left here who knew Winter's dad?" he asked.

Sister Ava pursed her lips, thinking. "I'm not sure. He was here under Father Luiz, before me. I can ask around."

If Father Luiz was anything like Sister Ava, then Tan could see why Winter's dad had turned out so well despite what he'd been through. Another thought occurred to Tan. "Do you happen to know Father Luiz's birthday?"

"That I definitely can find out. Why?"

"We're trying to figure out the passcode on her dad's phone,"

Tan said. Winter's eyes widened. "So we're looking for any numbers that might have mattered to him."

"Couldn't it just be random numbers? Mine are."

"It could be," Winter said. "But my dad didn't have a good head for numbers. He preferred ones he could easily keep track of."

"I'll make some calls," Sister Ava promised, and headed back to the kitchen.

Winter looked at Tan. "Great idea. What if we actually got it open?" She laughed suddenly. The sound of it filled him with a sense of rightness. He loved how he could make Winter laugh, and vice versa, even now. "I guess there really are silver linings in any situation."

"Fingers crossed."

"You know, I started coming here when I was Sana's age. I had crushes on all the older guys. I never imagined I'd be here with *you*."

"I'm glad I got to see the Cove, too," Tan said. "It helps me know you and your dad better."

She smiled. "I'll actually miss it when we go home."

She slung the green tote bag, which contained their wigs, onto her shoulder. Then she held up the old-fashioned metal key the nun had given her, obviously a match to the hefty front gate.

Rebecca joined them in the vestibule. Except for the pearls glimmering at her ears, Rebecca had shed the last of her original outfit. She looked oddly casual in jeans and an oversize navy Berkeley sweatshirt. Her hand was tucked in her pocket, where the pouch of coins was.

Tan and Winter looked soberly at each other. The Cove had been a temporary oasis.

Now it was time to face the heat.

Chapter 16

The Palace of Fine Arts wasn't an actual palace, but a sprawling beige-and-coral-colored monumental structure that had been built for an international exposition in the last century. These days it was a place where tourists as well as local families and couples liked to stroll. Its white dome shone brightly under the moonlight. Greek columns, lit by spotlights on the ground, alternated with well-groomed shrubs.

As they approached, Tan spotted a black van parked down the block, its windows as black as its sides. All was still, but a shudder rippled through Tan.

Was someone inside, watching them? Several someones?

"Amazing view," Winter said in a deep, touristy voice. Her face was framed by her short wig. Then, for their ears only, she whispered, "I think we're being monitored."

Rebecca's hand rose to her blond wig, then lowered again. They were just two guys and a girl out for a stroll.

"Stay close," Tan whispered.

The pathway leading into the monument was dark and deserted, as Liping must have known it would be at this hour. Adrenaline coursed through him as his body prickled with the touch of hidden eyes. His wig itched at the base of his neck. Were his hands too stiff? Where did he normally put them when he wasn't desperate to scratch?

"Where's the bench?" Winter whispered. "There are so many."

"He said it was between the theater and the rotunda," Tan said.

They moved toward the massive dome, passing stone figurines. Tan felt as if he were shrinking beneath their gazes and under the tall pillars.

To their left, the sleek black surface of a lagoon reflected the moon overhead. A small rowboat bobbed gently along the shoreline. Concrete terraces cascaded down like steps built for a race of giants and provided ample places for someone to hide or spring down on them. With the water on one side and the high walls of a theater on the other, there was no way out but backward or forward along the narrow path.

Exactly what Liping must have banked on.

Rebecca's hand was buried deep in her pocket, probably clenched tight around the coins. She rubbed her arm nervously.

"He said the bench was labeled 'Bill Chan,'" she murmured.

Tan inspected a bench of faux-wooden slats and curved metal armrests. No labels that he could see. He checked the next bench. And the next. Then he reached one facing a gorgeous view of the eight-arched rotunda.

"Is this it?" Winter whispered.

He tapped a bronze plaque in its center bearing Bill Chan's name. "He said to leave them underneath." Tan knelt and felt along the asphalt under the bench until his hand found a large, rough rock. He pushed it aside to reveal a small hollow.

Tan twisted to look up at Rebecca. "Becca, here."

He'd used her nickname by accident, but a flush came into her cheeks. Gripping the pouch tightly in both hands, she knelt beside him.

"Tan . . ." She rocked back on her heels. "I want to do the right thing."

Seriously? Was she reconsidering? He held back from wrenching the pouch from her hands and cramming it into the hole himself.

"He won't let us go without leaving them," he said as evenly as he could.

A rustling sound from the bushes made them all jump.

"Hope that was a squirrel," Winter whispered.

Then footsteps reached Tan's ears. And voices. From the opposite direction they'd come, an Asian American guy with spiky black hair and a long-haired girl in a sweater dress were Hansel-and-Greteling hand in hand down the pathway.

"Hurry," Tan whispered.

Rebecca leaned into him and placed the pouch in the hollow, and Tan set the rock back over it, hiding it from view. It was done.

"Come on." Tan stood. Every instinct in him wanted to break into a run, but he walked evenly back down the curvy pathway in the direction they'd come. He glanced over his shoulder, only to turn back into a low-hanging branch. It scratched at his face and snagged in his wig. He smothered an oath as he fought to free himself.

Then Winter grabbed his hand and pulled him toward the cover of a cypress tree. His wig yanked free, leaving a cool breeze to sweep through his sweaty hair.

"*Wig!*" he whispered, snatching it off the branch just in time. Behind the tree, Winter tugged him down, and Rebecca crowded in beside them.

"Look," Winter whispered. Her lips brushed his ear. He jammed his tangled wig back on as she gently parted the fronds to afford him a view of the pathway ahead.

Five men were walking stealthily along the pathway toward the bench—and them. The men, two in front, three behind, were uniformly burly. They moved with purpose. They had to be Liping's men. Winter's stricken expression confirmed she was thinking the same.

"Other way," Tan said, reversing directions. Almost immediately, he spotted two burly men coming from the opposite direction. Moonlight shone on a familiar hawk nose. It was Robin Hood and Little John.

"We're cut off," Winter whispered. Her grip on his hand tightened painfully and she pulled them closer together. The familiar strawberry scent of her hair tickled his nose.

Light voices tinkled in the air. The couple had sat on the Bill Chan bench and were talking, sitting so close together that Tan couldn't distinguish their individual silhouettes.

Tan's gaze swept the lagoon, searching for a way out. The black water lapped at the shoreline. Over the water. It was the only way. He pointed toward the rowboat bobbing on the waves. The voices quieted. The couple was now locked in a kiss, their heads moving together.

Tan tugged at Winter, who grabbed Rebecca. They raced off the path into the shadows and to the shore of the lagoon and the rowboat. Water soaked his shoes and chilled his toes as he tugged on the rope attached to the boat's stern, drawing it closer.

"Go!" he whispered, and Winter and Rebecca scrambled aboard.

Tan stepped knee-deep into the cold water and gave the rowboat a hard shove toward the opposite shore. It bobbed sluggishly forward. Tan heaved with his entire weight, his feet pushing off against the descending lagoon bottom. As it finally gave way beneath his sneakers, he began to swim.

"Get in, Tan!" Winter brandished a double-headed oar.

He grabbed the boat's side, causing the boat to sway violently. Water splashed into his eyes. When his vision cleared, Rebecca had retreated to the far end of the boat, curling up at its bow. But Winter rose to her feet and grasped the sides, steadying the boat with her weight.

She held out a hand. "Come on." Their wet hands were slippery, but Winter added her other to his and gave a mighty tug. The boat's edge bit into his chest and stomach as he scrambled aboard, knocking her off-balance. The two of them landed in a heap on the bottom of the boat with Tan's face pressed against Winter's bare stomach. She yelped softly, shoving at him.

"Sorry," he murmured. He untangled from her, snatched off his ruined wig, and stared back at the shoreline they'd just left.

But it was empty.

Then a guy's shout rang through the night: "What the—get your hands off me!"

It was the boy on the bench. The thugs weren't racing to the shoreline or swimming madly after their boat—they'd descended on the couple. Past the pillars, by the light of the moon, the couple was fighting on their feet. The boy was wrestling with two men. The girl was hitting another with her purse.

Tan was stunned. "Why don't they just take the coins and go?"

"What are they doing to them?" Rebecca asked.

"They think they're you and Tan," Winter whispered, stricken.

"Oh my God," Rebecca said, staring intently at the scene.

"We can't let them hurt them," Tan said. He raised his voice. "Hey! Douchebags, we're over here!"

He hadn't realized how deep his voice was until it echoed back from the monument. The shouting stopped. Men's voices rose in an argument as the guy and girl, hand in hand, fled down the pathway toward freedom. Tan was relieved. But now the thugs crowded the shoreline. They gestured excitedly at their rowboat, then doubled back toward the parking lot.

"They'll cut us off on the other side," Rebecca said.

"Not if we beat them," Winter said grimly. Her paddling quickened: tense, even strokes. Tan dropped into the cold water again and hung onto the back, desperately kicking the boat toward the opposite shore until a bump shuddered through it.

"Get off! Get off!" Tan urged, scrambling out of the water. "Run!"

Rebecca and Winter splashed onto the grassy knoll. Tan's sneakers made squelching noises as he raced toward the main street, where cars were passing by. The black van had moved into the parking lot. Rebecca flagged a yellow cab, but it sailed right by her. Another car honked, and she leaped back from the curb.

"Too busy here," Tan said tersely. "This way."

He pelted along the sidewalk in the direction of traffic. To his left was nothing but a vast emptiness that was the bay. Darkness and stars. A cab, coming from the other direction, threw blinding beams of light into his eyes. He flagged it down.

"Hey!" he yelled. The cab slowed. Checking for cars, Tan yanked open the back door, and Winter and Rebecca tumbled inside. He spotted the thugs emerging from between the Palace pillars. Then he dropped into the back seat beside Rebecca and shut the door.

"Fisherman's Wharf," Tan panted.

"You're wetting my seats!" complained the driver.

"Please," Winter said in a low voice. "Please, we need to get out of here."

"I can't take you like that."

"I'll pay you extra," Rebecca said. "Please! We need to go!"

The driver grumbled but stepped on the accelerator, and they rushed forward into the light traffic.

Tan looked out the window behind them. Robin Hood and Little John were climbing into the black van.

"Turn right," Tan snapped, low. The driver obeyed. Tan navigated him through a series of twists and turns and one-way streets until he was certain they'd shaken the thugs.

As Tan leaned back against the seat, he felt an enormous weight lifting. They'd barely escaped.

But the coins were finally out of their hands.

"He never intended to let us go," Winter said grimly. "I can't even think what they'd have done to us—or to that couple—if we hadn't stopped them."

"I can't believe Liping would try to kidnap me," Rebecca said furiously. "Something must be really wrong for him to go to lengths like these."

"They grabbed the guy," Winter said.

"What?" Tan blinked at her. So did Rebecca.

"Those thugs grabbed the *guy*. Not the girl. They're after *Tan*. Not you, Rebecca."

"Why would they be after Tan?" Rebecca asked, incredulous.

Yes, why? Tan's stomach constricted. He had nothing to do with any of this except that Rebecca had shown up on his doorstep. But even at Berkeley, the thugs had been about to haul him off—maybe Winter was onto something.

"Let's call Rebecca's dad from the Wharf," Winter said. "We can warn him Liping has his coins now, and tell him to take over from here."

Rebecca sniffed loudly. To Tan's surprise, she was near tears. The streetlights illuminated her puffy eyes, which were bleeding black mascara down her cheeks.

"Were you hurt?" Winter asked, concerned.

"No. No." Rebecca's mouth worked. Then she opened her palm and displayed . . . the three gold coins shining there.

"Rebecca, you—what?" Tan sat bolt upright, causing water to squelch around his toes.

"You were supposed to leave them!" Winter cried.

"I couldn't!" she said. "Don't you see? These coins are proof that my dad's hiding his money from the government. Liping's already threatened to report him. If I give him the coins, not only does he get all the money, my dad could lose everything." She took a shuddery breath. "My dad's an ass, but that doesn't mean I'm getting him jailed or killed."

"But we're telling him right now!" Winter said.

"And it might not be in time!" Rebecca heaved a shaky breath. "Look." She twisted to face Tan. "Liping handles all the small things—press, government, business relations. But when you add all that together, he has as much power as my dad and can move much faster."

"You let us come all this way!" Winter grated.

She turned back. "I didn't *ask* you to come—"

"You put Tan in danger!"

"I'm sorry. But I realized leaving the coins was the wrong call.

Whoever has the coins has the leverage." Rebecca's nostrils flared. "And I can't just turn all that money over to Liping. It's not his."

"Then turn it over to your dad!" Tan said furiously. "He's got the resources to take care of himself. We don't." His chest had tightened painfully. They were all still targets. Now more than ever.

The cab slowed to a stop. A salty tang wafted in through Winter's open window. A big ship's wheel hung on a rope-wrapped mast, labeled FISHERMANS WHARF OF SAN FRANCISCO.

Tan unlatched his door as Rebecca opened her wallet. She gave a small gasp, then dug through her purse. "I'm out of cash," she said, dumbfounded.

"What the hell?" Their driver's scowling face was suddenly between the front seats, glaring back at them.

Rebecca pushed her hair to one side, more flustered than Tan had ever seen her. She dug deeper in her purse but came up with only a small handful of coins. Not even enough for bus fare.

"Pay up, or I call the cops!"

"Here. Take these." Rebecca removed her pearl earrings and set them in the driver's hand.

"I don't want *used jewelry*," he said, disgusted.

"They cost five hundred dollars. You should be able to sell them for a few hundred, which is ten times more than our fare."

He continued to frown, but wrapped his fist around the pearls. "Just get out."

"Come on." Rebecca shoved Tan from the cab onto the sidewalk. He wasn't sure how they'd get back to the Cove now that they were out of money. But they'd find a way. They had to.

An orange trolley car clanged by, probably on its last route of the day. They swept up the sidewalk toward Pier 39, which was crowded with tourists eating clam chowder out of bread bowls. The barking of seals echoed off the wooden buildings, and the scent of frying fish reached Tan's nose.

"We need to find a quieter place to call Rebecca's dad," Tan said. And his parents, if they could find a pay phone. By now, they must be trying to reach him and Winter. They'd probably called the Kellers, who might have found the front door battered down. They would be worried not knowing where Tan, Winter, and Sana were. They might even have contacted the police themselves.

They stopped at a quieter intersection, near a gold-trimmed lamp that looked like a goblet on a sea-blue post. A convertible, its top down, nearly backed into it as it parked on the curb. The driver stepped out and headed for the ATM, leaving his keys dangling from its ignition. Tan would never leave keys in a car like that, but then again, there were all kinds of people in San Francisco.

Rebecca removed her phone from her purse. Her hand shook. "I can't talk to him."

"I'll do it." Winter held out a hand, then lowered it. "Or Tan. They've met him. They know you trust him."

"They hate Tan," Rebecca said. "They think he's a terrible influence."

Winter's eyes shone with outrage. "Seems to me that a lot of things were already wrong before you showed up in Palo Alto."

The girls locked gazes. Then Rebecca looked away. She handed her phone to Tan.

"It's true. I started lying and sneaking around." Rebecca's voice had gone soft. "But it wasn't Tan's fault. I had to lie. To survive. To have a life."

Winter bit her lower lip.

Tan slid his thumb to her phone's power button to turn it on. But to his surprise, the screen illuminated immediately, displaying her social media photo, with her head turned to the side so only her sleek black hair, lashes, and nose were visible.

"Did you just turn this on?" A pang of fear hit his stomach.

"No, why?"

"It was on already."

Rebecca stared at her phone as though it were a snake. "No," she choked out. "I haven't turned it on since you turned it off on the train yesterday."

"When did it turn on, then?"

"I don't know!"

"It matters! Liping could be tracking it. Was it on at the Cove?"

"I don't . . . maybe I accidentally turned it on? I turned it off as soon as I unblocked my dad," Rebecca said dubiously.

So the clock was ticking now, and had been for some time without their realizing it. Every second's delay was another second Liping's thugs could reach them.

"Should we call the Cove and warn them?" Winter asked. "Or we could come up with a reason to get the police over there."

"If there *is* a mole, cops won't help," Tan said. "We can't risk it. The less attention we draw to the Cove, the better."

He opened Rebecca's contacts and hit speed dial on *Ba*. He hit the speaker button, and the three of them leaned in, waiting for it to ring. "Talk fast. We want to shut down the signal as soon as possible."

A *click* sounded through her phone's speaker. No ringing. Tan sucked in a breath, but a robotic voice began speaking in Mandarin.

"It's his voice mail," Rebecca said. Her fist was clenched at her side.

"Maybe he's on another call," Winter offered.

"Wouldn't he pick up if he saw *you* calling?" Tan asked.

Rebecca's expression was uncertain. In that moment, despite everything she'd put them through and was still putting them through, Tan couldn't help feeling sorry for her. How could anyone live with the suspicion that the people who were supposed to love you the most might actually not?

"Let's try again." Tan redialed. Voice mail. Tan handed the phone to Rebecca. "Leave a message. Tell him to let you know when we can catch him."

"Hi, Ba." She put out her tongue to moisten her lips. "It's me. I need to talk to you about an emergency, but I need to leave my phone off. Leave me a voice mail with a good time to reach you."

She hung up. "Weird. I've always been able to ring through. Even if he was on another call and not picking up. I don't usually go straight to his voice mail."

"Can you call your mom?" Tan checked the street for pursuers. They needed to move again soon. But he still wanted to squeeze in a call to his parents.

Rebecca dialed and set her phone to her ear. She bit her lower lip. "Voice mail, too." She hung up without leaving a message. Her forehead creased with stress lines. "Something's wrong. I shouldn't be going straight to voice mail like this. Our lines are state of the art."

"Are their phones off? Or they're in a dead zone?" Tan suggested.

"It's early afternoon. And there are no dead zones in Shanghai, at least not where they go." Then she gasped. "What if they've set their phones to block *me*."

"What? Why?" Tan asked.

Rebecca held up her phone. "Because *I* blocked them."

"Your dad's staff might have done it, without them even knowing," Tan said.

"They could have. My parents wouldn't have checked if I was blocked. Why would they? The staff has always been one hundred percent devoted to them." She pulled in a quavery breath. "Liping could have done it. He has the keys to the kingdom." Rebecca's relief was palpable even through her fear. It was another shift in her understanding. There was a chance her parents weren't so indifferent after all. "I need to find a way to reach them. I need to warn them."

"Who else can you go to?" Tan asked. "Is there a family lawyer?"

"At this point, I don't know who I can trust." She squeezed her eyes shut tight, then opened them. "Our housekeeper's only been around a few years. Liping hired her. We have a few drivers, but Liping hired all of them, too. The wrong call could go straight back to him."

"You live in a nightmare," Winter said. "No wonder you left."

"That's what I've been telling you." She began typing on her phone, an email to her dad. But Tan already knew the emails would be blocked.

"Who else has access to your dad?" Tan urged. "Who else's calls would he pick up?"

She rubbed her temple with her fingertips. "There is one phone currently in North America that he'd absolutely answer."

A cold shiver ran through Tan. They'd tried so hard to run in the opposite direction, to avoid a face-to-face confrontation. But now—

"We need to get Liping's phone," he said.

The back of his neck prickled then. Spidey senses. Which had already saved them at least once. Tan's eyes darted around the square, searching for the source of the disturbance. The streetlamp illuminated a familiar hawk-nosed face.

The thugs. They were here.

The convertible hummed, still running before them. Tan didn't even think. He leaped over the passenger-side door and landed on the leather seat. He grabbed the steering wheel and yanked himself over to the driver's side.

"Tan?" Winter asked.

"Are you insane?" Rebecca cried.

"Hey!" yelled the car's owner, who was coming down the sidewalk, a churro in each hand.

"Get in!" Tan snapped.

Chapter 17

Tan yanked on his seat belt. Winter was already scrambling into the passenger's seat beside him. Rebecca climbed into the back seat. In the rearview mirror, Tan watched the thugs scan the crowd.

Then Robin Hood's eyes met Tan's in the mirror.

Tan stomped on the accelerator. The convertible shot forward, hurling Tan backward into the seat. He took a sharp left turn and careened the wrong way down a one-way street.

"You can't just steal someone's car!" Rebecca yelled.

"We're not keeping it!" His hands tightened on the steering wheel. The wind whipped his hair into his eyes and yanked at his shirt, but all of him was bent on getting them the hell out of there.

"That way!" Winter pointed, and he blindly took the turn. His entire body was stiff as he drove, checking his rearview mirror for pursuit. Winter was twisted at her waist, facing out the back.

"Did we lose them?" he finally asked.

Winter drew a quavering breath, sinking back into her seat. "I think so."

The wail of a siren pierced the air. Red and blue lights flashed in his rearview mirror. He swore. Should he pull over? Before he could make up his mind, Rebecca climbed over the seat back and squashed in between him and Winter. Kicking his foot aside, she slammed hers down on the pedal. The car lurched forward.

"Keep going!" she yelled.

"What the hell?" Tan yelled back.

"I'm not getting turned over to the cops!"

So much for her squeamishness about stealing a car. Tan swore as the light ahead turned red and he ran through it.

"We have to lose them before they call for backup," Winter said. She scanned the horizon. "Over there." She pointed to the Ferry Building along the wharf. The white clock tower was lit up from within. "Maybe we can catch a ferry to the other side."

Tan pulled up to the row of Roman archways, and the three of them hurled themselves from the car. Leaving the keys in the ignition, they darted into the building. A small crowd was spilling from a bookstore—an event had just ended. They blended in among the readers, cutting through to the back doors, and then the dock.

The salty tang of the bay tickled Tan's nose. A horn blew, sounding clearly through the night. In the harbor, light shone on the ferryboat, a white double-decker topped by a captain's bridge, with a sleek wedge-shaped nose painted in a gradient of blue stripes. Its horn sounded again.

"It's leaving soon," Tan said, darting forward.

"We don't have money for tickets," Winter said.

"We need to get on," Tan said.

He studied the crowd slowly filing through the turnstiles, sliding their tickets under a scanner. At the gangway to the ferry, another man was checking tickets. A few crew members in uniforms were headed up a second gangway.

"Come with me," Winter said. She darted toward an unlit trailer off to the side. Tan followed as she tried its door. It clicked open, and she disappeared into the darkness.

The ferry whistle blew, low and loud.

"What are you doing?" Rebecca whispered.

"Come in," Winter said. As Tan entered, she thrust cottony clothes into his hands. "Put these on. Hurry!"

They were navy crew uniforms. Unwashed, by the smell of them.

"This is ridiculous," Rebecca said. "We can just walk through the staff entrance?"

"Just put it on," Winter snapped. "We need all the help we can get."

Tan had already yanked the gold-trimmed pants on over his shorts and buttoned on the top. Winter and Rebecca finished at the same time.

Then Winter strode confidently toward the second gangway. No one was guarding it. But Tan still felt incredibly exposed as he followed Winter up the platform. It bobbed with their weight. They entered the ship into a narrow hallway that smelled damp and salty.

"You're late," said a woman in the same uniform. They were also very wrinkled, Tan realized. Not at all in keeping with the ferry's crisp image.

"We're off duty," Winter said apologetically. "We're headed home."

She set her hands on her hips. "You weren't supposed to board this way. You know that."

"The line was too long, as usual." Winter gave a sigh and massaged her forehead. "It's been a long day."

"Aren't they all?" said the woman wryly. "Okay. Enjoy your break," she said, and moved on past them.

"How do you do it?" Tan asked.

"I don't know," Winter said. "I just go by instinct."

The floor shifted under their feet. Through a round portal window, the shoreline moved away.

"We made it," Rebecca said with relief.

"Should we take these off?" Tan asked, plucking at his uniform.

"Yes," Winter said. "Fewer questions. And we're off duty, so it makes sense we'd change."

They stripped off the uniforms and hid them under the sink in the bathroom. Then they climbed a narrow staircase and took seats in the upper cabin around a small table. As the ferry sailed across the bay, Tan's thoughts raced painfully back in time.

They grabbed the guy. Winter's voice replayed in his head.

We need him alive, one of the Robin Hood thugs had said.

But why him?

Across from him, Rebecca was playing nervously with the gold coins. They flashed in her fingers. He stared at them without really seeing them.

Then the answer hit him. It was actually really straightforward. Rebecca needed him for the same reason.

"They want me to convert the currencies for them," Tan said. "They need me to get around the digital keys' security features."

Winter frowned. Rebecca's face was a study of confusion.

"They could go to anyone who works in crypto," Winter protested.

"My parents' digital-currency exchange handles almost a third of all cryptocurrencies getting converted to cash," Tan said. "Trillions of dollars flow through it. That's why the encryption methods on the digital keys looked so familiar to me. They were engineered by *my parents*." He rubbed the back of his head. "Technically, I came up with them." The Tan Encryption Scheme. The reason Dad had said DigitalWallet owed him a bonus. "The only ones who can decrypt them, besides the owners, are people who work at DigitalWallet."

"And you," Winter said, understanding dawning.

"And me," he conceded.

"But how did they even know about you?" Winter turned to Rebecca. "The only link is you," Winter said. "Did you ever mention what Tan's parents do? Where they work? About Tan?"

Rebecca bit her lip. "I talked about Tan's parents' work—after I went back. I mean, it was part of my life here. I suppose I wanted to impress my father. I even said once that you knew even more than your parents did. I didn't think it was a big deal."

"It shouldn't have been," Tan said. He was surprised she'd said any of that about his family. She'd definitely never said any of it to him.

"So those thugs were never after only you, Rebecca," Winter said. "They wanted the coins, but Tan's also been their target. All this time."

Tan's head spun. All this time, Rebecca had been so certain. He'd let himself be swept along with her, so much so that he'd ignored his gut warning him there was much more going on.

"So what now?" Rebecca asked. She pulled the coins from her purse, counting them with nervous fingers.

"I'm not unlocking anything for them," Tan declared firmly.

"They won't leave you alone," Winter said.

"Rebecca's dad is the only one who can stop Liping," Tan said. "Which means we need Liping's phone. Which means, we need Liping." He grimaced. "I'll call him."

Rebecca handed over her phone and Tan checked Liping's

number in her contacts against the one he'd written on his arm, but they were different. Tan dialed Crane's number.

"Maybe he's got a burner phone," Tan said, as the line began to ring. "Or a second number."

"You can't let on that we know what he's up to," Rebecca warned. "He'll strike out to protect himself. He has keys to our apartments in Shanghai. He could hurt my dad and even my mom."

"You said he'd do the minimum," Tan said. "I get the feeling he doesn't want to get his hands dirty himself."

"That was if he wasn't exposed." She gripped her hands.

"Well, we just need him to meet us somewhere so we can borrow his phone for a few minutes."

"He'll have guards."

"He's expecting us to fight him for the coins, not his phone." But the truth was Tan had no idea how they would get Liping to hand over his phone.

The distorted voice answered on the third ring. "Rebecca?"

"Hi, Crane. This is Tan."

"I gave you clear instructions." The voice hardened. "I want those coins put into place tonight as I asked or I'll take other measures."

Rebecca hunched closer over the table, listening intently.

He's definitely Liping, she mouthed.

"You also promised to leave us alone," Tan said. "But it sure didn't look that way."

"Change of plans. Turns out I need your help. We won't hurt you. We just need you to help us access what we want."

"I'm not your tool," Tan said coldly.

"You're not calling the shots," Liping said.

"Actually, I am," Tan said. "We'll bring the coins tomorrow

at noon to Union Square, where there are people around and you can't set your thugs on us. Meet us by the coffee shop. In person."

"You're in no position to negotiate," Liping said. "I have resources you can't even imagine. You're just a teenage boy and two girls, riding some ferryboat to hell. You've been slumming it, Rebecca."

Rebecca's gaze swept the cabin, eyeing the few people there.

"He can *see* us," she hissed.

Tan stayed in the same position, with his legs tucked under the table and one hand on his knee. But he scanned the ferry, landing on a security camera in the corner. He turned his back on the camera, his shoulders unbowed. They'd called Liping only a minute ago. Which meant Liping could almost instantly trace her phone within a few feet.

But Tan wasn't showing any fear if he could help it. "Actually, I *am* in a position to negotiate," he said. "I have what you want. I know how they work. And if you don't come tomorrow as I asked, I'll destroy the coins."

Rebecca gasped.

"You're bluffing," Liping said, but some of the edge had come off his voice. Tan hung onto the receiver grimly. Millions per coin. Mr. Tseng could afford to lose a few, but Liping couldn't afford to lose any. "Your little sister has a long future ahead of her—or at least she should. So if you don't cooperate with me, I'll find someone who will."

It was a threat to Sana. Tan's jaw clenched. To get Liping to come out himself, Tan needed to show Liping he was willing to play hardball.

"I warned you." Tan brandished the Swiss Army knife Lucia had given him, slid one of Rebecca's coins toward him . . . and stabbed it.

The crunch could be heard over the phone, along with Rebecca's gasp.

"Damn you!" Liping swore.

Winter was shocked, and to be honest, Tan was, too. He might have just destroyed access to a million dollars. But he *did* have power. And he shouldn't be afraid to wield it when he had to.

"Noon. Union Square." Tan laid a second coin beside the first one. He let his knife blade hover over it.

"No cops," Liping snarled. "I'll see them. And if you so much as scratch the other coins, I'll stencil little squares over your sister's dimples."

Tan's heart lurched. "You don't know where she is."

He regretted provoking him as soon as the words were out.

"Don't I?" Liping hung up.

Did he know? Even if Rebecca had turned off her phone immediately after unblocking her father, it had turned on at some point after that. The question was whether that had happened at the cathedral.

Tan tapped open Rebecca's app store. As Tan had feared, her app store was open to the last item visited: the sugar-filled icon of *Candy Crush*.

He felt a sinking inside him. "You don't happen to play *Candy Crush*, do you?" He showed her the game.

"No, what's that?" Rebecca asked.

"Oh no!" Winter gasped.

Oh yes. Tan was grim. So Rebecca's phone *had* been turned on at the Cove—by the only *Candy Crush* superfan Tan knew. Who, along with admiring Rebecca's sparkly fingernails, must have committed her password to memory, too. Sana.

The ferry was pulling up to the shore, where a few lit windows shone in shadowy buildings. Tan rose to his feet. He would have spread his arms wide and flown to Sana from there if he could.

"We need to get back *now*," he said.

Chapter 18

Tan pounded down the sidewalk along the high stone wall surrounding the cathedral grounds. It felt like an impenetrable fortress, with thick walls topped by broken glass cemented into the wall itself, to discourage people from climbing over. But his heart pounded painfully in his chest as he rounded the corner to the main gate. Winter pulled out her giant key and unlocked it, then they slammed it shut behind them.

Tan charged up the steps to the heavy front doors. The brass knob was unyielding under his tug—they were locked out. A hush had blanketed the whole space. Which could be a good sign, or a bad one.

Tan rapped with the door knocker. A thud echoed inside.

"Maybe Sister Ava's asleep," Winter said, catching up at last, the key clenched in hand. Her hair hung in tangles around her face, and she was breathing heavily.

"We should have asked for keys to *this* door," Tan said. But they hadn't expected to return so late. He didn't want to disturb Sister Ava, especially when all seemed quiet.

"She probably left a door open for us somewhere," Winter said.

"Should we try the back door, then?" Rebecca asked.

"If she doesn't answer soon." Tan tried the knocker again. Silence.

"It's good that it's quiet," Winter said. "It means everyone's probably safe. For now." She frowned. "But we still have to figure out how to get the passcode for Liping's phone. That's the big *if* here. It's not going to be easy."

"What about a finger scan?" Rebecca asked. "My phone unlocks both ways."

"Either way should work," Tan said. "I just don't see him standing still long enough for us to scan his finger tomorrow."

"How do we get the passcode, then?" Rebecca asked.

"If you call him, will he need to enter it to answer?" Winter asked Tan.

"No, but if he calls me back, he will. So tomorrow one of us needs to be positioned to watch him do it. With someone else close enough to grab it after he does."

"There's a raised platform around the statue in Union Square," Winter said. "I could look over his shoulder from there and not be noticed."

"And I'll be ready to grab it." Tan tried the knocker one last time.

"You can't get in that way," Lucia said from the yard, startling all three. Tan turned. Like a forest sprite, Lucia sat up on a large, flat rock, where she had been lying back in her pink nightgown, gazing at the stars. Her eyes were lit with curiosity. "Are you planning a sting operation?"

She must have heard their entire conversation. "It's nothing," he said.

"We don't want to involve you," Winter said.

"It sounded like a dumb plan," she said. "Grabbing someone's phone. They'll come after you. You obviously need me."

"You?" Tan asked. She was right that it was a dumb plan. They just didn't have a better option.

"Union Square is really crowded. Everyone bumping into one another," Lucia said. "I used to . . . work there. I'll get his precious phone, and he won't even notice." She rubbed the tips of her fingers together.

"Why would you help us?" Rebecca asked.

Lucia brushed a leaf off the front of her nightgown. "Because you're in the Cove," she said. "We stick together."

Tan and Winter exchanged a speculative look.

"It makes our chances of getting his phone a lot stronger," Winter admitted. "And Liping might not even realize it until we've reached Mr. Tseng."

If Lucia could pick Liping's pocket as smoothly as she put the knife in Tan's, her help would be invaluable. But she was Sister Ava's ward. And reckless. And Sister Ava had been kind enough to take them in, no questions asked. They couldn't abuse her trust.

Tan shook his head. "We can't put anyone here in danger." They might already have.

"I've already been in danger." Lucia rolled back her sleeve to reveal disfigured skin covering her forearm. She'd been burned at some point. "I've already been hurt," she added, letting her sleeve drop.

"What happened?" Rebecca asked, horrified.

"It was a long time ago. Point is, I know how to take care of myself. And I don't want *you guys* getting hurt. I mean, you're Sana's people."

"You weren't planning on sleeping out here all night?" Winter asked.

Lucia pointed to the roof. "There's a door up there. I climbed over to the tree house and came down that way."

"That's really high," Rebecca said nervously.

Tan looked at the branch hanging over the roof. It *was* long. "I'm not sure that limb can support my weight."

"Lucia or I could climb over," Winter said.

Light footsteps sounded on the other side of the double doors. The peephole in the door darkened.

"Who is it?" came Sister Ava's voice.

"It's Tan." He headed back up the steps, relieved.

"Is everything okay?" Sister Ava opened the door, draped in her tidy black robe that concealed everything but her face.

Tan took a breath. "Yes, but . . ." His voice trailed off.

Sister Ava's gaze drifted over his shoulder. Her brows rose in her smooth forehead. "Lucia, you're still not going to tell me how you keep getting out, are you?"

Lucia smiled. Sister Ava shook her head, drawing back to admit them. "Everyone's asleep. Sana included," she said. "Do you need anything else before you go to bed?"

"We can't stay," Tan said, stepping inside past her. "We need to get Sana and go."

"Oh?" Sister Ava said in a much less surprised tone than Tan would have expected. "It's the middle of the night."

"We're in trouble," Winter blurted.

"We don't want it to reach you and the Cove," Tan said. "We never meant to bring our problems here." He gestured at the backpacks and jackets hung on their hooks. "The Cove is supposed to be a safe place."

"Understood." Sister Ava ushered the others in, shut the door, and tugged down a thick wooden beam, securely fastening it with calm, deft hands. She turned to face them. "Well now, why don't you let me worry about that part and tell me what's going on." She folded her arms over her black habit and leaned against an archway over which the words were carved, FOR THE LOVE OF GOD. She looked at Rebecca. "I've been in this long enough to know when my charges might be in over their heads."

Her tone didn't leave much room for argument.

Rebecca took a breath. "My family in Shanghai runs a business empire. I needed to get away from them, and I took some antique coins when I ran away last week."

"The coins are actually digital wallets," Tan said. "They're carrying the digital codes to millions of dollars' worth of cryptocurrencies."

"And some people who work for Rebecca's family want Tan to get them access to it all," Winter said. "He has the skills to. He knows more about codes and ciphers than anyone else in Silicon Valley, except maybe his parents."

"Wow," Lucia said. Tan wanted to protest . . . But Winter was actually not wrong.

"People broke into Tan's house to get to him," Winter said. "That's why we're on the run."

"And you're worried they'll follow you here," Sister Ava said.

"They're tracking my phone," Rebecca said, holding it up. "They know we were here earlier today. I may have exposed you guys. I'm really sorry." She did look genuinely contrite.

Sister Ava's arms came unfolded. "It may surprise you to learn you aren't the first teenagers to show up on my doorstep with hooligans or even cops after them. Not just after contraband but to kidnap them, take revenge, even deport them. We've faced knives, guns, gangs, and ICE. I lost one kid who was sent back to an unsafe home." Her eyes tightened a bit with the memory. "After that, I realized I couldn't back down, and in every case, I've fended them off."

"By yourself?" Rebecca's eyes widened. She and Sister Ava were nearly the same petite size at five feet four inches.

Sister Ava smiled briefly. "When you grow up with no resources of your own, you learn to find them. So many have slept under this roof, so many who were let down by the systems that were supposed to protect us. Many of them continue to support the Cove out of loyalty for how it helped them. Just as I do."

"Tell them about the bomb shelter," Lucia urged.

"Bomb shelter?" Tan asked.

"This cathedral was built during World War II to withstand attacks that fortunately never came. It has a bomb shelter in the cellar, with a hidden entrance. I keep it stocked with supplies, water. If we need to, some or all of us can hide out there while I bring in reinforcements."

Whoa, Sister Ava was a badass. Winter looked equally impressed. Lucia smirked knowingly.

"So you can see, I'm quite capable of protecting my charges, including you four." Sister Ava securely snapped a second dead bolt into place. "You three and Sana will be far safer here than in some motel where your thugs might still trace you, no matter what precautions you're taking."

Tan's mind spun. It was one in the morning. Buses had stopped running. If they left, they would have to call a cab. They would have to find a motel to accept them at this hour and not raise suspicions. They couldn't be sure of the next time Liping would get wind of their location. And they were out of money.

"Anything I can help with?" Sister Ava asked.

A quick glance at Winter and Rebecca confirmed they were on the same page.

"Um, could we borrow a few cell phones?" He'd never heard of anyone borrowing a cell phone, but Sister Ava had so much at her disposal that it seemed worth asking.

"I have a spare iPhone the Cove kids share. It's an old model, so the software is glitchy."

They needed three phones. But one glitchy one off Liping's radar was better than nothing.

"Thank you," Tan said. "I assume the number is traceable to the Cove?"

She smiled. "Actually, no." It was a small reprieve. "Do you want to try your parents again?"

"In the morning," he answered. Had Mom, Dad, and Winter's mom already tried to reach them? Had they picked up from the strange messages Tan had left that all wasn't well back home?

Tan felt dizzy with the choices before him. He didn't know which route would lead to safety and which to destruction. Only that the stakes were impossibly high. And as he followed Sister Ava deeper into the Cove, he hoped with his entire soul that they'd never need to see the inside of that bomb shelter.

Chapter 19

A cold hand from behind wrapped itself over Tan's mouth.

Tan woke with a gasp, kicking out against his comforter. He was tangled up in it, and his back was sweating. A jasmine perfume tickled his nose. He turned his head. Rebecca's dark eyes glimmered inches from his.

She leaned in and put her mouth to his ear. "Come with me," she whispered.

"What's wrong?" He sat up.

Guy stirred in the bed across from him. Tan fell silent. Rebecca's gaze swept his chest, and he realized he was shirtless and in boxers. Embarrassed, he tugged on his shirt and shorts. He didn't want to leave with Rebecca, but he wasn't about to have a whole conversation with her right here. He slipped his feet into his still-damp sneakers, grabbed the Cove iPhone in its blue case, and followed Rebecca from the room.

She was dressed in her oversize hoodie. But under the large neckline, his *Mandalorian* T-shirt peeped out. She'd been sleeping in it. Because it was ratty and good for sleeping in? Or because it was his? Whatever the reason, he wanted it back.

She led him outside to the garden, taking a seat on a log not far from the tree house. He was surprised. She'd never been the type to sit on the ground, not even on blankets for picnics.

"Tomorrow's going to be . . . I don't know," she said. "And I wanted . . . to tell you I'll find a way to make everything up to you."

He wasn't sure why this conversation needed to happen in the middle of the night. Still, his nightmares were lingering, and it felt safer out here under the open sky. He settled onto the log beside her. "You don't have to make it up to me. We just need to end this."

"I knew you'd say that, but it's still important to me." She gazed up at the tree house. "It's amazing how many kids live here. All in two big rooms. My house in Shanghai has five bedrooms. One is mine. We have a summer home in the mountains and a winter one by the sea. My bedroom was even featured in *Vogue Asia*. They said it was a princess's room."

"It was probably bigger than my entire living room and kitchen combined," Tan said.

"My closet was as big as your living room. The photographer had a lovefest."

"But it wasn't paradise." He didn't actually know a lot about her life back home. He hadn't even known she was a billionaire's daughter until she'd skipped town and Winter told him.

"No." She pressed her palm to her temple. "My dad travels for work two hundred fifty days of the year. My mom usually accompanies him. I was raised by my nanny except for that year I came to the States. When Albert and I started dating, my parents were only too happy to push me into his family. The Young household servants became my new babysitters." An ironic smile touched her lips. "Like you taking care of Sana. Except not just for a week while my parents go on their first vacation in ten years. No, I've been babysat my entire life."

"It sounds lonely," Tan said. It gave him a window into the

girl who had come to Palo Alto and charmed his entire class, him included.

"You don't know how lucky you and Sana are to have each other and your parents," she said quietly. "Last year, when I was here, I knew your families were different from mine. I think that's what intrigued me most about you. Your family dinners. You ate with them almost every night. You *talk* to them. They cared about what was going on with you. All the details. They knew everything."

Tan's gaze flickered to the stars. "Well, not *everything*." Not about Winter. It struck him how much he'd changed since dating Rebecca—and getting ghosted. He'd been so much more transparent with his family back then.

"You were so anchored. And Winter got to be a part of it." She dropped her gaze to her shoes. "That's what I envied the most about you guys. All of you. I was just blowing with the wind."

Tan didn't know how to answer. There was truth to what she was saying, a lot of truth, but how did you agree someone else's family was horrible?

She looked up at the sky. "Beautiful, aren't they?" she said quietly.

The stars *were* beautiful. But it was getting late. It was on the tip of his tongue to say they should go back to bed when Rebecca laid her head on his shoulder and tucked her hands through his arm. She smelled familiar, even through the scent of the Cove's drugstore shampoo.

"The months I had in Palo Alto, with you, were the best of my life," she said.

They'd sat like this while they were dating, but they weren't dating now. He moved slightly away, but her head stayed firmly pillowed. He wasn't sure how to push her off without hurting her feelings. But things with Rebecca were over and had been for so long. Seeing her again, all the ways they were so different and had such different values, only confirmed that for him.

And now there was Winter, who had gotten him through those dark days after Rebecca vanished and helped to end them. And despite their months apart, his feelings for her were stronger than ever.

"The reason I told my parents so much about you and your parents," Rebecca said, "was that I wanted them to understand. That just because you came from—that you were—"

"From the wrong side of the tracks?" Tan suggested.

Rebecca's arms tightened on his. "You didn't date me because you wanted anything from me. You just—liked me for who I was."

"Rebecca . . . it was almost a year ago," he said, shifting a bit. He'd moved on. Now he was not-dating Winter, which to him was still everything.

"I wanted to stay in Palo Alto to study. I liked you—a lot—but my parents . . . they insisted I needed to be with a guy from my own world. That was the path set out for me. And my parents reacted exactly like I was afraid they would. They were so—loud about it—"

"Loud?"

"—and Albert seemed so . . . perfect for me at first. Until he became more insecure about us. Then he became more controlling. He said he'd never dated a girl as difficult as me. I was . . . too wild for him."

"You're not *wild*." Tan snorted. "Maybe Albert was just used to girlfriends giving in to him. You know what you want, and there's nothing wrong with that. I'm glad you got away from him."

"You see?" Rebecca said with feeling. She tilted her head to gaze up at him. Her thick lashes framed the tops of her eyes. "You've always . . . just known me, Tan. On my flight here, I was so nervous about seeing you again. But I wanted to. For months. It wasn't only that I needed your help with the coins. I really want you to believe that, Tan."

"I believe you," he said. And he did. Which surprised him.

Rebecca's hand tightened on his arm. "Why did Sana ask if I came back to marry you?"

He'd almost forgotten Sana's impulsive comment. *Because she's Sana*, was the answer. But before Tan could speak, Rebecca twisted toward him and pressed her lips to his.

Her mouth was surprisingly warm. Familiar. It brought back old memories of holding hands and walking through the Stanford Shopping Mall. Memories of himself as a younger, more naive Tan.

He pulled free, though her hand stayed on his arm. "Rebecca—"

Her eyes were stricken. "It's Winter, isn't it?"

"This isn't about Winter," he said. "It's about you and me."

"Will you . . . date her?"

It was none of her business. He just wanted to end this conversation and get back to bed. "Winter and I are totally different from each other. I'm a geeky science guy; she's an actor. We only hang out as much as we do because she happens to live in my house. But you and me—"

He caught a familiar strawberry scent on the breeze. It was faint and mingled with the scent of pine needles, but he would know it anywhere. Winter's hair.

Tan broke from Rebecca. Winter was behind them, ghostly pale in the moonlight and dressed in a borrowed shirt and jeans. Gazing at them with wide eyes.

"I was looking for Rebecca," she said in a strained voice. "Just wanted to make sure you were okay. I guess you are."

She turned and fled back toward the cathedral.

"Damn." Tan shot off the log. "Winter!" he called.

But Rebecca grabbed his sleeve, yanking him back. "Tan. Please—"

Tan wrenched free. Rebecca's eyes shone a little too brightly. A red flush infused her cheeks. But Tan had to set the record straight. Amazing that it took a moonlit night for him to see clearly what had been happening all along.

"Rebecca, you completely ghosted me when you left Palo Alto. You didn't even do me the courtesy of letting me know you were okay until I finally tracked you down. And the whole time we were dating, you kept trying to make me into someone else. Someone who had to buy a suit to wear to dinner with your parents."

Rebecca's mouth trembled. "I—I didn't realize you felt that way," she said. "I didn't know. I was—"

"And then you left the country—to get away from me!"

"My parents made me leave! It was just another way for them to control me. It wasn't really about you. I know I blamed you for it. I guess I thought they were right, at first. But . . . they were wrong. And so was I."

Hearing her say it—the feeling of release made his knees buckle slightly. Those excruciating months of getting ghosted had scarred him more than he'd admitted, even to himself.

"You were caught up in your own stuff. And you still are! Now you've come to me for help and put my little sister and my family and Winter's in danger. You've caused so much collateral damage and not even realized it."

"Wait. Tan—" She grabbed his wrist.

He tugged free again. He understood that her ghosting him had less to do with him falling short than her own churning through her complicated life.

But none of this changed anything between them now.

"You were right to leave Albert, and I'll never be the one to send you back into a dangerous situation," he said. "But you and I were over—a year ago."

He exhaled sharply. Winter. He needed to explain. He owed her that much.

"I have to go," he said, and strode toward the cathedral.

Winter's bed was visible from the doorway of the girls' dorm, but it was empty, the comforter flung back to reveal a dent in the mattress where she had lain. He whispered her name into the darkness, but there was no answer.

How much had she caught of his conversation with Rebecca? Everything he'd said about him and Winter—*we only hang out as much as we do*—if she'd heard it, out of context . . . but at least she hadn't seen the kiss, he hoped—

On a hunch, he headed toward the sanctuary. Moonlight through the plain glass windows illuminated the rows of pews. He found Winter seated in the second one, gazing up at the crucifix over the altar.

Quietly, he slid in beside her.

"My dad loved Easter," she said, not looking at him. "Even though he wasn't Catholic. He loved Mass, all the music and the whole ceremony of it. I never realized he got it here. There's a lot I don't know about him. So many things I never asked him, and now it's too late."

Tan laid his hand over hers, but she tugged it free.

"Tan, tomorrow—" Her lower lip quivered in the moonlight. Winter was never scared. But now she was. "If anything happens to you—"

He couldn't help himself. He wrapped his arms around her and just held her, resting his chin on her head. She was always looking out for other people. Her mom. Sana. She'd brought them here to the Cove. She'd even looked out for Rebecca, despite Rebecca's disdain. And she'd been looking out for Tan since the day they met.

"Nothing will happen to me," he said, releasing her at last.

She'd held herself stiffly through his hug. Now she kicked off her piano-shoes and tucked up her legs, still not looking at him. In the shadows, her profile blended into the sanctuary. It was fitting, because that was what she was to him: a sanctuary, just like the Cove. When he was with her, he believed they would prevail. And they could.

"Winter, there's nothing between me and Rebecca. I know it didn't look that way—"

"You don't have to not-date her because I'm so judgmental."

"Huh? Judgmental?"

She finally turned to him. Her face was still shadowed, but he could make out her eyes, the tip of her nose, and the curve to her lips. "I've been asking myself, did I call 911 because I really wanted to help her? Or because I didn't like having her around?"

"Only you would even question yourself like that," Tan said. It was both frustrating and something he admired about her. She had integrity. She wanted to be consistent inside and out, and she wasn't afraid to ask hard questions, even of herself.

"I know I've been on your case about her. But there's a reason you guys got together in the first place. I guess the truth is, I wasn't willing to see her good qualities before. I mean, she's still out of touch, but she's connected with the kids here in her own way and shown there's another side to her. So maybe it's a possibility, you guys getting back together."

"Getting back together?"

"I mean, look what you're doing to help her. You're going all out. Risking yourself, your family even." Her throat bobbed with a hard swallow. "I know it's complicated, but it says something about how you really feel about her, doesn't it?" She looked away. "You're taking on Rebecca's problems, no matter what the cost to you. And she automatically turns to you for help." Her voice was low. Resigned, like she'd sounded about her dad's locked phone. "Tan, you were crazy for her. Seems like you still are. I mean . . . she's . . . so glamorous. That's not me. It never will be."

What? Winter was almost always right, but she was so wrong about this.

"It's not even a comparison," he said forcefully. "And what about you? You take on everyone's problems. Your mom's. Mine. Rebecca's. You sacrifice yourself for everyone else and don't give it a second thought."

Her eyes widened. He folded his hands over his knees. He didn't know where they went from here. It was too much to figure out the state of his heart and the state of their futures all at once.

"You should check voice mails," Winter said finally.

His brow furrowed. "I don't have my phone." Which she knew.

"You can access them remotely, dork," Winter said. "Call your own number, hit Pound, and put in your pin."

"Pin? Do I even have one?"

She gave an exaggerated sigh and elbowed him in the ribs. "For a genius, you can be so dense sometimes."

He pulled out the Cove phone. It was ancient. He turned it on, and its cracked screen glowed. At least it worked. Tan dialed his own number. He had one guess at a pin. Winter watched his fingers as he typed it.

"Hey, that's—"

"You have three new messages," said a robotic voice.

"—my birthday," she finished weakly. "That's totally not secure! You need to change it."

"You weren't supposed to look!" he said. But she was smiling now. And so was he.

The first voice mail was a spam call about insurance premiums. The second voice mail made Tan's heart lurch.

"Hey, Tan," Dad's cheerful voice boomed. "We're back from our hike. I got your voice mail—just calling you back."

"Hope you're having fun!" Winter's mom chimed.

"Let us know what else you'd like from Hawaii!" Tan's mom said.

If only it were that easy. The third voice mail was also from Dad. "Tan, I got a voice mail from you from another number, but it was garbled. Everything okay? Sorry if my reception is spotty. You can reach us tonight at the Waikiki Beach Marriott."

The voice mails ended. "He didn't even get my last message," Tan said. He dialed Dad. This time, the phone rang but went to voice mail. No surprise—Dad wouldn't answer a number he didn't recognize, either.

"Dad, it's me," Tan said. "I'm borrowing this phone to reach you. Someone wants me to help them steal a bunch of digital keys. I need your help. Call me back here, okay?"

He hung up, frowning. He needed them. They were the experts. Maybe they'd even run into things like this before. He looked up the Marriott in Honolulu and dialed.

"Aloha, Marriott Waikiki," came a friendly baritone.

"Hi, are James and Liz Lee there?"

"Yes, they just checked in this afternoon. Let me ring their room." Tan met Winter's eyes. The man returned. "I'm sorry. They seem to be out. Can I take a message?"

"Yes, please have them call Tan back at this number."

He hung up. His body felt stiff from not moving. But at least he'd gotten to a live person. He knew where their parents were tonight.

"You okay, Tan?" Winter asked.

"I guess they're trying to reach us, too."

"I'm almost glad they don't know what's going on. My mom's been through enough already." Her eyes shuttered briefly. By the glow of moonlight, her face was soft and luminous. She rose, pressing her feet back into her shoes. "I should go to bed," she said.

She started to leave, but he grabbed her hand. She paused, startled, looking down at him.

"What is it?" she asked in a guarded tone.

He tugged her back down beside him. Their legs pressed tightly together and her arm warmed his, the touch of her body sending electric pulses into him. He took a deep breath and took the plunge.

"There is no comparison between you and Rebecca," he said. "I've had to do this for all of us. Not just her."

Winter bit her lip. She didn't believe him.

"And you and me—look, ever since prom, we've been walking on eggshells. I hate that I didn't even know you were auditioning for *Hamilton*. Or thinking of going to London for the summer."

She tugged her hand free, though her leg stayed tightly wedged against his. "You could have asked. That's not my fault."

"I wasn't saying it was."

"You just stopped talking to me," she said. "After prom."

"Because you said we had to take a step back."

"Take a step back, yes. Not become total strangers." This time, she scooted away from him. "And I was right, wasn't I? I mean, look at us now. We can't even communicate properly."

"Because we've been avoiding each other!"

She averted her gaze. How had they gotten to this point? Months of dodging her in the hallways. Wondering how to behave around her and feeling like he wasn't doing it right. He ran his Winter-warmed hand through his hair, frustrated.

"I wish we'd never gone to prom together," he blurted.

His words hung between them like the echo of a bell.

"Well, I know it was my fault," she said stiffly. "You were on the rebound. Your ex was out of the picture. And I basically strong-armed you into going with me."

He was stunned. "That's totally not—not how I see it."

"You said it yourself just now to Rebecca. We only hang out so much because we live under the same roof."

So she *had* heard him. But her version of prom couldn't be further from his. And that *was* his fault. He'd been too afraid to show her how he felt. He had to tell her. They were about to face Liping, and who knew what would happen? He had to tell her the whole truth of his heart.

He opened his mouth to let it all come pouring out. "Winter. You have it all wrong. I'm not crazy about her. I'm crazy about *you*."

There. He'd said it.

She just laughed, not unkindly. "Tan, I *saw* you and Rebecca—"

But the crash of glass breaking at the far end of the sanctuary shattered the rest of her words.

Chapter 20

They'd smashed in a window. What struck Tan most was not the loudness of the sound, but the quiet of it. They were pros. He and Winter heard them only because they were sitting in the dark not more than fifty feet away.

As the silhouette of a broad-shouldered man hoisted himself through the window, Tan yanked Winter to the floor. The tiles were cold under his hands and feet, but he'd already broken out into a sweat. He crawled between the pews to the aisle farthest from the broken window. Winter moved so silently he turned his head a few times to check on her. She was right on his heels, the paleness of her face the only visible part of her.

From the sanctuary's opposite side came more sounds of glass tinkling. A thump as someone heavy dropped to the floor. The creak of a floorboard, footsteps, low whispers. Tan peered around the edge of a pew. The window now gaped with a star-shaped hole. Moonlight shone on two burly men helping a third, hawk-nosed man—Robin Hood—climb inside. The silver hilt of a gun glittered.

Tan's stomach tensed. They were here for the coins, obviously, but Liping had threatened Sana. Tan needed to get to her and to warn Sister Ava and the Cove kids. And what about Rebecca?

He'd left her outside—would she walk straight into Liping's men?

And was the man here himself?

Winter hefted a pew Bible, nudged Tan, and mimed tossing it across the room. Tan understood. He took it from her, rose to his knees, and heaved it at the front of the sanctuary.

Thump! The Bible hit the wall and fell to the floor.

"Who's there?" demanded Robin Hood.

They started toward the altar. Tan crawled swiftly toward the back doors. His senses felt on overdrive. He could hear the men moving and fumbling in the darkness away from them.

Tan shoved the door open, and he and Winter raced out into the nave. He shut the doors and locked them fast, trapping the men in the sanctuary—but not for long.

Tan and Winter sped past the rows of coats and hooks and ran upstairs to the bedrooms, where Tan pounded on Sister Ava's door. Her voice sounded from beyond, then it flew open and Sister Ava appeared in her nightgown. Her thick black hair flowed down over her shoulders, and the vine tattoo on her right arm bloomed with red roses. It was the first time they'd seen her without her nun's habit, but she looked exactly like who she was: an older sister to the teens in her shelter.

"Sanctuary," Tan gasped. "They broke in. Guns. We locked them in, but we need to get everyone to that shelter."

Sister Ava grabbed a walkie-talkie from a table just inside her door. "I'll call for help. Let's get the kids downstairs."

"We can't call the cops," Tan blurted, his legs already carrying him toward the boys' room.

"I have other resources," she answered. Tan didn't have a chance to ask what her plan was before she vanished around the corner.

In the boys' room, Tan didn't dare shout or flip on the lights, so he moved from bed to bed, shaking shoulders and legs and tugging on blankets. Most of them were unwilling to wake up.

"You have to get to the shelter," he kept urging. "Sister Ava's moving everyone there."

When he finally emerged, he found Sister Ava shepherding bleary-eyed kids down a stone spiral stairwell. Her flashlight cut through the darkness. "This way," she said. "Hurry."

"Tan, I don't know where Sana is," Winter said, white-faced. "I don't know if she left earlier. All the girls got out so fast. By the time I got to her bed, she was gone."

A cold fear seized Tan. "Could Liping have gotten to her?"

"I don't know."

"Maybe she went downstairs with the others," Sister Ava said.

Tan hurried down the spiral stairs, passing on the tighter inside, studying each kid he passed. But he reached the bottom—a basement built of cold stones—with no Sana in sight.

Sister Ava led the kids through a rectangular doorway.

"In here," she whispered.

It was a large storeroom lined with shelves loaded with massive cans of peaches and applesauce. Guy and Perry began to unfold a pile of folding chairs and set them up. Jaxon grabbed blankets. "I'll make some beds in the back for everyone."

"I need to find Sana," Tan said. He grabbed a flashlight from the shelves.

"No, wait, Tan," Sister Ava said, but he was already running down the hallway, shining the light into rooms. He didn't dare call out, for fear of leading Liping's men to her. He'd almost reached the girls' room when Winter caught up to him.

Tan passed a wall lined with windows and heavy porcelain vases. Outside, two small forms were sitting on a rock behind the cathedral, both dressed in matching pink nightgowns. Sana and Lucia. Stargazing. Far enough from the front that they wouldn't have heard the break-in, either.

But then, from the right side of the building, two men dressed like shadows rounded the corner.

"They'll see them!" Winter hissed.

Tan grabbed a vase in both hands and hurled it through the window. The glass shattered.

"Sana! Lucia—*run*!" he yelled down.

They sat up, looking wildly around. Lucia pointed at the men coming toward them. She grabbed Sana, and they slipped off the rock. Tan had to keep the men distracted while they got to safety.

"Hey, guys!" Tan yelled down. "You here for these coins?"

He thrust his closed fist through the window, holding it aloft. They must be able to read the lie in his voice—but no, they did an about-face and headed back toward the front of the cathedral.

"They're coming for us," Tan said. "Let's go." He took the stairs two at a time with Winter, through the common room and back outside the side door. They moved quietly on the pine needles until the main gate came into view. But a pair of burly thugs were now guarding the gate. Heavy wool blankets were draped over the wall above their heads, muting the protective barrier of broken glass that lined its top. They must have climbed over. Tan's skin prickled with a sense of foreboding. Clearly, Liping meant to keep them all trapped inside the cathedral grounds until he got what he wanted.

Heavy, rapid footsteps were drawing near. As the men appeared around the corner, Tan grabbed Winter's hand.

"The tree house." He ran for it, tugging her along. He shoved her toward the wooden ladder hammered at intervals into the large trunk, and climbed right behind her so the backs of her jeans scraped his nose. He wished this were a rope ladder he could pull up after himself, but that was exactly the exclusivity Sister Ava hadn't wanted.

Tan tumbled into the unfinished tree house beside Winter, and they both sat up. Hammers, a box of nails, a saw. He peered over the edge down on the men searching the courtyard. Moonlight cast an eerie glow on a familiar face: Liping.

The man slipped a hand into the pocket of his black unzipped jacket. He wore jeans and sneakers and looked so . . . normal. Thick hair and a solid physique and an air of competence—the kind of guy the head of an empire would want around.

"Crane, I'm up here," Tan called.

Liping froze between two pine trees, glancing in Tan's direction. Surprise on his face. He started toward them.

Winter made a soft sound in her throat. "We're trapped," she whispered.

Tan studied the branches of their tree. It was intertwined with the branches of other trees, but the limbs were all too delicate to support their weight. All except one.

He squeezed her elbow. "Go that way," he whispered back. He pointed to the limb that hung over the cathedral roof, which Lucia said she'd used earlier. "Get back inside and make sure Lucia and Sana got to the shelter."

She grabbed his hand. "What about you? Aren't you coming?"

"We need to keep Liping away from the Cove until Sister Ava's help gets here." Fingers crossed that they would. "Lock the roof door behind you so Liping can't follow if he gets up here. Lock every door you can to delay them."

Winter's eyes opened wide. "But then you can't follow, either."

If Liping managed to climb up here, Tan wasn't letting him through. "We have to keep them all away from the shelter as long as possible."

Tan tugged his hand free, laced his fingers together, and offered them to Winter's shoe.

"I don't like leaving you here," she said, but let him boost her onto the thick, overhead limb. He watched anxiously as she crawled toward the cathedral rooftop. He felt cut off from her, unable to touch her or talk to her. He wouldn't be able to reach her now. But neither would Liping. He breathed a sigh of relief when she landed safely.

They *weren't* bad at communicating. And he wished he'd said so when he'd had the chance.

The scrape of a shoe on wood below warned him. Fifteen feet down the length of the trunk, Liping was climbing the ladder. Tan tossed the hammer down. It scraped the side of the tree and landed with a *thunk* on a fallen log.

Liping froze. Their eyes met for the first time. Liping's cheeks were soft, his face almost angelic. But his glittering black eyes told a different story. They were narrowed with determination. He might only be the number two to Mr. Tseng, but Liping was also a man who wasn't used to losing. The air crackled with tension between them.

"I wouldn't come any farther if I were you," Tan warned. "I have a pile of hammers up here and really good aim."

Liping searched Tan's face, as if gauging whether he was bluffing. A smirk quirked the corner of his lips, but then he dropped back down to the ground. Tan clutched his last hammer, trying to read an unpredictable man. Liping fell back with his men, who were muttering among themselves. But Tan didn't have any room for his bluff to be called. He had to keep stalling for as long as Sister Ava needed.

And maybe stalling was also how Tan could get Liping's passcode. Liping was just below him. Close enough that Tan might be able to read his fingers entering it into his phone.

Tan breathed a prayer that Liping didn't use a finger scan. He pulled out the Cove phone and dialed Liping's number. Down below, Liping studied his own cell phone, which had lit up with Tan's incoming call. The soft white light gleamed against Liping's face.

He held it to his ear. "Is that you, Tan?"

Tan hung up.

"Tan, I don't like games," Liping said.

His phone lit up with the dial pad for his password. Tan leaned forward, straining to see. Here was Tan's bird's-eye view of Liping's passcode—exactly what he wanted—but the pad was too far for Tan to make out with his naked eye.

But maybe not for his phone. Tan held its camera lens out over the edge, filming Liping's fingers as he typed. He hoped the camera wasn't as nearsighted as it was ancient.

Liping set his phone to his ear, then Tan's phone buzzed with Liping's incoming call. He sat back on the boards and answered.

"I figured it would be easier to talk like this," Tan said. "It seems we're at an impasse."

"We are not at an impasse. You're stuck in a tree. You'll come down and hand those coins over to me. We'll walk over to my van, where I have some equipment, and you'll unlock them."

"You seem like a guy used to giving orders," Tan commented.

"I've been studying you. Good kid from a good family. Raised well. Good grades. You give a damn, and you won't be responsible for something unfortunate happening to your sister, to those kids, or to this cathedral. Not to mention you have a bright future. Too bright to lose."

"So you targeted me because I give a damn?" It was creepy to hear his life story from this man's mouth. A guy whose very line of work was understanding people and getting them to do what he wanted.

"With too bright a future to lose," Liping repeated.

"The cops are on their way," Tan said, hoping that was true.

"The cops are in my pocket."

"You mean Rebecca's father's pocket. Without his resources, you'd be nothing, right? Isn't that what this is all about? You going from nothing to something?"

Liping had found a helmet. He set a foot on the ladder and began to climb.

Tan snatched up the second hammer and dangled it over the edge. "Stay back!"

Liping kept climbing.

"I told you to stay back!" Tan yelled.

No dice. A trickle of sweat rolled down his back. If Liping called

Tan's bluff, Tan doubted he could go through with this. Bashing in a guy's head just wasn't in his DNA.

Below, more of Liping's men were drawing closer to the base of the tree.

Then, to Tan's horror, Winter appeared behind them, holding up what must be a borrowed phone. He sat up hard, bumping his head on a limb. Winter was supposed to be in the bunker with the others. But she was here—he hoped that meant Sana and Lucia were safe. But now he felt helpless to stop her from walking right into the midst of Liping's men.

"Smile, because you're all on camera!" Winter said, filming them all.

Liping snarled an order, and began to descend the ladder. Robin Hood grabbed for Winter's phone. She dodged him, then landed a kick that earned a grunt. He tackled her and then the two of them wrestled madly for the phone. Robin Hood finally yanked it free and smashed it on the ground.

"Hey!" she shouted.

The men were closing in on her. Tan was already scrambling, falling down the ladder, scraping his knees on every rung. But the tree was high and he was too far away. Too slow.

Then the side door in the cathedral wall burst open.

Out charged Jaxon and Guy, wild-bed-haired both, with Jaxon in pajamas and Guy in the old shirt and striped boxers he slept in. With a yell, they rushed the thugs.

Tan couldn't believe it. Sana's friends had come to their rescue.

More men charged from the shadows toward Jaxon and Guy. The Cove boys dodged. They were good, but these men were pros. Despite their bulk, they were nimble and agile—and Tan had seen a gun earlier. A blow landed on Jaxon's jaw. Two men closed in on Guy. Tan spotted Liping backing away, his phone still in his hand: their lifeline to Rebecca's dad.

Tan was still fifteen feet off the ground. But now all he could see was Liping's phone. With a prayer in his heart, he let go of the rungs and fell.

Chapter 21

Two men blocked Tan's path as he rushed Liping. Perry tackled one, and Tan grabbed for the other. He tried for a headlock the way Master Kwon had taught him, but the man had forty pounds on Tan. Tan found himself flipping horizontally through the air. He landed flat on his back with a painful thump that knocked the wind from him.

Keep moving.

Liping's black sneakers stepped into view. Tan swung his leg, knocking Liping off his feet and onto his face in the dirt. Tan rolled to his feet. He dived for the phone in Liping's hand. But then Robin Hood grabbed Tan from behind, forcing him upright. Little John closed in and the two immobilized him.

"The coins!" Liping scrambled up and frisked Tan, turning out his pockets. "Where are they?"

"I don't know," Tan lied. Liping shoved his phone into his jeans pocket. It was out of reach. But Lucia—she could help. Tan's eyes roamed the yard, where the Cove kids were fighting Liping's men. Lucia was nowhere in sight. She was probably in the shelter with Sana.

Then Tan glimpsed a familiar face wearing a floral scarf—Maria, the grad student from Berkeley. She stood with her arms wrapped around her elbows, almost hidden behind a group of Liping's men.

What was she doing here? Last he'd seen her, she was breaking her hard drive, shooing them from her lab, and readying to board a flight. Now she looked strangely dwarfed among Liping's men. And terrified. Tan cursed himself. None of this had been any of Maria's business until Tan made it so.

And now—what did Liping want with Maria?

A musty wool blanket was tossed over Tan's head, turning his world dark. Iron arms gripped him around his waist, pinning his arms to his sides and then lifting him bodily off his feet.

"Let go!" His voice was muffled. His heart hammered against his chest as he was flipped onto his side, lurching with his captor's gait.

"Let him go!" Winter shouted, but her voice was farther away than he expected.

They were taking him away. But where? He strained to orient himself, to make sense of the sounds of struggles: grunts, blows, Cove kids shouting. His foot clanged against metal—the cathedral gate. The brighter light of the streetlamps poured through the weave of the blanket. They must be outside the cathedral property now.

Tan redoubled his struggles. An engine roared to life. Tan was dropped onto a humming, feltlike surface that vibrated beneath him. Twisting around, his feet made contact with a fibrous wall.

I'm in a trunk. He lashed out with all four limbs. His shoes struck the lid just before it closed.

"Shut it!" Liping ordered.

Hands forced him down, but he kicked wildly. He had to keep them from shutting him in.

A fresh commotion erupted, and the hands released him. Tan flung the blanket off and gasped for fresh air.

He sat up in the trunk of a sedan parked outside the cathedral gate. A motley group of people were barreling down the sidewalk toward Liping and his men. A beefy guy in the lead sported a headful of gray braids over a tie-dyed shirt and shorts. One tall woman, still in pajamas, was flexing a bat.

Before Liping and his men could move, the Cove kids boiled out from the gate. Sister Ava was right behind them, cutting a striking figure in the moonlight in her nun's habit. The newcomers and the Cove kids didn't have guns of their own, but they faced off right there on the sidewalk against Liping and his men, outnumbering them two to one.

"You can do this the easy way or the hard way," said the tie-dye man.

The new group appeared to be a neighborhood watch. The friends of the Cove Sister Ava had alluded to. Liping's mouth twisted. Lines deepened on his forehead. Tan's eyes dropped to Liping's side, where the silver gun was waiting. Inches from it, Liping's fingers jerked slightly.

The silence pulsed as Sister Ava waited.

Her crew of people waited.

Liping's men waited.

Liping's voice broke the silence. "*Zǒu ba.*" He gestured curtly to his men, who climbed into their cars.

Tan scrambled to rise from the trunk. His whole body felt bruised. Jaxon held out a hand, helping him out and onto the street as Liping and his men slammed their doors and roared off. The vacuum they left behind was almost visceral. Tan's knees wobbled.

"You okay?" Jaxon put a steadying hand on his shoulder.

"Thank you," Tan said, dazed. "I'd be driving off to God knows where if not for you guys."

"You learn pretty fast how to look out for yourself when you have to," Jaxon said. Guy nodded grimly.

Winter threw her arms around Tan, pressing her face into his shoulder. She smelled good. Like strawberries and chocolate and mint. She was warm, but her entire body shook, and so did his. For a moment, they just held each other, until Tan's heartbeat slowed to something closer to normal.

"Is Sana okay?" Tan asked.

"She's okay." Winter finally pulled back, giving Tan a view of Sister Ava's crew arranging themselves by the gate.

"Thank you," Tan said as he reached them.

"We're here to help," said the tie-dye man. He and the woman shook his hand, then returned to planning their protection.

"Who are they exactly?" Tan asked, moving back into the yard.

"Neighbors and friends of the Cove," Winter said. "People who relied on this place at one point or another. People who Liping—or the Tseng empire—have zero influence over."

"Is it redundant to thank God for a nun?"

A choked hiccup laugh came from her lips. "Tan—I was so worried for you."

"I was worried for *you*," he said. "Did anyone get hurt?"

"No. Everyone's okay."

"It could have been worse." They'd had a reprieve, but Tan didn't believe for a moment that it would last.

"You should have dropped that hammer on Liping, Tan," Winter said seriously. "He wouldn't have shown you mercy. He'd have thrown you out of the tree."

"He really didn't want to wait to meet tomorrow, did he?" Tan said.

"Maybe he has his reasons."

A thought struck Tan then. "Damn, we didn't get to his phone."

He'd been so focused on not getting hauled off, not that they'd really had a chance.

"That means we still have to meet tomorrow," Winter said soberly.

Sana and Lucia emerged from the cathedral's front door with a few of the other kids. Sana spotted Tan and raced toward him.

"Sana!" He swept her up in a hug.

"We had to hide in the basement!" Sana pouted. "I missed all the fun!"

Tan expelled a breath. "Fun is *not* the word I'd use."

The door to the shed opened, and Rebecca crawled out, tugging off her black hoodie. So she was unharmed, too, thank God.

"I've never seen Liping like this," she said quietly. "He looks . . . so determined."

"You look like you were playing hide-and-seek," Sana said, laughing.

Rebecca gave her a small smile. "When I was younger, I'd hide for hours in places like this." She gestured at the shed. "I'd hide right before dinner. Or an event. Testing to see if my parents would even notice."

Sana frowned. "Of course they did."

"No, actually."

"No one came to find you?" Sana's eyes were round with shock. "Tan always looks for me."

True. Although Sana was giving him too much credit. Tan had spent countless *annoyed* minutes searching for Sana . . . because there wasn't any other option. He had to find her. Of course he had to. But that was exactly Rebecca's point.

"This trip," Rebecca said. "It's another hide-and-seek. Although I didn't mean it that way. Not intentionally. But deep down, I *wanted* them to come looking for me." Rebecca sat heavily on the pine needles and leaned back against a log. "And no one did."

Sana sat beside her. "Maybe because you don't have a big brother," she said seriously. She took Rebecca's hand, the way their mom often took hers when she was unhappy. Rebecca's lip trembled. Tan understood something then, too. Sana hid so often because she *wanted* Tan to come looking for her. That was her world: When she hid, he would find. And she craved that special interaction . . . And so, it seemed, did Rebecca.

"Where will you live when we go home?" Sana asked. "Are you going to live with us, too?"

Rebecca caught Tan's eye and looked away quickly. "No, of course not." Rebecca sniffed, wiping her nose on the shoulder of her sleeve. "I just don't want to go back to Shanghai with my tail between my legs."

Tan didn't want her forced back, either. Despite everything she'd put them through, he wanted her to win. He glanced at Winter, who was watching Rebecca. A mix of emotions flashed across her expressive face. Sympathy. A trace of wistfulness.

"My dad had to rebuild his life after his parents passed away." She knelt beside Rebecca and set her hand on her shoulder. "My mom and I had to rebuild our life after *he* did," she said. "And you'll rebuild yours, too. One safe space and person at a time."

"You can make it work here if you really want to," Tan said to Rebecca. "You just have to be willing to give up the cushy life you planned for."

She gave him an uncomprehending look. "What do you mean?"

"If you truly want freedom, you can't be dependent on your parents for money. You're eighteen tomorrow. You can choose not to go back to them, and they can't force you."

"Honestly?" Winter said. "I've never even had a hundred dollars to spare in my life. Neither has my mom. That's why we're renting rooms in Tan's house." She took a breath. "The important thing is you find people to care about." Her eyes caught Tan's briefly. "And who care about you," she added.

Rebecca took that in. She rubbed her hand across her eyes. "So what now?"

"We still need Liping's phone. I tried to get his passcode." Tan checked the video he'd taken of Liping entering the digits on his phone. He enlarged the screen until he could almost make out the numbers. It was enough to see the silhouette of Liping's thumb darken and pause over each circle on the keypad.

"One-eight-six—damn," he said. "It blurs on the last three digits."

"Can we improve the resolution?" Winter asked. "We use AI enhancers to do that for yearbook."

"I could try," Tan said. Winter showed him an app in the app store, which he applied to his video of Liping's fingers. It improved the resolution slightly, but not enough to make out the last three numbers.

"Maybe the number means something," he said. "Like a birthday or anniversary."

"It's not a month or day combination," Winter said.

"Could it be a year? 1860-something?" he asked.

"I don't know." Rebecca spread her hands. "The 1800s in China were bad years. Opium War. Famine. That's when all those young men came to America to build the railroads. I doubt it's those. It could be a random number."

"What are his interests?" Winter asked. "I've been working on my dad's passcode for a long time now."

Rebecca frowned. "When I was little, he owned a collection of spaceship models. He hired a maid to keep them dust-free."

"One-eight-six . . . ," Winter mused. "Could it be one-eight-six-two-eight-two? The speed of light?"

Tan played the video again. "It could be!" He played it again. "Yes, I think it is. You just happened to know that?"

A smirk touched her lips. "I've considered every special six-digit number out there."

"Let's hope we got it, then," Tan said. "We have the coins. I think we can assume the meeting tomorrow is on." His stomach clenched. He could still end up in a trunk before this was all over.

"I want to come to the meeting," Sana said.

"What?" Tan said. "This isn't a field trip."

She glowered at him. "I *know* that!"

Not again. He had zero patience for another fight tonight.

"I need you to stay here," he said.

"He broke our door! He broke the Cove! *I want to come help!*"

"No, Sana!" Tan yelled. "Your help isn't really help, so just—stop pretending it is!"

Sana's face turned the shade of a red pepper. She burst into loud wails that echoed off the cathedral's stone walls. "I miss Mom and Dad! You *lied*! You never took me to Barnes and Noble even though you *promised*. I want to go *home*!"

Bursting into sobs, she took off for the cathedral. Tan gritted his teeth, but Winter laid a soothing hand on his arm.

"I'll talk to her." She hurried after Sana.

Tan sank onto the bench he'd painted with Winter. Cookies at Barnes and Noble felt like eons ago. Sana had just made a huge declaration of Tan being her awesome big brother, and here he was yelling at her.

Winter returned. "She's with Sister Ava now. She'll be okay. We should all get some sleep soon."

"Thanks, Winter," Tan said. He didn't know what he'd have done without her this week. Probably died by now. Winter took a seat beside him and he allowed himself a breath. It was long past bedtime for them all. The other kids were slowly starting to drift back inside.

After a few minutes, Sister Ava joined them, carrying a roll of duct tape. She surveyed the tree house with a sort of steely determination in her eyes. One of the lower rungs had broken off, and a long gash ran down the trunk where the hammer must have scraped. But the tree house itself remained strong and intact. Sister Ava taped a large *X* over the lower rungs.

"The kids are so proud of this fort," she said.

"That's because it's theirs," Rebecca said, low.

Sister Ava held up her phone, displaying a video for Tan and Rebecca. "This wasn't your first encounter with these people, was it?" she asked. "Is this you two?"

It was a video of him and Rebecca fighting off their attackers at the train station. Tan remembered the passengers aiming their phone cameras at them.

"Tonight was their third attack," Tan admitted. The video

had been viewed by thousands of people. Word might even have reached his parents or Rebecca's. He hoped so, but it was a slim chance.

"These guys were professionals," Sister Ava said gravely. "And your friend, Maria, seems very badly shaken."

"You met her?" Tan asked.

"Yes, she slipped away during the fight and filled me in. I offered her some tea. She's with Lucia and Sana in the dining hall now."

"Thank you," Tan said.

"So what's next?" Sister Ava asked.

He'd apologize to Maria in a bit. He pulled out the Cove phone. "Now that Liping knows where we are, I might as well try my parents again."

Tan's call to his father, again, went to voice mail. "Dad, please call. We're in trouble. It's serious." He hung up, frustrated. "Why isn't he picking up?" Tan dialed his own voice mails.

"You have two new voice mails," said the robotic voice.

Tan's heart lurched in his chest. "I hope it's them." Tan put the phone on speaker.

"Tan, sorry we missed your call." Dad. Thank God. "I tried that number you called from, but it doesn't have a voice mail set up. We're back in our room at the Marriott, so give us a ring back. Mr. Keller said you guys aren't home and the door's been broken in. We called the police—what the—how did you get in here?"

Tan's father's voice broke off. Winter's mom was yelling in the background.

"Who the hell are you?" Tan's mom demanded.

"What's happening?" Winter asked, her brown eyes widening.

"I don't know!" Tan said.

243

Over the phone beat thumps and shouts and muffled voices—the sounds of a struggle. Tan's hand hurt from gripping the phone so tightly. Thank God Sana was with Lucia and couldn't hear this.

The second voice mail began. A familiar AI-distorted voice came on. The voice of someone who should be locked in a jail cell right now.

"Tan Lee. Listen very carefully," said Liping. "My team in Hawaii has three parents in custody, and you have three coins."

"What?" Tan gasped. "How?"

"We can do a trade," Liping continued. "Three parents for three coins."

Tan felt frozen in time. In his mind, he watched the thugs breaking down their hotel door, just as they did at their house. Only this time, there was nowhere for their parents to run.

"And let me be perfectly clear: If you call the cops or anyone, we break a parent. If you sic your nun or her people on us, we break another parent. And we can keep going. Break another. And—oh, by then, we'll have run out. Damn."

"Tan?" Lucia asked at his elbow, startling him. She thrust a note into his hand. "The Watch asked me to give this to you." *Tan Lee* was printed on the envelope in a feminine handwriting he didn't recognize. From Liping?

"Where did Sana go?" asked Lucia as Tan ripped it open.

"Wasn't she with you?" Winter answered, suddenly concerned.

The writing was shaky. As though the person had jotted it at lightning speed with a trembling hand.

I'm sorry, Tan. Crane cornered me. I'll keep your sister safe. He said to meet him at 10 AM tomorrow. Union Square.

The message swam before his vision. He read the words twice. It was from Maria. Maria was here, and now she was gone. A pressure was building in his chest. It erupted as he raced for the gate, in a voice he didn't recognize.

"Sana!" he roared. "Sana! Sana! Sana!"

Chapter 22

Tan barely remembered the next few hours. He barely remembered charging out the gates, madly dialing Liping only to hit voicemail again and again. Or how he got to the International House, or how long he banged on the glass doors with both fists until a bleary-eyed student opened it.

Winter found him madly kicking Maria's doorknob. She took hold of his arm with a warm hand and gently tugged him away. The Berkeley campus police were there, uniformed and imposing with their official badges. "I called them," Winter explained, as they first knocked, then picked Maria's lock and flung the door open.

But Maria's room was empty.

Tan returned to the Cove, shaking. He was aware of Winter's steady presence beside him, her hand gripping his, but his mind spun with his sister.

Tan had pieced together the story. The Watch had let Maria leave hand in hand with Sana. Sana had led the way. She said they were off to help Tan get rid of the bad guys. They hadn't believed her, but none of them had any reason not to trust that Maria—a victim herself—wasn't taking Sana somewhere safe. *Tan* had trusted Maria. And underestimated Liping.

And Sana—was she frightened? Did she know by now that she'd

been taken? That her big brother would do everything he could to find her? She knew he would. She'd said it herself. He always looked for her, and when she hid, he found her. She'd never once doubted him, and he would make good on that. He would take back his last, furious words to her.

When they returned, they spotted Sister Ava deep in conversation with Rebecca on the common room couches. Their backs were to Tan and Winter, who were approaching through the hallway.

"Lucia says she can't wait to find a family of her own," Rebecca was saying.

"You cannot underestimate how powerful family is."

Rebecca shook her head. "*Guówài de yuèliàng gèng yuán.* 'The moon is always rounder in other countries.' Here you'd say 'the grass is always greener on the fence's other side.' You never had a traditional family, and so you long for one."

It was harsh, but Sister Ava didn't even flinch. "I did have one," she corrected her gently. "They were killed in a car accident when I was a year younger than you are now."

Rebecca's face reddened. "I am sorry," she said, and it might have been the first time Tan had ever heard her apologize with such sincerity. "But you're happy now."

"Yes. I realized over time that my calling was to this shelter, to be family to those without. Just as the good Lord has been to me."

"Honestly? Lucia may actually have more of a sense of family here than I've ever had," Rebecca said, low.

Sister Ava laid a hand on her arm. "Sometimes we need to mourn what we will never have."

Rebecca's chin trembled. Then Sister Ava spotted Tan and

Winter. She rose swiftly to her feet, her black habit whispering. "I promised you safety," she said. "And I've failed your sister."

"It's not your fault," Tan said, and he meant it.

"He's desperate now," Rebecca said soberly.

"Well, we can't send cops after Sana," Winter said. She squeezed Tan's hand gently, then released it. "Should we try the cops in Hawaii?"

"It's too risky," Tan said. "We don't know where they're being held, and if we interfere, they might get hurt." He couldn't even imagine what their parents were thinking right now. They'd gone to Hawaii for a well-deserved vacation and a conference. Now they were hostages for reasons they might not even know. His mom would be having panic attacks.

Tan felt completely helpless. Liping wasn't answering calls. Mr. and Mrs. Tseng weren't answering calls. He had no choice but to wait until their designated meeting time tomorrow.

Winter paced the common room, clenching and unclenching her fists. Lucia sat on the window ledge with her hands thrust deep into the kangaroo pouch of her bulky green hoodie. "She said she was your friend," she kept saying. "We believed her."

Lucia had been the last of the Cove to see Sana. They'd gotten snacks with Maria in the dining hall. Lucia went to the bathroom. When she returned, Maria and Sana were gone.

"Maybe he threatened her family, too," Tan said. "Enough to make her risk everything like this. We have to get through to Rebecca's dad. He's the only one who can help Sana and our parents."

"If the Guójiā Ānquán Bù doesn't get to him first," Rebecca said bleakly.

Tan gave Rebecca the Cove phone's number and then entered

hers into it. "The plan's still the same. We get Liping's phone tomorrow. You call your dad."

Rebecca pursed her lips. "Okay."

"I'm coming with you guys." Lucia turned from the window, her expression fierce. "Sana is my friend, and she's part of the Cove. I'm coming, and I'll get this asshole's precious phone from him and get him put away forever."

Tan locked gazes with her.

"Sister Ava can't stop me," Lucia answered his unspoken question. "If you don't let me come with you, I'm coming anyway. I'll be safer if we go together."

A hard lump swelled in Tan's throat. Lucia cared about Sana. So much.

Tan looked to Winter. She was sitting on the back of the couch, blinking back tears. She gave him a tremulous nod yes. His chest ached. He wanted to hold her tightly. So much had happened since their talk in the sanctuary, and he hadn't had a chance to process the conversation they'd begun there. And he wouldn't still—not until they came out on the safe side of tomorrow.

And they would. Tan would fight with everything he had in him to get there. For all of them.

Turning to Rebecca, he held out his hand. "I need the coins."

"What?" She clutched at her pocket, taking a step back. "I can handle them."

"Our parents' lives are on the line," he said. "Your dad is surrounded by bodyguards protecting him. Our parents have no one except us, and these coins are their only hope."

Rebecca didn't budge.

"I need to be able to count on you to make the call to your dad,"

Tan continued. "It's Liping's word against ours. We both know he won't listen to me. But we need his help, and that call is also your chance to warn him that Liping is after him, too."

After a moment, she reached slowly inside her pocket. "This was never your fight to begin with."

Winter expelled a breath through her nose.

Tan was still waiting. Rebecca swallowed hard. "Okay. Once we get Liping's phone, I'll call him."

She set the coins in Tan's hand, and he pocketed them. They had no choice but to count on one another. And he had to hope, for Sana's and all their parents' sakes, that Rebecca wouldn't have another change of heart before then and betray them all again.

Chapter 23

Union Square was a large open block surrounded on all four sides by massive historic buildings, with white-striped crosswalks passing over streetcar tracks, department stores, and a five-story Barnes and Noble bookstore, with a facade of red bricks and paneled windows, and a green awning spread over three dark wooden doors.

Despite the cheery space, the morning sun felt cold on Tan's face as he and Winter entered the central square. It was one of the more popular places in the city. Tourists flowed up and down the sidewalks: old people, young people, a student group. It was both comforting to not be alone and terrifying. Liping had broken into the Cove. He'd kidnapped four people. Was he desperate enough to endanger all these people? None of them, including Rebecca, knew Liping well enough to predict his next move.

"Do you think he's here yet?" Winter whispered. Her lips barely moved.

"We're about to find out," he whispered back.

Rebecca and Lucia had arrived on the bus ahead of them. They were nowhere to be seen as Winter and Tan approached a tall pillar in the center of the square, topped by a Goddess of Victory statue, brandishing a trident and wreath. Tan hoped that meant victory would be on their side today.

He turned on his Cove phone, which he'd shut off earlier in

case Liping was tracing it, too. The plan was for Tan to meet with Liping and ask for proof that their parents and Sana were safe. While Liping was distracted, Lucia would pick his pocket. She'd get his phone to Rebecca and—if his passcode really was the speed of light—Rebecca would call her dad. Winter was here as backup. For everything that could go wrong. Which was a lot.

Timing was key. Tan needed to persuade Liping to let their families go before he realized his phone was gone. Then they needed Rebecca's dad to intervene before Liping could retaliate or make contingency plans. Rebecca wasn't sure how fast he could act, but she believed he could get help to them within an hour.

Tan's insides were knotted into a hard mass. He could only cling to Maria's promise that she'd do her best to keep Sana safe. But if her own family had been threatened, who knew what she'd be forced to do?

Tan studied the passing people. "See them anywhere?"

"Nope," Winter answered tightly.

Winter stopped at the statue, pretending to read a placard. Tan moved on to the coffee booth that was their meeting point, a red-and-white stand with a row of five black stools arranged before it. A barrel-chested man in a Hard Rock Cafe shirt was sitting casually on the far left. He wasn't looking at Tan directly, but Tan felt the prickle of his interest.

The man was watching him.

Tan's hand tightened around the coins in his pocket. From this angle, Tan could see everyone entering and exiting the area. No Liping. It was a few minutes past the hour. Would he still show up? He had to. He had all the cards. But Tan had the coins.

A group of tourists walked by. Tan was shocked when Liping

materialized beside him, a businessman in a black suit. He ordered a cappuccino, standing close enough that their elbows brushed.

"Beautiful day, isn't it?" Liping asked.

Liping was holding his phone in his hand. Which was a problem for Lucia. Tan felt as if he were staring daggers at it. He forced his eyes up to Liping's face. In daylight, Liping looked older than he had at night in the shadows. He had thick, graying hair that hung over a face that had seen a lot of sunlight. His black blazer covered his pockets.

Four large men strolled into the square and arranged themselves around the statue. They were of different ethnicities and dressed in collared shirts over slacks, as though they worked at one of the tech office buildings downtown. But at the back of the group was the familiar hawk nose. Robin Hood. Liping had brought plenty of reinforcements. Plenty of eyes and ears, too. Tan hoped Lucia had noticed them, too.

"Let my sister and our parents go," Tan said, keeping his voice low.

"Coins first. Then family."

On the other side of Liping, an elderly gentleman took a seat and ordered a black coffee. The situation felt explosive. Tan wished he could warn him to get away while he still could. But the last play had begun.

Tan held up his Cove phone, which was already ringing. "I want to confirm they're safe."

"Where are the coins?" Liping asked.

Tan's call went to Dad's voicemail. He hung up.

"You're not protecting the Tsengs, are you?" Liping asked. "You don't owe them a dime, let alone tens of millions."

"Yes, but you probably do. Or at least, you owe someone tens of millions. Isn't that right, Liping?"

He let the name drop casually. A card played to keep Liping off-balance. Liping's eyes flared briefly, but if he was surprised Tan knew his real identity, he took it in stride. "We're the same, you and I. Both rejected by Old Man Tseng. Neither of us good enough. Both of us infinitely smarter."

"We're nothing alike," Tan snarled. He pointed his Cove phone at Liping. "Tell me what number to call."

Liping tucked his phone into his pocket, securely under the flap of his jacket. "I need an earbud," he said, and Tan tossed him one of his, fitting the other into his ear. "Use FaceTime." Liping gave him a number. Tan dialed it.

His phone screen opened onto a tidy hotel suite with a red-and-beige-striped couch and round wooden table. Winter's mom's face appeared. Too far from the screen to be holding the phone herself. Her cheeks were splotchy, but her head was held high.

"Tan!" She blinked at him. "Are you guys okay?"

"Fannie!" It took all his willpower not to call Winter over. His parents were just behind her. Dad's face was bruised. Mom wore a floral print dress and sat strangely still in a chair by a window over-looking a grove of palm trees. A man who reminded Tan of James Bond stood with his arms folded at the back.

The parents all spoke at once. "Are you hurt? How's your sister? Is Winter safe?"

"Everyone's safe," he said. The fibers of his body felt taut, ready to snap. But why was Winter's mom blinking so oddly? Was she in pain?

Four quick blinks. Two more. Then one slower blink.

It was code. Morse code. The Woos really had adopted the Lee family and vice versa.

Hurry.

Tan's heart pounded harder.

"Release Ms. Woo," Liping snapped. The James Bond guy opened the door and beckoned for Winter's mom to walk out. She didn't move, but glanced back at Tan's parents.

"Fannie, go!" Mom said. "Get yourself someplace safe."

"You assholes won't get away with this," Winter's mom said. She walked out the door, and James Bond shut it behind her. Then Tan's screen blanked out.

"There," Liping said. "One parent free. Two to go. I'm a man of my word."

"How do I know they're not grabbing her back right now?" Tan asked.

"No more delays!" Liping shifted forward, deliberately, revealing the glint of silver inside his jacket. Tan could smell the coffee on his breath.

A trickle of sweat rolled down Tan's back. He had no proof of anything and no way of forcing it. And Winter's mom had entrusted him with a message. *Hurry.* She was telling him that Liping wasn't bluffing. That their situation was dire. Liping could even shoot him right here and take the coins off his dead body.

At least the others were safely out of range.

At least things couldn't get worse.

Then he heard a voice that proved him very, very wrong.

"Tan, I'm here!" Sana cried behind him. She climbed onto one of the stools, and now she leaped, flinging her arms around his neck and swinging her entire weight like a monkey.

"Sana!" He tried to tug her loose.

"I hid from Maria! She's over there." Sana pointed vaguely toward the street. "She can't find me!"

Of course she couldn't. No one could keep up with Sana when she was bent on hide-and-seek. Especially since Maria wasn't a trained operative and whose heart wasn't in the kidnapping. But she'd made good on her word. Sana was unharmed.

And Liping was frowning at Sana, distracted. One of his hostages was on the loose.

From the corner of his eye, Tan saw Lucia, nondescript in a black hoodie and jeans and with a floppy sun hat hiding her face. She slipped away from Liping and vanished into the crowd. Tan hadn't even noticed her arriving. Which could mean only one thing: She'd gotten his phone.

Then everything happened at once:

Liping lunged at Tan.

The elderly customer splashed his hot coffee on Liping's back, who yelled and spun around.

Tan shoved Liping hard, sending him tumbling into the stools and clattering to the ground. His gaze flashed to the elderly man's warm hazel eyes. So like Father Luiz.

Then Tan grabbed Sana's hand. "Run!" he yelled.

Chapter 24

Hand in hand with Sana, Tan raced from the square. He skirted tourists, sculptures, tour guides holding umbrellas. The crowds slowed him, so Sana had no trouble keeping up—but neither did Liping and his men, who pounded closely on their heels.

He shut his phone off. He was risking their parents' lives by running away like this.

He could only hope that the coins still in his pocket—Liping's need for them—would keep them safe. And that Lucia would get Liping's phone to Rebecca in time for her father to save them all. But in the meantime, he couldn't lose Liping. He needed to keep him close and stall for time.

Sana skipped along beside him. She was afraid, but more excited to be back with him. She probably didn't even know their parents had been kidnapped, and he wanted to keep it that way . . . But was that fair to her?

Then Tan spotted the Barnes and Noble with its green awning, just down the street. An idea struck. For how he might be able to save their parents. He grabbed Sana's hand. "Sana, what's the name of your board game back home? The pink one we bought at Barnes and Noble?"

"It's *Pirates* in Pink," she corrected him politely. Without her usual eye roll.

She caught sight of the store rising before them. Her eyes widened, and her lips moved without sound, shaping the name of her favorite store.

Tan almost laughed. The hysterical, teary kind of laugh.

"Let's go to Barnes and Noble," he said.

But as he started forward, a hissing sound filled the air. A canister rolled toward Tan's foot, spraying out a yellow mist. A yellow smoke rose up, stinging his eyes and distorting his vision. It clogged his throat, setting him coughing. A shoulder bumped roughly against Tan, knocking him into the brick wall that rose up beside him.

The square was in chaos. Tourists and people in business attire ran screaming into traffic. Horns honked. Then directly before him, human shadows materialized from the smoke.

Robin Hood and Little John.

Robin Hood's hand closed on Tan's arm. Tan flung him off, kicking into the vicinity of his groin. His foot made contact, and he heard a startled curse.

"Tan!" Sana yelled. Little John had seized her by the arms and lifted her off her feet, but Sana was twisting like a wild cat. Tan raced to her. Grabbing his shirt at the shoulder, he drove his fist into Little John's face.

With a yell, Little John dropped Sana. Tan caught her against his hip, slowing her fall. Then he grabbed her hand and ducked beneath the smoke.

Tan ran blindly, dodging shadows and people. Sana was so short the smoke mostly billowed over her head, but she was also more likely to get trampled.

Then Sana yanked him sideways. "In here!" she cried. He

followed her to familiar, heavy wooden doors set with a grid of square windows. He hauled the nearest one open and stumbled into a sanctuary with greenish-gray carpet . . .

"Barnes and Noble," Sana said with reverence.

Tan spared a moment to take in familiar dark wood bookshelves and tables stacked high with books and a sign that read NEW RELEASES. Journals and pens and stationery. Rows of magazines.

But behind him, others from the street were cramming in, jolting by. He shielded Sana and moved deeper inside, clearing the way. Store guests were gaping at the crowd surging in.

Then all the lights went out. A scream went up around the store.

A panicky guy with a STUART name badge over his green Barnes and Noble sweatshirt was running for the cash registers, his badge bouncing on his chest and keys fumbling in his hand.

"Lock it," Tan grated out. "Lock the doors."

Stuart's mouth trembled. It shaped soundless words. He didn't seem able to move, so Tan grabbed the keys and locked the doors.

"Make an announcement," Sana urged. "Like for story hour."

Stuart's hands shook as he reached for an intercom. "Attention, Barnes and Noble customers." His voice boomed over the speakers. "There is an active security issue in the square. We are going into lockdown. Please stop where you are and take a seat. Please do not go near the windows or try to leave the store until we can provide further instruction."

Emergency lights overhead cast a faint glow. Tan caught his breath. All these poor book-reading customers and employees were now caught up in an international intrigue that had nothing to do with them.

"I've called 911," Stuart said. "Help is on its way."

"I wouldn't count on that," Tan said. "Keep the doors locked. Stay low to the ground until you can get everyone out." He grabbed Sana's hand. He had to hurry. The locked doors would keep Liping and his men at bay for only so long. "Help me find your game," he said.

They'd never been in this particular Barnes and Noble before, but Sana had a radar for the kids area. She led Tan into the games section, where she scoured the shelves. Tan scanned for the title, but he was lost in the vast selection. He'd never looked closely at her game box cover. Never cared to.

"Here it is!" Sana dived forward, tugging the shrink-wrapped box free. "Look! It's different! Better!"

It was a deluxe version. Pirates in Pink. Featuring a dragon-slaying pirate girl on a quest through a world of magical creatures. The kind of game Tan had to admit he'd actually enjoy playing. He just hadn't looked past the very pink cover and AGE 7+ label.

Tan ripped open the box. "Where are the coins?" he asked, dismayed.

"In here." Sana spilled them out from a pink pouch with a drawstring. "They're dragon's gold." Up close, they were slightly shinier than Sana's set, which had gone through her grubby hands for months. But they were the same gold color and about the same size and weight, with the same squares in their centers. Taking out his knife, he stabbed one in about the same spot as he had before.

Then he closed his hand around them.

"These are perfect." It really was no wonder Sana had mistaken them for her own game pieces. Now, if only Liping would do the same. Tan knelt down to hug his sister. "I'm glad you're here."

"I helped," she said wonderingly. Her stunned expression tore at his heart.

"More than you know," he said, his throat tight with emotion. "You really did." She'd had their parents' numbers at her fingertips when they'd needed them. She'd won over the Cove. Now this critical decoy. He'd missed so many chances to tell her that. Worse, he'd yelled at her the exact opposite.

Still kneeling at eye level, he held her by one narrow shoulder. "I'm so sorry, Sana. I've been a terrible big brother."

"It's not your fault." She set her small hand over his fist, clenched around the coins. "They're the bad guys. Not us."

Five going on eleven. If only everyone could see as clearly as Sana and be as forgiving.

Sana looked sober and serious for once.

"That man outside was a *very* bad man," she added.

"Yes, he was," he said. It was time to come clean with her. She deserved that much. He set his hand over hers, holding it tightly. "And you have to be brave, because he's got Mom and Dad and maybe Fannie."

Her lips trembled as she took this in. "Not with Maria?"

"Not with Maria. In Hawaii."

"Will they be okay?"

"I'm not sure," he said truthfully.

She threw her arms around his waist and buried her face in his lap. He stroked her sleek hair, which was damp from sweat. He felt a gut-wrenching stab of love for her. After all this—getting her feet cut up, forgetting to feed her, missing his chances to be kinder, and letting her get kidnapped right under his nose—she still trusted him. Loved him. And he loved her. That love had always been there. He just hadn't felt it like this.

This must be a glimpse of what his parents felt. Knowing you'd do anything to protect someone, and hoping against hope that it would be enough. This was what it meant to really watch over Sana—and all of them. Keeping Sana out of the direct line of fire, and stepping it up himself.

"When this is over," he said, "I promise, we're getting that cookie."

She smiled through her tears. "Okay, Tan."

They returned hand in hand to the front of the store. The clerk was relocking the doors after a few frightened girls, who vanished into the back. At the checkout counter, Rebecca was sitting on the floor beside Winter, her long black hair slightly tangled and her head on Winter's shoulder. Winter's arm was slung comfortingly around her. Winter's freckles stood out more sharply than usual on her pale face.

"There you are," Winter said. "I saw you and Sana duck in here."

At the sight of Tan and Sana, Rebecca hastily dried her tears and sat up. To Tan's surprise, Jaxon and Perry were also sprawled nearby. Guy was crawling on hands and knees toward them.

"What are you guys doing here?" Tan blurted.

"Lucia told us Sana was in trouble," Guy said.

"I'm not in trouble," Sana said, and Guy held out a fist for a bump.

Tan's throat ached. But then he looked around. "Where *is* Lucia?"

Winter and Rebecca gave him blank looks. "We thought she was with you."

"She has Liping's phone. She's probably still out in the square, looking for you guys."

Winter scrambled to her feet. "We need to find her."

"Yes, she's our way to Rebecca's dad now." Tan flashed the Pirates in Pink game tokens. "These are for Liping." He tucked them carefully into his right pocket. The real coins were in his left one. "I'll buy us time for my parents until you guys can get ahold of Rebecca's dad."

"Once we do, he'll be able to help your parents right away," Rebecca said.

"I'll need your phone again," he said, and she handed it over. "I need Liping to come to me. His men should be able to track your phone."

"We'll go find Lucia," Winter said. "She can't be far." She extended a hand to Rebecca, helping her up.

"Please hurry," Tan said. "Go out through the back."

Winter squeezed Tan's elbow gently as she passed him. "Good luck," she whispered.

Then the two of them headed out the back of the store.

Tan turned to the Cove kids. Barnes and Noble was in danger of turning into a war zone, and he didn't want anyone else becoming Liping's hostages. They had to get everyone out of here. Sana included.

"Jaxon, Guy, Perry, Sana, I need you to evacuate everyone. Same way as Winter and Rebecca."

Guy held out his hand, and Sana took it.

"I'm helping," Sana said smugly. She took Perry's hand, and the four of them faded into the store, herding customers along with them. "Time to go!" Tan heard Sana say.

Tan was all alone now. The lights were dim. The rows of shelves and tables of books eerily abandoned. He could hear the soft churn of the air conditioner. His stomach cinched. Who knew whether he'd see Winter, Sana, or any of the others again?

But it was time to stop hiding. And time to start seeking.

So Tan put his thumb to Rebecca's iPhone and turned it back on, sending a homing beacon out to Liping.

Chapter 25

The glass panel of the door shattered loudly this time. The tool was a large ice pick. Glass spilled onto the carpet with a muted tinkle—but there was no one but Tan to hear it. And Robin Hood, whose hawk nose filled one of the square panels. Beyond the glass windows, Union Square itself was cleared of the smoke bombs, with no signs of cops—no surprise, 911's dispatch had never arrived.

Robin Hood's fleece-padded arm reached through the broken panel and groped at the lock. But there was no latch or key. With heaves of his pick, he destroyed the remaining glass panels and wooden lattice frame and climbed through.

Across from the panel of doors, Tan waited in the dim light by the new-books table. He feigned calmness, despite his racing heart. In his right pocket, his thumb ran over the nick he'd created in the fake coin.

BAM. The door busted open under a heave of Robin Hood's meaty shoulder. Then Liping stepped inside, backlit by sunlight.

His silver gun glittered in his hand.

Liping walked into the heart of the store, stopping opposite Tan. Six of his men ranged like a row of tanks behind him. Including Little John and the guy in the Hard Rock Cafe shirt.

Great, we're all here, Tan thought grimly.

"Now I need my phone back, *and* the coins," Liping said in a pleasant tone. He gestured with his gun.

Tan was acutely aware of the vast emptiness of the store behind him. He tossed the stabbed game coin at Liping, who greedily snatched it out of the air.

"That's for Fannie," Tan said, keeping Liping's focus on him, not the coin. "Now I need you to release my parents."

"My phone," Liping said. "In exchange for Sana. We have her again."

He was bluffing. Sana was on the run with Guy, Perry, and Jaxon. They would have texted him if there was a problem. But Tan still felt a shiver go down his spine.

"I don't have your phone."

"Then a coin. A whole one. Fair is fair."

Tan took his time fishing a second coin from his pocket. But he was losing control—Liping's men were spreading out, moving deeper into the store. In seconds, he would be trapped. They would search him and take the real coins. Then kill him.

"Stop stalling!" Liping barked.

Tan threw the coin wide, toward the register. It sailed over the counter toward a stack of outward-facing books. Swearing, Liping chased after it.

"You don't get the last one until you let my parents go," Tan said. Then he turned and ran.

He aimed for the back door. He passed the information desk, bolting down the central aisle between the sections of shelves. But the thugs were everywhere. Tan dodged an oncoming one, sliding into the travel section. As he emerged, Little John came at him. He ran down the aisle, but more men charged at him from opposite book aisles.

They were hemming him in. Blocking his access to the back door. The escalator was narrowly within reach, but Robin Hood was racing toward him. Tan knocked a stand of new releases into the man's path, then leaped for the escalator. He took the moving stairs two at a time, swinging himself onto the second floor. The thugs stayed close on his heels. He ran without a plan, on to the third, and then the fourth. The pounding of feet behind him grew fainter. If he could put distance between them, find a place to hide . . .

But the escalators ended on the fifth floor, which was full of low shelves of music records. With nowhere to hide. He backed into a potted tree, barely catching it before it crashed. Below him, the clatter of footsteps on metal treads drew closer.

Then Tan spotted a small wooden door at the rear. Racing toward it, he burst through to a short set of steps to another door. Tan jiggled its rusty latch frenetically until it opened. He stumbled out onto a rooftop terrace.

The sun beat down on him, and a breeze gusted through his hair. The rooftop was empty and flat, ringed on all four sides by a low brick wall, with just a stack of plastic pails in a corner. He was standing outside a small brick dormer that housed the stairwell from which he'd just emerged. He slammed its door shut, leaning against it, but there was no lock on this side. It was only a matter of time before Liping and his men came looking for him here.

Tan was trapped. And it was a long way down.

Somewhere in the distance, a bell tolled the half hour. Tan

moved to the roof's edge. Union Square teemed with people oblivious to what was happening inside Barnes and Noble. A police car was coming down the street, although without the blue and red flashing lights or sirens. And it simply passed the building by. Tan felt a dig of fear. By now, customers and even the store headquarters must have called the cops. He had to hope some cops would get the message and answer the call of duty—in which case, if Liping and his men were still in the building, *they* would be trapped, too.

And what about Lucia? Had Rebecca and Winter tracked her down yet?

The stairwell door burst open. Liping appeared, followed by Robin Hood and Little John, Hard Rock Cafe, and a fourth man. They blocked the doorway.

Liping's lips pulled back in a snarl, and he opened his hand, revealing the two gold coins shining on his palm.

"This isn't what I asked for," Liping said, starting toward him. "Where's the third?"

Tan felt a trickle of sweat roll down his back. At least Liping hadn't realized the coins were double fakes.

"Have you released my parents?" Tan asked.

"Turn over that last coin *now*. Or the question becomes moot."

Tan reached into his pocket. Then the deafening roar of an engine shook the air. To Tan's utter surprise, a helicopter was approaching. It descended on the far side of the roof. Its blades kicked up a terrific wind that tore at Tan's shirt and hair.

What the hell was a helicopter doing here?

"Give it to me now!" Liping yelled.

Tan tossed the third coin at him. Liping caught it in the air.

From the helicopter's open door, a wiry man in a blue dress shirt leaped out. He was holding a chrome laptop under his arm and a small silver device in his hand. He jogged over to them and handed the device to Liping, who appeared completely unsurprised to be taking a meeting by helicopter.

Liping placed one of the gold coins in the silver rectangular device. Tan recognized it—the reader Maria had used in her lab. Just as Maria had, Liping linked the reader to his laptop with a cable.

Little John and Hard Rock set up a folding table before Tan, and Liping set the laptop before him.

"Now," Liping said. "I need you to decrypt the keys before we go. All of them."

Things were clicking rapidly in Tan's mind. It wasn't an accident Tan had ended up on the rooftop. Liping had deliberately forced him up here for this private rendezvous. And that helicopter was his getaway.

The reader lit with a yellow light, churning as it tried to read the coin. Tan needed to keep Liping from realizing the coins were fakes as long as possible. Until he persuaded Liping to let his parents go, or Rebecca's father intervened for them.

"Don't I get a chair?" Tan asked. He moved before the laptop, hiding its screen from their view, as Liping snapped his fingers and Robin Hood grabbed an orange plastic bucket, dumped its contents onto the floor, and set it face down before the table.

"Your seat, Your Royal Highness," he sneered.

Out of their sight, Tan closed out the reader's application. He didn't know what it would show him. Probably "no data" or an error message. Tan slowly took a seat. He opened a web browser, improvising as he went along. He typed in the address for the DigitalWallet website. Liping leaned closer, his breath hitching eagerly.

"I need space to breathe," Tan said coldly.

Liping's brow rose slightly, but he took a step back.

"Whose name do I create the account in?" Tan asked.

"I don't need you to create an account. I just need you to decrypt the keys."

"It will take a while," Tan said.

"You have ten minutes. Which means your parents have ten minutes."

Ten minutes. Tan bet that in ten minutes, whatever means Liping had of warding off the cops would wear off. Tan hoped so. He busied himself opening a programming app, still debating how he would make Liping believe he was giving him access to tens of millions of dollars. Because every instinct told him that once he turned over the real currencies, Liping would hold all the cards, and Tan would have no other way of saving his parents. He could generate a bunch of fake alphanumeric digits . . . But Liping wasn't letting him or his parents go without confirming the money was in his possession.

"It's upside down," Tan said with disgust. "You don't even know how to use this." He reached for the reader with one hand and slipped his other into his pocket for the real coins.

He opened the reader and removed the fake coin, then pretended to examine it as he swapped it for a real Tang coin. His hand shook slightly. The real coin felt exposed and vulnerable sitting there in the reader.

Tan had told Rebecca it would take him days to decrypt the coins. He'd believed that was true. It took him six minutes for this first one. A list of alphanumeric digital keys began to populate on Liping's screen.

"Test it," Tan said. "I'll read it to you."

Liping took back the laptop. He opened his account, copied the top alphanumeric key into his account and watched his page greedily. A five-digit dollar amount flashed. Tan felt a cold sweat breaking over him. The one key had unlocked over ten thousand American dollars. Real ones. Times as many numbers on this list, and his original estimate had been right. There were millions of dollars on each coin. More even.

"Decrypt the rest," Liping said triumphantly.

The digital keys continued to populate on Liping's screen. Tan slowed the work as much as he could, until he reached the end of the list. He felt as though he'd been downloading dollars for Liping for an eternity, that by now, Rebecca could have flown to her father in Shanghai and back. But in reality, only nine minutes had passed.

"It's done," Tan said with dread. He reached for the reader, but Liping slapped his hand aside with a painful sting.

"I'll do it." Liping pocketed the coin, then placed his second coin in the reader. Seizing the momentary distraction, Tan switched his program to a pseudorandom number generator, adjusting the settings to create sixteen-to twenty-digit false keys.

Then he pretended to run the reader on the fake coin.

A second list of digital keys began to fill Liping's screens. They repeated the drill with Liping's third fake coin. Liping impatiently circled Tan as he worked. Tan felt as though he were made of fiberglass, ready to snap under the stress of waiting for these digital numbers to grow in their long column. The clock chimed the three-quarter hour. Tan was far over his ten-minute allotment, but with every minute, Liping's wealth appeared to grow on his screen, reaching into the hundreds of millions.

Another trickle of sweat rolled down Tan's back.

What was taking Rebecca so long?

Or what if her father's reinforcements had arrived, but found Barnes and Noble empty, and simply left?

"Are you done yet?" Liping peered over his shoulder at the screen.

Tan jumped slightly. "It's done." He showed Liping the end of the long list of keys. Then Tan shut down the laptop and stood, shoving it into Liping's arms.

"Now what about my parents?"

Liping merely tucked the laptop under his arm and headed for the helicopter. The man who'd arrived with the laptop and Robin Hood and Little John formed up behind him. The rotor picked up speed, kicking up a huge wind that sent his bucket clattering over the roof. The other thugs were disappearing back down the stairs, leaving Tan alone on the rooftop.

"Hey!" Tan called. "Hey, we had a deal!"

Liping kept walking. Tan might as well have been invisible. And Tan's parents were still captives. Tan was out of time and options. Had Rebecca's dad already released his parents? Had he sent help to Tan?

He reached for Rebecca's phone just as it buzzed in his pocket. His heart lurched, and he pulled it out to a blue text bubble from Lucia:

8;9;19;0;16;8;15;14;5;0;9;19;0;4;15;21;2;12;5;0;5;14;3;18;25;16;20;5;4
23;5;0;14;5;5;4;0;8;9;19;0;6;1;3;9;1;12;0;19;3;1;14;

Tan felt a surge of relief. Lucia was using code, which meant she knew Tan had Rebecca's phone, which meant Rebecca and Winter had found her. Which meant they had finally reached Rebecca's dad. They could end this nightmare now. Tan rapidly decoded the message in his head.

And what he read instead was this:

TAN: *His phone is double encrypted. We need his facial scan.*

Facial scan.

Facial scan . . . facial scan!

Tan swore. They needed Liping . . . who was now strapping himself into his getaway helicopter.

Tan pelted toward the helicopter as it ponderously rose a few inches off the floor.

"Liping!" he yelled, frantically typing back to Lucia: *ROOF NOW.* "Liping, those coins are fake!"

Inside the chopper, Liping turned to look back. His expression was shocked. Tan thrust his arm skyward, holding Mr. Tseng's gold coins aloft. The real ones.

"*Your money is fake!*" Tan screamed.

Liping dug into his own pocket and pulled out his game tokens.

A man like Liping probably always had a strong control of his emotions. An ability that made him an asset to the Tseng empire. But now those emotions shifted rapidly from disbelief to surprise to fury. He hurled the coins off the roof.

Pocketing his coins, Tan flung himself onto the copter's landing skid. The roar of the chopper was deafening. He grabbed a bar with one hand, heaved himself up and into the open doorway, then grabbed Liping's shirt. Liping was already fighting with his seat belt buckle.

As the helicopter rose into the air, Tan and Liping tumbled back toward the rooftop.

Chapter 26

Tan landed on his shoulder. A jolt of agony ripped through his body. Then Liping's full weight was crashing down on him, pinning him on his back to the rough floor. Fingernails scraped Tan's hands as the two of them fought for access to his pocket—and the coins. With a rush of fury, Tan wrenched free. He staggered to his feet, gasping for breath.

Robin Hood and Little John had leaped down from the helicopter, which was awkwardly hovering, trying to land again. The two men advanced on Tan, who backed away.

He needed to keep Liping here until Lucia, Winter, and Rebecca arrived with his phone. Tan had no idea how he would best three grown men without getting tossed over the roof himself. But he wasn't going without giving this fight everything he had.

"You want them?" He flashed Rebecca's coins again for all three men to see.

Then he shoved them into his mouth.

Liping swore. The coins tasted like salt and metal on his tongue, but Tan kept his teeth firmly clenched around them.

Then Tan tucked his chin, as Master Kwon had taught him, and charged Liping.

Liping took the full blow of his shoulder, staggering back. Tan let his fist fly at Liping's nose, earning a satisfying crunch. Warm blood splattered onto Tan's cheek. Liping grunted, and his grip slackened. That was for Mom. He hit him again for Dad. Then for Fannie.

But if he beat Liping's face too badly, the facial scan wouldn't work. He altered his aim, but Liping twisted away, and then Robin Hood and Little John pinned Tan's arms behind his back.

Two more men were jumping from the helicopter, their faces hidden in gray balaclavas.

Tan glowered at Liping, who was wiping the blood from his face. Liping came toward him. "I've eaten too much shit for too long to let another little shit like you ruin everything." Liping landed a hard blow to Tan's stomach, sending a rush of bile into his throat to mingle with the coins.

Then his hand closed on Tan's neck again. His breath now reeked of onions, but the stench vanished as he pinched Tan's nose shut, trying to force him to open his mouth. Tan bit down hard, fighting for breath.

"Open up or I'll break your teeth!" Liping snarled.

Darkness began to cloud Tan's vision.

Then swift footsteps sounded in the stairwell. The door flew open. Tan twisted to see Lucia in her black hoodie leap onto Robin Hood's back, arms around his neck, kicking him wildly with her heels.

"Let him go!" she yelled.

"Lucia," Tan croaked through his clenched teeth. He jerked free of Robin Hood's grip, then grabbed Liping's hands, still around his throat, fighting his hold.

"Put me down!" Lucia yelled. Little John had seized Lucia around the waist and was yanking her off his partner. She kicked wildly. She swung her sun hat into his face. She let out a cry that could be heard across the bay.

Then Lucia dropped like a stone, and Little John collapsed beside her. Guy was standing behind them, a hardcover dictionary raised in his hands. He tackled Robin Hood next as Jaxon piled into Liping's other men, and Lucia rushed over to help. Fights broke out in the periphery of Tan's vision.

"Liping!" Rebecca shouted. In a whirl of flying black hair, she and Winter dashed through the dormer's entrance. Winter's eyes flared wider as she took in the melee. "You'll wish you were in a nice safe jail after my dad gets ahold of you."

"Ow!" Liping's hands suddenly fell from Tan's neck. Tan dived forward into freedom. He twisted back. Liping's hand had flown to his own head, and Winter was pulling back from a baseball pitcher stance. On the rooftop floor, a metal object clattered away.

Liping glowered at Rebecca. Tan read the reckoning that crashed over his face. Rebecca knew who he was. Which meant her dad would know, too, eventually. Which meant Liping's career in the Tseng empire—and his days as a free man—were finished.

A flash of silver sprang into his hand.

"Look out!" Winter cried.

Tan lunged for the gun. A blast by Tan's ear set his entire head ringing. A brick overhead shattered, sending pebbles showering down. A searing pain laced his arm, but he grabbed the hand with the gun and smashed it against the brick wall until the weapon fell.

Tan threw his arms around Liping's neck, forcing his head down until Liping was staring at his own feet. Liping struggled, but Tan hung on tight in a headlock that would have made Master Kwon proud.

"Winter!" he yelled over the coins still in his mouth.

Winter thrust Liping's phone screen under his immobilized face.

"What the hell?" Liping yelled. "My phone!"

"It's unlocked!" Winter cried.

"Hand that back!" Liping redoubled his struggles, but Tan held tight.

Winter thrust the phone into Rebecca's hands. The white glow of the screen illuminated Rebecca's face as she intently navigated the buttons. She dodged Robin Hood, who was coming at her, and ducked behind Guy, who crossed his arms over his broad chest and stared down the man as if he were a librarian on duty and the man was talking too loudly.

Rebecca lifted Liping's phone to her ear. She waited, her jaw clenched.

"He's not answering!" she cried. Robin Hood's eyes flitted rapidly among them, assessing the situation.

"Try your mom!" Winter yelled.

Rebecca dialed again.

"Wéi, Liping?" came a woman's voice. Robin Hood whirled on his heels to flee through the dormer, but Winter stuck out her foot and sent him sprawling into Guy's and Jaxon's arms.

"Ma!" Rebecca shrieked. "It's me."

Chapter 27

Rebecca's mother got her father on the line in seconds. The call was brief and to the point. "Ba, Liping's been trying to take the cryptocurrencies stored on your Tang coins," Rebecca said. "He's here in San Francisco, threatening to kill me and my friends to get to them."

"San Francisco?" Her father's voice was clipped and brisk. Tan could hear him even ten feet away. "Where are you exactly?"

Rebecca looked to Winter and Tan for help.

"Union Square," Winter supplied, and Rebecca repeated it for her father, along with the Barnes and Noble name.

Liping was still struggling in Tan's headlock. Jaxon gripped Liping's arms more securely. Lucia and Guy were grappling with Robin Hood and Little John.

Winter dashed back inside the store. She returned with a roll of nylon ribbon and swiftly bound Liping's wrists behind his back.

"His legs," Tan said. Liping kicked out, but with a kick of his own, Tan knocked Liping's feet out from under him. As Liping landed face down, Tan sat hard on his upper back, pinning him with his weight.

"Get the hell off me," Liping snarled.

Tan spat the coins back into his hand. "Ugh." He wiped the

279

salty tang from his mouth as Winter bound Liping's legs. His arm was bleeding from a long cut where the bullet must have grazed him. His ears still hurt from the roar of the helicopter. A shudder ripped through him belatedly. It could have been worse, so much worse.

Guy and Lucia were binding Robin Hood and Little John's arms to their sides. The helicopter, and the rest of their thugs, had melted away.

Rebecca was still on the phone. "Why are you in California?" her father was asking. "Liping told us you had gone on a vacation with Albert."

"Vacation?" Color came into Rebecca's cheeks. Her eyes fluttered with surprise and sought out Tan's.

"He didn't know," Winter whispered.

"I would *never* go on vacation with Albert," Rebecca flared.

But some of her anger had abated. That her parents had believed she'd gone on vacation with Albert meant they didn't know her— but it was a lesser evil than not caring altogether.

"We were wondering why Liping was in the States," Mr. Tseng said. "Stay put. I'm making sure Liping and his men are handled."

Mr. Tseng's crisp voice went silent. Rebecca held the phone to her chest and turned a cold gaze on her father's man, still lying under Tan's weight.

"You gave me my first Barbie," Rebecca said. "I wouldn't have believed this of you."

"You don't know anything about me," Liping said. "You're a spoiled princess who has never had to work a day in her life. How was shopping in Paris?" His voice dripped with sarcasm.

Rebecca flinched, but kept her voice steady. "I know you had free rein over the entire Tseng empire and household. Every single door was open to you. And that wasn't enough for you."

"And why would it be?" Liping's head came up sharply. "Your family never believed I had any ambitions of my own. Everything else came from that."

"I'm sorry about that. But that doesn't make your choices anyone's fault but your own."

"Look out," Winter said warningly.

Tan turned in the direction of her gaze. Four athletic men were emerging from the rooftop doorway dressed in black yoga pants and shirts. Two were bearded. One was blond. They weren't the same men who'd been with Liping, but they carried themselves in the same alert way.

Like undercover bodyguards.

"We'll take over from here," said the blond man. "Hello, Liping."

Liping shifted suddenly under Tan. "I'll kill you all," Liping said softly, for Tan's ears only.

They were screwed. Tan couldn't keep the men from wrenching Liping out from under him. Liping surged to his feet and held out his bound hands to be released. His gaze fell on Tan, sharp and triumphant. With a sharp zip, the blond man tore a piece of duct tape from a roll on his arm.

And slapped it over Liping's mouth.

Liping's eyes widened. Even through the tape, Tan could hear the swear words.

"Ms. Tseng?" The blond man inclined his head respectfully. "Your father asked us to make sure he doesn't bother you anymore."

Rebecca was hanging on to the doorknob. Now she released her grip and returned his nod stiffly. "Thank you."

He started to haul Liping toward the door. Liping searched wildly for help, but Robin Hood and Little John were bound just as tightly—and being dragged out by the other three men.

As Liping passed Rebecca, she put out a hand to block them.

"I told you you'd have been better off with the police," Rebecca said.

Sunlight fell on Liping's lined face—creased with sheer terror. Then the guards moved him and the others swiftly on, and they were gone.

The Cove kids, Rebecca, Winter, and Tan shared a collective exhale.

"You okay, Lucia?" Guy asked. Lucia was dabbing at a bloody scratch on her arm.

"I'm good," she said. "Thanks for showing up."

"We're the Cove," Guy said. "We show up. That's what we do for one another."

She smiled. "Remind me to return your Magic cards when we get back."

Guy blinked. Frowned. "You little thief."

"Hello, Rebecca?" Mr. Tseng was back on the phone. "Is Liping restrained?" he asked calmly.

"Yes, your guys have him," Rebecca reported.

"What about our parents?" Tan asked.

"Baba, Liping's holding my friends' parents captive in Maui," she said. Tan gave her the hotel details, and Rebecca passed them along.

"I'll take care of it," Rebecca's dad said.

"Call me back when their parents are released." Rebecca hung up.

"Let's get his log," Tan said before she could shut off Liping's phone.

Winter let out a breath. "Good idea."

Tan snapped a photo of the list of phone numbers Liping had called in the past few days. Most of them started with 650 and 408—Bay Area numbers.

"The mole or moles are in here somewhere," he said grimly. "I'll get this over to my cousin to investigate."

"My dad will take care of Liping," Rebecca said. "He has no allies here now, not even the police."

"What do you mean 'take care of'?" Winter asked.

"This was a personal attack, and my dad will deliver a personal response. He'll extradite Liping to China."

"What will your dad do to him?" Tan asked.

"You don't want to know," said Rebecca. And shuddered.

"Wow," Tan said. "I thought this before, but now I know for sure. Your family is *terrifying*."

"Liping chose this," Rebecca said. "It's not easy to breathe when every step you take is already predetermined. I know that better than anyone. And Liping did everything my dad wanted. He basically . . . canceled himself for twenty years . . . waiting for his moment to strike." She shuddered again. "I'm not turning out that way."

"There's a lot to figure out." Winter gave her elbow a comforting squeeze. Rebecca hadn't cried talking to her parents, but now her eyes reddened.

Then Rebecca's phone rang in Tan's pocket. "It's your dad again," he said, handing it to her. He held his breath.

Rebecca's face flooded with emotion as she answered. They spoke in Mandarin. Her eyes met Winter's and Tan's, and she gave them a thumbs-up.

"Does that mean they're okay?" Winter asked.

"They're okay."

Winter grasped Tan's hand tightly as they waited for Rebecca, who continued in Mandarin for a minute longer.

Mr. Tseng's voice rose. He was obviously unhappy, but Tan couldn't tell if he was upset about Liping or at Rebecca. She remained calm and resolute.

"Albert hurt me. I tried to tell you. But you obviously didn't listen or understand," she said. "You made me feel like I was a spoiled brat who deserved whatever Albert dished out. And I didn't."

His answer was stiff. Mr. Tseng was a man who wasn't used to being crossed.

"It's not about money, Ba," she said. "It's about so much more than that. I'm not coming home. And there's nothing you can do to stop me."

She hung up and turned to them. Her face was a study of conflicting emotions—resolve, a tinge of sadness, but also triumph.

"Your parents have been released," she said. "They're safe. They said to let you know they're coming straight home."

"Oh my God, thank God," Winter whimpered. "They're okay. They're okay," she kept saying.

Tan wrapped his arms around Winter, and they held tight, hearts pounding together. Tan had no words. Only feelings too big to fit inside him.

When they finally broke apart, Winter turned to Rebecca. "I can't believe how fast your dad's people got to them."

A glimmer of pride touched her eyes, though it was mingled with pain. "He moves faster than anyone I know."

The six of them headed back inside, down the escalators to the deserted main floor. As they reached the shattered front door, it flew open.

"Tan!" Sana cried. She raced in and threw her arms around his legs. He knelt to squeeze her hard.

Perry jogged up behind her, panting slightly. And behind them both came Maria, her expression devastated and resigned, and behind them, a herd of cops in navy uniforms with silver stars gleaming over their left breast pockets.

Tan finally let go, and Winter swiped at the dampness on her cheek, and then Tan's, laughing a bit.

"I'll deal with the cops," Winter said, and moved to intercept them.

Maria was coming closer. "I'm so sorry," she said in a low voice.

"We're not turning you in," Tan said.

"I've already turned myself in," Maria said, lifting her chin. She gestured to the cops, who were spreading out into the store. "I've committed a terrible crime."

"*Liping* committed a terrible crime," Tan said firmly. "We'll tell the police the whole story. He forced all our hands. And you kept Sana safe." He didn't know if that would be enough to help Maria. But he would do his best.

Maria trembled. "Your nun was very kind," she said, then walked away.

"We're okay with the cops," Winter said, returning. "Although they want a debrief after they fingerprint and all that." She hoisted Sana into her arms, groaning, "When did you get so big?" They both smiled at Tan.

Rebecca watched them with a wistful expression. She wrung her hands uncertainly. "Could we talk?" she asked Tan.

Tan glanced at Winter, who set his sister down. "Sana, I saw a balloon man on the corner," Winter said, and they headed outside hand in hand.

Tan followed more slowly with Rebecca, who twisted her hands even more. "When I thought my parents were ghosting *me*—I felt—I must have hurt you really badly when I did that to you last year."

He hadn't expected this. "It did hurt," he admitted.

Her hands whitened, but she pressed on bravely, like she wanted to get it all out before she changed her mind.

"I wanted to say, I'm sorry. For everything. And for getting you guys into this *mess* . . ."

"It's all over now," he said. And not just this wild chase.

"I know," she whispered. She bowed her head briefly, shuttering her eyes.

"Will your dad try to force you home?" he asked gently.

Rebecca shook her head. "He owes me for what I've done for him. He won't drag me back. He was able to help us, but I'm still not going back, and if I ever do, it will be on my own terms. Besides, I've been eighteen in Shanghai for three hours now. I'll be eighteen here in twelve."

The clock read a few minutes past noon.

"Happy birthday," Tan said. Winter and Sana were returning with three balloons bobbing overhead.

"Happy eighteenth," Winter said.

Sana handed Rebecca the balloons, and she accepted, smiling ruefully. "Never imagined I'd kick off adulthood like this."

"What will you do about money?" Tan asked. "You still have two coins. I can help you with them."

"My dad already cashed out the cryptocurrencies," Rebecca said. "There won't be any evidence for the Guójiā Ānquán Bù. Even if they wanted to pin him down, which they don't. And he'll cut me off. He said he would, and he'll make good on that. But of all people, I should know it's not all about money." She laughed softly. "I wanted a bed in Sister Ava's shelter more than I ever wanted the bed in my own home. I'd even take the tree house. Actually, that would be the best option of all."

"It's a good place," Tan said.

"Maybe you can work something out," Winter said.

"I wouldn't want to just take up space there. Maybe I could keep volunteering in exchange for room and board, like Guy." She rubbed a smudge of green paint on her hands. "I'm not a very good volunteer," she said uncertainly. "I don't know if they'd go for it."

"Ask Sister Ava," Winter said. "I bet she'll find a way you can be helpful."

Rebecca smiled tentatively. "I think I might."

Then Winter squeezed Tan's hand. "Ready to go home?"

He squeezed her back and knelt to scoop Sana into his other arm. *Oof.* Winter was right—she *was* heavy. All that good Cove eating. He tweaked her nose and she giggled.

"I'm ready," he said.

Chapter 28

The house in Palo Alto was in shambles when Winter and Tan, Sana riding piggyback, finally returned. They had been gone only a bit more than forty-eight hours, but Tan felt like a long-lost traveler stumbling onto the shore of his homeland. Despite the wide yellow tape labeled POLICE LINE DO NOT CROSS wrapped around the entire stone wall.

"So much for keeping this all on the down-low," Winter joked. "The whole neighborhood knows something was up."

Tan broke the tape and unlatched the front gate. "At least the police are back on our side."

"But it's still creepy that Rebecca's dad's empire can reach into them like that."

"That's why I'm getting that list of Liping's phone calls to my cousin."

"At least we've improved state security," she said.

"Silver linings," he answered.

Beyond the wall, the front door was splintered and swinging open. Broken glass from the window glittered in the grass. Tan found their house numbers, the lucky "eight" and "eight," on the ground behind a bush. One had broken in half at its waist. Which made it "four," which was bad luck in Chinese. And bad luck had definitely hit the Lee family home this weekend.

Tan followed muddy shoe prints inside, passing the fallen Chinese screen that normally covered the wall in the entryway, passing the overturned couch and the kitchen whose pots and pans had been emptied onto the floor. Liping's thugs had done their best to find them. But it didn't appear as if anything had been stolen.

"Hello Kitty!" Sana swooped the doll into her arms from the wreckage.

Tan laughed. Another silver lining. "We must have dropped her before we even got out!" He looked at Winter. "Maybe we can find your necklace?"

"It's worth a shot," she said.

Tan gave Sana another piggyback ride, and the three of them returned to the shed. But though they scoured the grounds carefully for a good half hour, they turned up nothing. Winter's necklace was gone.

"I'm sorry," Tan said finally. "I know it was a present from your dad."

"It kept us safe," Winter said bravely. "He would have been glad for that."

Sana was asleep on Tan's back by the time they returned home. Tan tucked her into bed. Then he and Winter inspected the damage. Dad's sensitive garden had wilted without water. In the bedrooms, the closet doors stood open, with clothing thrown onto the floor. Tan's bed had been stripped, and his comforter lay trampled with a large black shoe print in its middle.

Sana's room was the least touched. When Tan walked by, her light was back on and she was at her shelf, pulling out a stash of Oreo cookies.

"Hey, where did you get those?" Tan asked suspiciously.

"In the cupboard," she answered without batting an eye. "Want one?"

She ate two while Tan checked the locks on her windows. He checked the locks on all the windows and on the back door. It would be a while before he'd feel safe without locks and bolts and maybe a few dozen security cameras pointed in every direction. But at least they were home now.

He returned to a trail of cookie crumbs through the hallway—leading to Sana's guilty face.

"Sana," Tan said sternly. "The whole house is a mess, and the front door is destroyed. The least we can do is not let Mom and Dad come home and clean up after us."

Sana scrambled to clean up her crumbs and dumped them into the trash.

Tan tousled her hair. "Nice work," he congratulated her.

He helped her wash up, brush her teeth, and get tucked back into bed. Then he and Winter removed the broken door and set it against the outside wall, under a shelter from the rain. They went back inside and righted the overturned couch and chairs. Winter pulled the vacuum cleaner from the hallway closet while he got out the mop. It felt good to do ordinary things. This was what his week was supposed to have been. Side by side, cleaning the house together in a sort of domestic tranquility.

He worked his way down the hallway, kneeling with a cloth to wipe away the muddy tracks. When he returned to the living room, he found Winter plumping up the couch cushions. It was nearly midnight. They both planned to go to school in the morning, to return to normal life as quickly as possible. But he didn't feel ready to split up for bed yet, and Winter didn't look like she did, either.

"I plugged in my dad's phone," Winter said, indicating the older model resting on the lamp table. "But Father Luiz's birthday turned out to be the same as my grandma's, which I tried last year. And Sister Ava couldn't find anyone who knew my dad well. So I'm back to the drawing board."

"That's disappointing," Tan said.

"Yes, but I'm glad I got to spend time at the Cove again. And with you there, too. It really is a special place. It meant the world to him, and I see why now."

"We can keep up the Woo family tradition of volunteering there over the holidays. If you don't mind the Lees crashing."

Her face lit up with her smile. "I'd love for the Lees to crash."

Then a thought struck Tan. "Hey. What's the cathedral's address?" In his memory, he could almost read the silver numbers on the plaque beside its gate. There had been quite a few of them. More than the double 88 of his home.

Winter's eyes widened. "I'll look it up." She hopped onto her laptop and googled the cathedral. "294568 Berkeley Avenue." She looked up at Tan. "Six digits," she whispered.

With trembling fingers, she entered the number into her dad's phone.

His phone unlocked.

Winter sat heavily on the couch. She didn't look through his phone. She just held it, shaking. "I've been trying to open this for *over a year*," she said.

"Then what are you waiting for?" Tan joined her, and she leaned into him so he could look with her. And breathe in the scent of her hair without interruption.

Her dad's wallpaper was a photo of the three of them: Mr. Woo with his arm around Winter's mom, and a young Winter smiling between them.

"You were cute back then," Tan said.

"Back then?"

"And now."

A smile of pleasure tugged at her lips. She opened his photo album and began scrolling through his collection.

Besides the photo in the Cove, Tan had seen only a few photos of her dad. He still wasn't present in most of these—but Tan could see the man behind the camera. There were goofy photos of Winter hamming it up with an ice-cream cone mic. Catching a gummy bear he tossed her with her mouth, just like the shrimp-catching video Tan had caught at prom. Even at the age of ten, she was a great actor. Tan pointed it out.

"He was the first one to suggest I become an actress," Winter said.

Tan flipped through photos of the three of them on a windy beach. He paused on a tender photo of Winter and her mom passed out on an airplane together, with Winter's arm tucked around her mom's and their mouths soft.

Tan found himself swallowing against a lump in his throat. "He loved you guys so much."

"I still miss him," she said softly. "So much. And my mom—she looks so tough, doesn't she? She got my dad through the hardest days in the hospital."

"She's still tough," Tan pointed out. "She blinked Morse code at me when Liping called her. She let me know they weren't bluffing."

"She did?" Winter's brow rose. "She learned that with Sana."

"And she got her law degree faster than some people get their driver's license."

"Well, maybe not *that* fast." Winter frowned thoughtfully. "I guess she's a lot tougher than I give her credit for."

Her head brushed his shoulder as she bent over the album again. They looked at all the photos, all the way back to Winter age eight, where the photos began. They took their time to savor them.

"These are priceless," Tan said, leaning back at last. "I'm so glad we got to them."

"Me too," Winter said fervently. She set his phone down on the coffee table and turned to face him. "I think I should go to London this summer."

He felt a squeeze in his chest. But it was an incredible opportunity for her, and he would never stand in the way. "Of course you should go. Look at those photos of you. Your dad would have wanted you to go. I'm sure your mom will want you to go."

"I was thinking that just now. I've been too protective of Mom."

"*I* want you to go, too," Tan said.

"You do?" She blinked, surprised. Maybe a little hurt.

"I'll miss you like anything." He took her hands and held them tight. "But I'll survive."

"Survive!" She laughed. "Now who's the overly dramatic actor?"

"And I want you to do more things for yourself, and not only for other people."

Her hands tightened on his. They were so much smaller, but larger than Sana's. They felt good nestled between his. Like they belonged there.

"When you guys first moved in, I was worried our house

wouldn't be home anymore," he continued. "I still remember the first time I saw you. You were wearing your purple bandanna. You were holding your backpack over one shoulder, and you looked like you wanted to bolt."

She smiled. "I was nervous, too, when I heard our new landlords had a kid my age. I hoped you wouldn't be a jerk. Prayed, actually."

He laughed. "Did I live up to your towering expectations?"

She squeezed his hands back. "And much more."

"And about prom—I've been wanting to set the record straight. You didn't strong-arm me. I *wanted* to go with you. Not to mention you kicked my ass back into gear. Prom was . . . magical."

The word landed on her like the touch of a wand. "Magical?"

"Magical," he said firmly. "But then you said we should back off. And you were right. About the power dynamics. I don't ever want to be *that guy*. But I didn't like it. And after a while, I figured, maybe it wasn't so magical for you. That you living with us was a real reason, but also a great excuse . . . for you not to be with me."

Winter trembled. "I thought we just got carried away that night. When I said we had to stop, you said it wasn't a big deal. I thought . . . it meant nothing to you." She gave a small laugh. "I guess you felt you had to say that. You're an even better actor than I am."

He smiled. "That's saying a lot."

Months of getting ghosted had made him fearful it would happen again . . . with Winter. And so, at the first hint of that possibility, he'd pulled away. To protect himself. He'd refused to believe the evidence before him. That she still cared for him. A lot. Winter wouldn't ghost him, but even though they were still living under the same roof and seeing each other every day, he'd practically ghosted *her*.

But the truth was, she had been and was always there for him, when he was lost and in his darkest moments. Now he would build a new future, and he wanted it to be with Winter. And even though speaking up now was opening up a new uncertain world—his parents' reactions, her mom's, and even their friendship could change—he wasn't letting her get away without her knowing how he really felt.

"Winter, I'd say I love you like a sister, but that would be a lie. I want to be with you—not just as your friend, either. I've felt this way for a long time now. And I'm willing to wait as much longer as we need to."

"I've been lying, too," she admitted.

He moved toward her, just as she did him, and his arms encircled her waist. Their mouths brushed, a bit clumsily. Then again with more certainty. They pulled apart shyly, holding each other's gazes. The kisses had been brief. Without the intensity of The Kiss of prom.

But all the magic was still there.

She put a finger on his lips, where her own soft lips had just been, and traced lightly around them. "So now we know where we stand."

Tan expelled a ragged breath and folded her hand to his chest. "Yes."

"But this doesn't solve anything," Winter said.

He'd never been more clear in his head. That was the thing about having his life and everyone else's on the line. It crystalized what he really wanted.

"We need to tell our parents," he said. "It's time we figure this out."

Winter touched his cheek. No more words were needed. That was how it was with Winter. How it had always been, until he'd done his best to hide from this connection they shared. But Tan was done doing that . . . and by the look on her face, so was Winter.

This time, when their mouths met, it wasn't light or hesitant. They moved together, hungry and ferocious. Tan crushed her against him, and then Winter shoved him over, pressing him into the couch and following with her entire weight. Her elbow dug into his shoulder, and his hand tangled in her shirt, and she yanked on his hair—all the pent-up wanting exploding between them until Tan suspected they might not be able to stop—

A car door slammed outside. Tan groaned as Winter lifted herself from him. His body protested, and Winter's eyes glinted mischievously. Her hair tickled his cheeks as she leaned in to give him one last kiss on his mouth.

"To be continued," she whispered.

Outside, voices moved swiftly toward the broken front door.

"—can't believe we made that flight," Dad was saying.

"Oh no!" Mom cried. "It's even worse than I imagined."

Winter and Tan stood as Mom and Dad spilled inside, followed by Winter's mom. Mom and Dad were sporting tans. Their necks were deep in floral and brown leis. With a cry, Sana came rushing from her room and hurled herself at everyone.

For about ten minutes, no one could understand a word anyone else was saying. There were hugs, tears, more hugs. Winter's mom laid a lei of brown nuts over each of their heads.

"I got these on our first day, before—" She broke off. "Kukui nuts. They represent good luck, which we seem to be sorely lacking. But I just think they're lovely."

"They are, Mom," Winter said. "And we are lucky. We have each other." She hugged her and pushed her dad's phone into her mom's hands. "Look. Tan cracked the passcode. It was the shelter address where he stayed as a teen."

Winter's mom's breath caught as she scrolled through the photos. "Oh, Noah." She fingered the pearl pendant at her throat.

"He had to rebuild his life completely after his parents died," Winter said. "That's something I came to appreciate while I was at the Cove."

"He did rebuild it, didn't he? He had us." Fannie looked at the broken front door and then at Tan's parents. "And we will rebuild again—all of this."

"We will," Mom said. "I'm just so thankful you all are safe."

"We are, too," Tan answered. "Though it wasn't much of a vacation for you guys."

"We got in that waterfall hike," Dad said. "But we'll be giving our conference talk virtually from here."

Their parents were a little worse for wear. A purple bruise still bloomed on Dad's cheek. Winter's mother was jumpier than usual. Tan's mom was in the worst shape, with new tense lines around her eyes. But they were all alive, bones and bodies intact—and their suitcases were full of macadamia nuts.

Mom poked her head into the kitchen, the bathroom. Everything was sparkling.

"The house looks great," she said. "If not for that door, I wouldn't believe it was broken into."

"I've got a new pen pal. Her name's Lucia," Sana said. "We can write each other in code."

"Amazing." Dad folded Sana into his arms and held out an arm to bring Tan in as well. Tears welled in his eyes. "We have so much to catch up on."

Mom, Dad, and Winter's mom talked about their time in captivity. Everything was shared. No attempts were made to brush over anything.

"They treated us well enough," Winter's mom said. "They needed what they thought your parents had in their heads to access Mr. Tseng's funds. So they couldn't push us too far."

Winter's face paled as she took that in. She squeezed her mom's hand. "They could have hurt *you* badly."

"I supposed I was the dispensable one," she admitted. "After they released me, a guy stayed on my tail to make sure I didn't alert the cops. Your friend's people got there just in time."

"We were most worried about you three," Mom said.

"How did you get the shiner?" Tan pointed to Dad's cheek.

"It's nothing now," Dad said.

"He fought them off when they broke in," Mom said proudly. "It took three of them to hold him down."

Tan shuddered. It could have all ended so badly. "That's my dad," Tan said shakily. "Gardener, chef, and black belt wannabe."

"I think we'll need several years of therapy to process what happened," Dad said, his voice equally shaky.

"At least we're safe." Mom tucked her arm into his. "And DigitalWallet is very interested in hearing about what happened. What you dealt with is exactly the risk cryptocurrencies face without government protection."

"There's still a lot to figure out," Dad said. "But by stopping

Liping from running off with those keys, you averted a destabilizing crisis for the whole industry."

"Extra credit for Tan," Winter said with a shaky laugh.

Tan laughed, too. Then he took Winter's hand and folded his fingers through hers, earning surprised looks from all three adults.

"We have something else to share with you," Tan said. "Besides everything that happened while you were gone." Tan took a deep breath. "Ever since we went to prom together, Winter and I haven't really wanted to be just friends."

"Oh?" Mom's eyes fluttered with surprise. Dad was quicker to get it. The surprise—and softness—in his eyes gave Tan even more courage to continue.

"We really like each other," Tan said. "At least, I do." This should have felt super-awkward. But it just felt right.

"I had no idea," Winter's mom said. "I was thankful you got along so well, but then you seemed to drift apart."

"We were trying to keep apart," Tan said.

"Is this how you feel, too?" Tan's dad asked her.

Winter's fingers tightened around Tan's. She met Tan's gaze. "I do."

Winter's mom laughed, but her eyes were wistful. "I'm even more thankful now."

"Well, we need to deal with us," Winter said, pointing to her and then to Tan. "Mom, I know you love hanging out with Tan's parents, but I think it's time we move out."

"Oh!" Fannie toyed with her necklace before letting her hand fall. "I'd thought about it when I finished my degree. But you were enjoying living with Tan and Sana so much, and you're an only child. I didn't want to take this from you." She gestured at the whole Lee family. "But now that I've graduated and have my first real law job, maybe it *is* time for us to have our own place again."

Winter laughed. "I've already spotted the perfect place. I saw a rental sign in their lawn. You know that house with the shed down the road?"

"The hide-and-seek shed?" Sana asked.

"Yep," Winter said. "I noticed it belongs to a duplex. The front unit is just the right size for us."

Winter's mom blinked. She smiled a bit mistily. "Well, that's the best possible graduation gift I could have imagined."

Chapter 29

"So what happened to Liping?" Tan asked Rebecca two weeks later. Rebecca was visiting from Oakland, and he and Winter had grabbed a bubble tea with her before heading to the science fair to present their project on encryption. Which Tan was confident they would nail.

"Don't worry about Liping," Rebecca said. "He won't make trouble for anyone again." She looked like a different person in a blue cable-knit sweater over well-worn jeans. She even carried herself differently. More relaxed. They all had a lot less to worry about now.

"I can't say that I feel sorry for him," Winter said, touching the scar still healing on Tan's arm.

"How are your ears from the helicopter?" Rebecca asked.

"Still ringing," Tan replied. "But I'm getting better."

"I'm glad," she said. "Nice headline in the *Chronicle*, by the way. PALO ALTO TEENS THWART BANK ROBBERY—ONLINE! Everyone in the Cove was reading it. I got lots of love for knowing you guys." She smiled, and so did Winter.

"That's pretty funny," Winter said.

The article had featured a video of Tan forcing Liping into a headlock. Even Master Kwon, who wasn't online much, had seen it. And was so proud he'd printed it out and pinned it to the bulletin board at the studio.

"That write-up was a little overdone," Tan said.

"But it helped with our neighbors whose scooters we lost," Winter reminded him.

"True. They dropped the charges they threatened to press. And the police dropped all charges against Maria. Her visa's safe."

"Glad to hear that," Rebecca said. "And thank you for keeping my name out of it."

"All the moles have been arrested, too," Tan said. "Four of the calls on Liping's phone log traced back to the local police departments. One was to an FBI agent."

Rebecca whistled, which Tan had never heard her do before. "Liping is an embarrassment to his country," she said. "The Chinese government won't look kindly on that."

"My cousin and his fellow cops uncovered a dozen moles," Tan said. They were a surprisingly diverse group of people, from every ethnic background. "None of them were working just for your dad. They were leaking classified information to buyers on five continents. Now the police are investigating how they were hacked so badly as an organization."

"Did you ever find out why your dad had spies everywhere like that?" Winter asked.

"I asked my mom," Rebecca answered. "It's not exactly that he has people planted. It's that people everywhere owe him favors. And he—or Liping acting on his behalf—could call them in anytime he wanted."

"Well, my cousin got a promotion for running them all down," Tan said. "But I wouldn't say he owes it to your dad."

"He owes it to *you*." Rebecca smiled. "Something for everyone."

"Well, Tan applied for an internship at the CIA to investigate all things related to cryptocurrencies," Winter said. "So that's one final silver lining—that he got off his butt for his dream job."

"I wasn't on *my butt*," Tan said with dignity. "The application just opened last week."

Winter nudged him. "It took people kidnapping you to exploit your cryptography prowess for you to believe how good you are."

Tan smiled. "Glad we can laugh about that now."

"Your government would be fools not to take you," Rebecca said. "Oh, and before I forget . . ." She handed Tan his *Mandalorian* shirt, and Winter a slip of paper. "Lucia told me you were shopping for a purse for your mom."

"Oh," Winter said, surprised. "Yeah, I mentioned it."

"This is a great vendor in San Francisco that just opened her shop. She's a friend of Sister Ava's. Big leather bags that last forever. I like her designs, and the prices are really reasonable."

Another something new about Rebecca. Tan had never once heard her talk about reasonable prices. She caught his eye. "They're really well designed," she said, as if reading his mind. She turned back to Winter. "I thought maybe you might want to check it out."

"Thank you. My mom will appreciate that. Her bag is literally falling apart." They exchanged a tentative smile. "So let's get to the good stuff. How is it living at the Cove? It's not exactly the resort you were planning to set yourself up at."

A slow smile lit Rebecca's face. It might have been the happiest Tan had ever seen her.

"It's not the life I planned to have when I left home. Sister Ava said the universe's plans for us are often better than the ones we have for ourselves. Even if the path there can be painful."

"I love that," Winter said.

"Come by sometime. We finished the tree house, and I did this whole opening ceremony with Jaxon cutting the ribbon. The kids loved it. The library has become *the* place to hang. I wrote my first grant application for the Cove and received a pledge for a donation of a dozen new computers."

"That's a perfect role for you," Tan said.

Rebecca glowed. "It feels good to be useful," She shifted in her seat, showing off the blue paint splattered on the calves of her jeans. "I'm even painting. The clothes somehow feel more meaningful when they're covered in paint."

"I get that," Winter said.

"Well, your dad's life changed for the better after the Cove."

Winter's eyes softened. "Yes, it did."

"Sister Ava convinced me to write my dad, about everything," Rebecca said. "So I wrote a letter. Everything I've been feeling about him. He hasn't answered, and it won't be warm fuzzies anytime soon, but it's a start." Rebecca rubbed a hand on the leg of her jeans. "I'm living on hand-me-downs, and I miss having my own bedroom, but I've never been happier," she confessed. "There's something about life in the Cove that I used to see in your families. And wished I had."

"Our families are pretty special," Winter agreed. "And I'm glad you're finding it, too."

"And what about you two?" Rebecca lifted her chin toward their clasped hands. "How's it going?"

Tan smiled at Winter.

Epilogue

Sana rattled the dice in her cupped hands, then sent them clattering across the coffee table. Tan stopped one, Sister Ava–style, just before it plunged off the edge into oblivion.

"Yes!" Sana advanced her pawn over the remaining colored blocks. "I won!"

It was the week after Winter and her mom had moved out. Tan and Sana were kneeling on the rug, playing Pirates in Pink. Board games were so much more detailed and complex than when Tan was younger. The game was full of treasures—rubies, diamonds, emeralds . . . and, of course, gold coins. Tan had gotten to be quite the expert. But he was no match for Sana.

"Well played," Tan congratulated her. "This calls for a cookie run."

He helped Sana into her jacket and grabbed his off the coat-tree by the door. Outside, the December air nipped at their cheeks, but the sun was bright. They took the Caltrain to San Mateo, got a chocolate chip cookie from Barnes and Noble, and rode the train back home, with no need to race from one car to another to throw off pursuit. It was luxurious.

"I need to help Dad with dinner," Sana said as they reached their stop in Palo Alto. "Now that Winter and her mom are gone, he's only got me."

"What about Mom and me?" Tan asked, pretending to be offended.

"You guys burn everything," Sana said seriously.

Tan laughed. "Sad but true. All right, let's get you home." He squatted beside her, and she climbed onto his back. "Oof. Pretty soon, you'll be too heavy for me to piggyback. Which means," he grunted as he rose to his feet, pretending to stagger, "I better get it in as much as possible." Sana laughed.

Tan dropped Sana off at home, then hopped on his bike and headed down the street and around the block to the Woos' duplex on Misty Lane. Winter opened the door, wearing a purple checkered bandanna in her hair.

"Tan, hey!" Her face lit up. "I've got news. I got cast as Eliza in *Hamilton* for the spring production!"

"Congrats!" he said. "I knew you could do it."

"All that practicing with you helped. A lot." She opened her arms, and he moved into them. The thing about Winter was she was always warm. Her skin radiated heat. And so did the rest of her. He was content to stay there, but he'd come on a mission.

"Show me around the new pad?" he asked, pulling back at last.

"I thought you'd never ask." She smiled and led him into a tastefully decorated hallway with a large vase full of fluffy peacock feathers and a gilded mirror. Winter's iPhone sat in a stand, playing pop music from a playlist. Tan had never seen the Woo family decorations, since they'd always just lived in the Lees' home.

"I love it," he said. "It's very Fannie and Winter." An enlarged framed photo of Fannie, Winter, and Winter's dad on the beach hung over the mantel in the living room. And on a side table, among a collection of photos of Winter and her mom, was a recent selfie of Winter and Tan in the Cove tree house.

"We don't have a fireplace, but the place feels homey," she said. "Safe. Like your place."

"Safe." That was how he felt with Winter.

Even though she was a person, she was his Cove.

As Tan started back into the hallway, a familiar song began to play. The song they'd danced to at prom. Winter put her hand on his chest, stopping him inches from her. Her face tipped up toward his. He could understand why Sana loved being found in the game of hide-and-seek. After being lost, he'd found Winter, and she'd found him.

"Did you dress up to visit me?" she asked. Her eyes sparkled up at him. A warm breeze gusted through the open front door.

"Would I do that?" He raised a brow.

"The question is, would you admit it if you did?"

He smirked. "I did."

She returned his smile boldly. Then he encircled her waist, and she wrapped her arms around his neck, and she kicked the front door shut as they pulled each other into a kiss with no boundaries.

Acknowledgments

This book takes place in San Francisco, where I make my home, but it was primarily written during my year in Vienna, Austria! As my first published novel outside the Loveboat universe, this novel has a special place in my heart and my library.

My heartfelt thanks to Marissa Meyer for inviting me to join her amazing anthology *Serendipity*, which led to "The Idiom Algorithm" short story that led to this novel. To our editor, Liz Szabla, who found a way for Tan and Winter to continue their journey in a story that had never existed before. Thank you for your vision and for trusting this story would find its way.

To my brilliant beta readers and writing community: Stacey Lee, for your thoughtful feedback as always, and for loving this one more than the Loveboats! Sabaa Tahir for brainstorming with me in Austria on a train ride from Vienna to Salzburg. Eileen Tucci, for your spot-on instincts and comments through multiple drafts. You are going to have an incredible career! Anne Ursu, I couldn't send another novel into the world without you. A.M. Jenkins, my fairy godmother, thank you as always for our conversations. Derrick Hsu for sharing your expertise on cryptocurrencies. Thank you, Cathy Yardley, Catherine Yeo and Kate Vandermel.

To my agent, Jo—I can't believe we're on our fourth novel!—and her fabulous team at New Leaf. To Kristen Pettit. To all the teams at Macmillan who have touched this novel and helped to launch it into the world.

To my siblings, who've reminded me of those "group stories" I used to tell at night, about us kids on adventures in a world without grown-ups . . . well, years later, here is my grown-up version.

To my family and community.

And to the One above, who loves all kids.

Thank you for reading this Feiwel & Friends book. The friends
who made *Kisses, Codes, and Conspiracies* possible are:

Jean Feiwel, Publisher
Liz Szabla, VP, Associate Publisher
Rich Deas, Senior Creative Director
Anna Roberto, Executive Editor
Holly West, Senior Editor
Kat Brzozowski, Senior Editor
Dawn Ryan, Executive Managing Editor
Kim Waymer, Senior Production Manager
Foyinsi Adegbonmire, Editor
Rachel Diebel, Editor
Emily Settle, Editor
Brittany Groves, Assistant Editor
Ellen Duda, Designer
Helen Seachrist, Senior Production Editor

Follow us on Facebook or visit us online at mackids.com.
Our books are friends for life.